Before Ryan Was Mine

The Remembrance Trilogy

PREQUEL

by

KAHLEN AYMES

TELEMACHUS PRESS

Cover Designed by Telemachus Press, LLC

Cover Art:
Copyright © Strawberry Mood/130041314/Shutterstock.com

Published by Telemachus Press, LLC
http://www.telemachuspress.com

Visit the author blog site:
http://www.kahlen-aymes.blogspot.com

ISBN: 978-1-941536-93-3 (eBook)
ISBN: 978-1-941536-94-0 (paperback)

Version 2014.12.13

Dear Readers:

After all of the love and adoration that has poured in for Ryan and Julia, I have been inundated with requests for more of their love story. I thank you for that. I write for you, but you inspire me to write. I am humbly grateful to each and every one of you who take time out of your busy lives to spend time with the characters my words create. I can't express how much it means to me to know you love these two that much. I also love them dearly, and I hope it shows.

This prequel, though written after *The Remembrance Trilogy* was completed, may be read before or after the series. It's a series of scenes, in chronological order, that tell the story of their college years... A peek at how they met and became "Ryan and Julia."

Whether you are a new reader, just meeting them, or someone who knows them well, I hope you enjoy their beginning...

Thank you, again, from the bottom of my heart.

~Kahlen

Dedicated solely to my readers...

RYAN IS MINE

And yours.

Before Ryan Was Mine

The Remembrance Trilogy

PREQUEL

~1~

The Beginning

Ryan ~

The biggest moment of my life found me unexpectedly. It crept up softly, and settled around me like a fuzzy blanket. A mere whisper; it hit me like a sledgehammer. At the time, I knew it was significant, but I didn't realize just how those few seconds would change absolutely everything. How could one brief glance leave such an indelible stamp on the remainder of my life? It would become a contradiction; an unstoppable force that would send me reeling out of my control, churning and shredding my emotions, but creating the most incredible contentment I'd ever feel. Contentment that could wrap me up in a warm, safe place or devastate me to the core and leave my heart in shambles. It would become years of want and pain, lust and love... It would hurt like the deepest hell but become the most euphoric and precious ecstasy I'd ever know.

It would wreck me. It would *make me*.

I'd never forget that day, that moment; that glance. The auditorium was huge, like a massive theater, with throngs of young bodies milling around trying to find seats; bustling with activity. Only, it wasn't the premier of Harry Potter or one of those damn Twilight movies. It was Stanford University and Psychology 101, required curricula for practically every undergraduate student.

Ugh, my brain protested. No matter what your major, whether you were pre-med or planning a future on Wall Street, you had to take some dumbass form of psychology for your liberal arts requirement. Boring as hell to me, but whatever. I had plans to attend med school, and this course was the most basic psych class. Normally, I had no interest in basic anything, but it was the next best thing to skipping it, which I'd choose if I could. I'd heard it was super easy, which explained why so many students enrolled. Community Health Psychology—even the title was vague.

Aaron had taken it the semester before and whined the whole time because he wasn't lucky enough to take it with the most preferred professor in the department; Dr. Gerrity. We'd heard to make the course tolerable, he was the only choice for instructor. I would have taken it with my brother, but the class was closed by the time I'd gotten around to the scheduling session. I didn't make the same mistake this time, but my enthusiasm was at an all-time low, despite landing one of Gerrity's classes.

I scanned for a seat toward the back, near the main entrance. The hell if I wanted to participate, anyway. I just wanted to show up, sign in, take the tests, and ace the fucker. That was my plan. *Cha'ching!* That's what was expected; by my parents and myself; so that's what I did— ace shit. School was always easy and, good or bad, the knowledge made me slightly arrogant about it.

I fully expected the first two years of undergrad to be fluff and loaded up on credit hours so that later, when I had lab, my ass wouldn't be dragging. I'd even gotten special permission from the dean to take three hours beyond the max class load. My father and I discussed it and decided it was better to have more out of the way, early on, so I could take more difficult courses that would secure my future plans—Harvard Medical School—

after I'd declared my major sophomore year. We'd shared the same goal for as long as I could remember. You didn't get there by taking the bare minimums in anything and if Dad had done one thing, he'd drilled that into me; work your ass off and never expect success to be handed to you. So far, I hadn't had to work that hard, if I were being honest. But, I knew it was only a matter of time. He'd gone to Harvard years earlier and while that would help, neither of us expected an easy in. Anyway, I wouldn't want it that way. I'd earn every piece of it or it wouldn't mean shit.

My parents offered the same opportunities to my adopted brother, Aaron. When we were ten his parents were killed in a car accident, he moved in with us, and we grew up together. He was the best friend I'd ever had.

Aaron struggled and had to work harder than I did; always had. I felt bad that it was more difficult for him and tried to help whenever I could; especially with math. So far, we'd only had to take first semester calculus, which to me was just a repeat of my senior year in high school. This semester was trigonometry and I wasn't looking forward to that at all. It was the most boring part of my requirements, other than this liberal arts crap, but whatever, it was necessary.

"I hear Dr. Gerrity is hot. Let's sit more toward the front so we can get a good look," a girl with short, black hair and a red mini-skirt giggled as she moved past me.

Apparently, she had her own reasons for taking this class. I rolled my eyes. *For fuck's sake!*

I was a red-blooded male and as such, I wasn't immune to the opposite sex. I'd had it easy in that arena with no shortage of girlfriends or willing partners. Sometimes they were too willing… to the point of annoying. Mini-skirt girl was pretty, but my eyes landed on the back of another young woman walking behind the one who was hot for the professor. She had long, flowing dark hair that looked like a shiny, slick river of dark chocolate as she moved. It was smooth and looked very soft, dropping almost to the middle of her back. My eyes moved lower toward her denim-encased ass. Her waist was small and the curve of her hips flowed deliciously out to place emphasis on the bedazzled pockets I was staring at. There was an "M" embroidered on one side. My lips twitched in the start of a grin as it struck me; "M" was for Matthews. It had to be a sign. I needed to talk to this girl or I'd regret it. Regardless, if it meant something or not, didn't matter. *It was a sign,* my subconscious argued as I talked myself into it. I grinned because I couldn't fucking help myself.

I picked up the backpack I'd just placed in one of the seats near the aisle and followed the two women further down. For all I knew, she could be a troll and I should rein in my eagerness until I knew for sure. How fucking disappointing would that be? A troll with a stellar ass, maybe, but I hadn't seen her face. Then she spoke, her voice soft, almost musical, but adamant. I knew I had to meet her.

"Ellie, he's old, and I don't wanna sit in the front. This class is gonna suck as it is. We'll have to join discussions up there, and you know how much I hate this shit."

"Please?" her friend lamented.

"No! I can't put up with you and the others batting their eyelashes at Dr. Gerrity. It's embarrassing!"

Even though her words might come off as whining, somehow, it didn't seem way. The same words from someone else would have, but with this girl it was more like a statement of fact: a verbal bitch-slap; to the point and without drama. I loved it.

She stopped and half-turned and I got the first glimpse of her profile. My heart paused for a beat. She was stunning: high cheekbones, delicate features with a slight blush to her cheeks and dusky pink lips. Her skin seemed flawless—creamy perfection. If it weren't for her casual dress, I'd have placed her from some highbrow, rich-bitch, old money crowd. Her breasts were full, but not overly large for her frame. I sucked in my breath to start breathing again. Yep. I definitely needed to find out who she was. Good thing I wasn't the shy type.

"Look, if you want to go ogle the dude, go ahead, but I'm staying up here."

I smiled, stifling a laugh. Definitely not highbrow. I was elated. She moved into a row about six ahead of me and I searched the surrounding seats. There was one open just behind her to her right. It would give me the prefect vantage point to observe, undetected. There was something about her that intrigued me. I could almost see her intelligence as if it were written like a sign on her shirt. *"Mouth breathers and bottom feeders to the left."* *Damn.* I could *not* stop smiling.

People brushed by me, and I was knocked in the shoulder as a larger guy passed. I barely noticed, my focus still on the girl as she moved into the row of seats I'd targeted.

"Sorry, dude," he mumbled.

"No problem," I said and casually waved him away as I moved toward my objective.

The red-skirt girl stopped and visibly stamped her foot. "Julia!"

Her name flew around in my brain with the speed of a hummingbird around a tree full of orange blossoms. It suited her to a T. *Beautiful*, but without the need or desire to shorten it into something less dignified; like how Grandma Matthews had reduced my Aunt Elizabeth's name to Betty. I never understood how the hell Betty came from Elizabeth anyway.

"What?" The girl with the pretty name simply looked at her friend—perplexed—and stopped, flopping down her book bag and taking her seat. She patted the one next to her with a teasing smile. "You'll have plenty of time to get into the professor's pants later. Just think of all the opportunities to discuss this bull-shit in his office. Of course, it might be difficult trying to con-vince him why you're so passionate, since psych has nothing to do with your major."

"Jeesh, Julia! Fine!" Her friend relented and threw her body down in the seat next to Julia, as I moved into the one behind them and sat down. Leaving my backpack between my feet, I opened it and pulled out a notebook and a pen. Afterward, I was free to observe the girls the last few minutes before class began.

My hand went to my mouth as I leaned on my elbow to watch and listen.

"Just look around." Julia motioned with her hand. "There are plenty of hot guys who aren't geriatric." She shrugged. "Choose," she said with a small giggle, digging out her notebook and a pen. "Besides, what about Jason?"

"Nope. He's *your* boyfriend."

"Ugh," Julia groaned, "I know. Tasty, that one," she said, tongue-in-cheek. The two of them burst out laughing, and I found myself wondering about this poor bastard, Jason. Julia's laugh was infectious. I saw how the people around her noticed her, most of the men doing a double take. I didn't bother trying to hide my admiration and watched her openly. "Not bad looking if he could just keep his mouth shut."

A pretty blonde next to me was staring wide-eyed at me as I listened to Julia and her friend's conversation. I glanced at her briefly, preoccupied, when she began speaking. "I'm really look-ing forward to this class. I took a college credit course online from UCLA in sociology and I just loved it."

I huffed inwardly, trying to concentrate on Julia's words. "I'm pretty sure psychology and sociology are on two different planets," I answered, dismissing her.

"Well, it's an *ology.*" She shrugged carelessly. "So, I'm sure I'll love this, too!" the blonde said. "I'm Rita."

Okay, this chick was way too enthusiastic; making my brain hurt and the nasal quality to her voice was irritating. It was all I could do not to laugh out loud. Did she just fucking say what I thought she said? It's an *ology*? My eyes widened against my will. *Okay.*

"Ryan," I mumbled. I pulled the text out of my backpack and feigned interest in it as if it were Gray's Anatomy. Now, *that* was interesting. I'd spent hours as a child, pouring over the pictures and pages of the copy my father kept in his study, memorizing the structures and systems of the body. It was then we knew med school was in my future. Like father, like son.

I glanced at Julia as a guy on the other side of her made a move toward her. Something in my gut didn't feel right, and I shifted uncomfortably in my chair. The guy was standing there, grinning and openly gaping at her foolishly, asking her name and stammering like an idiot when she told him. *What a douche.*

Finally, after a couple more minutes of meaningless chatter and Julia's obvious indifference, he left her, defeated and minus her phone number, to go find his seat. Julia pushed her hair behind her ear, and I found myself looking for the pulse in her neck, wondering if her skin smelled sweet and if the blood rushing just beneath the surface would make it warm under my mouth. I took in a deep breath.

"Why are we taking this class again?" the girl named Ellie asked. She was sitting directly in front of me and leaned into Julia.

"It's required, though I'm not sure for what. It has little relevance for my marketing degree."

I couldn't help myself, and I wanted her to notice me, so I leaned forward and spoke.

"Or, anything else, for that matter," I interjected softly.

Sparkling green eyes shot to mine for the first time, and I was instantly sucked in. There was deep blue-green around the irises, lightening to jade, then resuming the darker shade around the pupils; utterly captivating. She paused, a small smile spreading out on her full lips. She had two barely-there dimples that showed up when she flashed her white teeth as her face lit up. She was gorgeous, though now I could see she had very little make-up on.

"Yes, well, I think we picked this class because my friend here is warm for the professor's form." Her perfectly manicured brow shot up, and she laughed softly when her friend shoved her in the shoulder.

"Thanks a lot!" Ellie protested, throwing a glance over her shoulder at me.

Julia was still looking at me, her eyes skirting over my face. She looked away, nervously glancing at her watch. I could sense her discomfort and then it became my own. I wanted to ease it.

"I picked it because it was the least offensive psych class and might have a slight relevance to my pre-med program." Yeah, it was cocky, but I needed this girl to know I wasn't some brainless idiot, wasting my mind and opportunities, like that last loser who was just trying to pick her up. I knew I was being an asshole when I mentally dissed him, but I didn't care.

Rita continued to stare in open admiration. "Wow, med school. You must be really smart."

Julia and Ellie smirked at me, Julia's eyes widening in feigned innocence. "Yeah, you must be *really* smart!" she shot out in a veiled attempt to tease me about Rita's obvious effort to divert my attention back to her. No way in hell that was going to happen. Julia was beautiful, but, also witty and intelligent. I found her engaging and intriguing.

Ellie burst out laughing, and Julia batted her eyelashes at me, openly mocking the other girl's comment. "I'm only teasing. I'm Julia and this is my best friend, Ellie."

"Hi. I'm…" I began to introduce myself only to be cut off by the start of the class. *Fuck!*

The professor noisily adjusted the microphone on the podium at the front of the class before his gruff voice began rattling off the syllabus for the course. He might as well have been reciting a grocery list for all the attention I paid him. Thankfully, Rita was the type to take rigorous notes. It would be easy to get her to lend them to me if needed, or better yet, maybe I'd have to make a study partner out of the vivacious brunette who now held my rapt attention. It was stupid. I never got all giddy over women but what I was feeling was magnified by the three times she glanced over her shoulder at me and burned me with those intense green eyes and a sly smile. My stomach did little flip-flops, my palms were sweating and my heart sped up. I wanted to know more. Much more. I couldn't wait to speak to her, but the damn class droned on for 45 more minutes. It seemed like ten years.

When it ended, I'd already loaded my stuff in my backpack and remained seated until the two girls in front of me rose from their seats.

"So Ryan, do you live on campus?" Rita tried to make conversation as we waited for the people to my left to shuffle out in front of us. I was essentially standing next to Julia, while she waited in her row and I could smell her perfume wafting up like a musky dessert filled with vanilla and something that made my heart slam against my ribs.

I shoved a hand in my pocket. "Nope." I threw the answer over my shoulder with no other explanation and looked down at Julia. Her smiling eyes found mine, and she bit her lip to stifle a laugh. She knew I was blowing Rita off and she approved.

I ignored Rita's comment and spoke instead to the object of my new fascination. "So, as I was trying to say before, I'm..."

"*Ryan*," Julia interrupted. As long as I lived, I didn't think I'd ever forget the first time this woman said my name. "Um... yeah, I heard. Before."

I smiled. "Yeah. Where you from?" I asked.

"Kansas City. At least, my mom lives there. My dad is closer. San Francisco."

We inched our way toward the aisle as the students filed out.

"Oh, is that why you chose Stanford?"

"No. I mean, partly. It was the reputation, and my crystal ball said I was going to meet the greatest people here."

"How's that working for ya?" I chuckled as we finally made it to the end of our row. I waited for her and Ellie to exit, allowing them to move ahead of me.

"It was rough at first, but things are looking up." She leaned in and nudged my arm with her shoulder and electricity shot through me like a lightning bolt. She was quite a bit shorter than me. I could have rested my chin on the top of her head, and I found myself wanting to do just that. I nudged back instead, and she laughed softly.

A smile slid across my face again, the damn thing seeming to settle permanently on my lips. I was giddier than I'd ever been in the presence of a girl, but I felt at ease and comfortable, too. We slowly climbed the stairs toward the exit of the lecture hall, and I realized in literally seconds we'd be outside, and if I didn't say something quick, I wouldn't see her until the next class two days from now. I shook my head. Just because she made me hard beneath the belt and all soft and gooey inside didn't mean I had to get stupid.

Ellie turned as we poured out with the stream of other students from the auditorium into the foyer of the building. "See ya later, sweetie," she said to Julia. Her gray eyes darted from me to Julia and she smiled devilishly, like the cat that swallowed the canary. "Nice to meet you, Ryan."

I panicked slightly, even knowing there was a chance I wouldn't see them both on Wednesday—there was no assigned seating, and the hall was huge—I could easily miss her in the swarm of students. My backpack thrown over my shoulder, I rubbed the back of my neck.

"Bye, hon." Julia hesitated as Ellie left us. "Um…" She pointed in the direction of the library but hovered, not stepping in its direction. "Do you have another class now? I was going to go read the assignment in the library."

It was the first week of classes and most of the work would be reading, except the trigonometry and chemistry class I had next hour. I nodded, pulled my sunglasses out and shoved them on. "Unfortunately, I do." I hoped she felt as disappointed as I did that we couldn't keep talking. "Chem."

"Oh, that's right. You're a science snot." Her lush lips smiled, as she squinted in the sun and lifted a hand to shade her eyes.

I chuckled at her teasing. "Guilty. My entire family is, except my mother. Tell me about the 'M' on your butt."

Her eyebrow shot up. "What?" she asked incredulously.

"The 'M'," I stammered. "On your butt. On your back pocket." This was as good a way as any to make sure she knew who I was, even if it was a little awkward.

She frowned, not understanding, then astonishment flooded her features, her eyes widening. "You were looking at my ass?"

"Well, I couldn't see your face." Shit, this was weird. I felt out of my element, nervous and ridiculous. I couldn't believe I'd just mentioned her ass. I laughed uncomfortably, hating myself for not being smoother. "My last name is Matthews. We have to be friends now. You're branded. It's a sign." I was seriously attracted to this girl, but I wanted to know her mind more than I wanted to get in her pants. The thought left me stunned as I wondered if I could be friends with someone I was so in to.

"Ah." Her head nodded once as realization of what I was doing dawned on her. She raised her eyebrow and nodded to indicate someone was hovering behind me. I turned to look. It was the other girl from the lecture hall.

"So, I'll see you Wednesday?" Rita asked awkwardly, stammering slightly. I'd forgotten all about her and didn't realize she was still around.

I shoved one hand in the front pocket of my jeans and opened my mouth, then shut it again. Rita wasn't the one I wanted to sit next to during the next class. "Um... I guess?" I inwardly grimaced as my eyes locked with Julia's. I came off rude and that was unfortunate, but I wanted to speak to Julia, and I was running out of time before my next class.

"Okay." Rita answered shortly then turned away, disappointment clear on her face.

I returned my attention to Julia.

"The jeans are branded, for sure. Miss Me-s. Lots of girls have 'M's' on their butt's," she challenged with a grin. "Are they all branded? 'Cuz, you don't look like the kind of guy who lacks female companionship. Obviously." Her eyes darted to mine then she nodded toward Rita's retreating back.

I bit my lip and my hand swiped through the side of my hair. The last thing I needed was Julia thinking I was a user. "I think there might be a compliment in there if I dig deep enough," I teased. "Look, I wanted to meet you. So, sue me."

Our eyes met and held again, and I almost blurted out that I wanted her number. I told myself to get a grip. I never acted this dumb in front of a girl.

Julia rocked on her heels and glanced at her watch. "You're gonna be late."

"I'd blow it off if it wasn't the first class of the semester. I really want to talk to you some more." Suddenly, I was happier than hell that I didn't get into Gerrity's class last semester. I already liked this girl more than most I'd met at college and I'd only spoken to her for a few minutes. There was just something about her. Not the way she looked, though she was beautiful, but I wanted to know about her life, to invest time in her. It was a gut feeling, but this girl was going to be important to me, she was a long-term investment. "So maybe you could agree to meet me outside the lecture hall on Wednesday and we can sit together. Then this class might be bearable?"

Julia's smile widened immediately, and she nodded. "Okay, sure. I'll make sure my ass is branded. But that other girl will be bummed."

I smiled back and wished I had more time to get her number. "Oh, well. Good. See ya."

"Uh huh. Bye, Ryan." She waved awkwardly and started off toward the library.

I turned in the opposite direction, took three steps and stopped. "Hey, Julia," I called over the others walking between us. "If you can wait an hour for lunch, I'll be in the Student Union snack bar."

A brilliant smile flashed, and I waited, knowing I would have to run to my class now. Something wouldn't let me leave without knowing I'd see her later.

"Sounds good."

My heart sped up, and the silly smile returned and didn't budge the whole time I ran across campus. Anticipation made my heart race more than the exercise. This was stupid. I met girls all the time and most of the time I couldn't give a shit. There were always more girls to meet, and a missed opportunity usually wasn't a big deal. Julia was a big deal to the point I couldn't wait for this hour to get out of the fucking way. I burst through the door to my class and breathlessly found a seat at the back, flopping down quickly amid glances from the others around me. Yeah… this girl was gonna be important.

Julia ~

Wow. Just wow.

My face hurt from smiling, and dang if the book in front of me could hold my attention. It didn't help that this shit was boring as hell; it was made worse because my mind was full of the guy I'd just met in the class. He was like a magnet—too gorgeous not to notice, and I'd seen him take the seat behind me right before that blonde girl started talking to him. My heart had plummeted, thinking she'd mean I'd miss any chance of meeting him myself, and I'd have to resort to the high school tactics of trying to sit near him for the next class. The only problem was, the auditorium was huge and chances were good I'd never find him. Which was why it was so great when he'd taken it upon himself to butt into my conversation with Ellie.

I saw Ellie checking him out, too. Who wouldn't? Tall, easily over six feet, built, golden skin and sun-kissed hair, brilliant, dark blue eyes, and that *face*. There were no words for that face. Strong jaw, killer dimples, bright white smile, straight nose, and that tiny cleft in his chin. Beautiful couldn't cut it. And, to top it all off, he was nice. I mean, *really* nice. Even though he'd been checking me out, for the first time in a long time, I felt like a guy was really interested in what I had to say. *Matthews*. Ryan *Matthews*. Matthews with an "M." On my ass. I laughed softly to myself, pleasure shooting through me like fireworks. Sure, the sweet persona could be a ruse to suck in unsuspecting victims. I'd seen that crap often enough, but something inside me told me he was different. I intensely hoped he was.

I glanced at the clock again and gave up trying to read the textbook in front of me, flipping it shut and unzipping my black backpack to slide it inside. I still had fifteen minutes until I was supposed to meet Ryan, and I felt a little nervous. He was so pretty; surely, there were a bevy of women vying for his attention. What if he didn't show up? My stomach dropped before I could stop it, but I hoisted the heavy bag of books over my right shoulder and slowly made my way toward the Student Union. I didn't want to get there too early and look like an anxious jerk standing around waiting. I didn't want to order lunch without him. Ugh. I was overthinking this way too much. It was crazy, but something about him was unnerving and comforting at the same time. He seemed really genuine, so I didn't know why I was acting so ridiculous. Maybe it was the way every woman who came near him stared.

I found the bathroom and made my way inside; weaving in and around all of the women coming out, all with book bags made for a tight fit. My eyes widened as I took stock of my reflection in the wall-to-wall mirrors over the sinks, and quickly dug out the hairbrush and lip-gloss I kept in the front pocket of the backpack. Normally, I wasn't one to retouch; I reapplied a light glaze of the gloss on my lips and smoothed my hair slightly. I didn't want to appear overly anxious to Ryan and I chastised myself as I made this small deviation from my usual routine. I replaced the items in my bag and smoothed the dark denim over my thighs.

When I left the bathroom, I stopped to scan the snack bar. It was nice, set up like a restaurant with wooden booths and several tables with chairs. Ryan hadn't said exactly where inside I was supposed to meet him and my eyes scanned the room. No sign of him yet, but the Student Union was large and there were a lot of students walking through, hovering around tables, and at the end of a few of the booths. I felt self-conscious; walking around like a moron, looking into booths and glancing around like I was lost. Many sets of curious eyes met mine while I wandered around seeking the striking blue gaze of the man I met two hours earlier.

I caught sight of him quickly pushing in the front entrance doors, his eyes scanning the room. He didn't see me right away but was rapidly set upon by a group of students: a dark-haired man and two women—one with long blonde hair and one with cropped red locks. I was anxious and my feet wanted to move toward him, but I hesitated as I watched the group engage him. His gorgeous face split into a grin and he nodded, the blonde's hand coming out to wrap around his bare forearm. He was wearing jeans and a long sleeved white T-shirt, the cuffs shoved up to show strong muscle and golden skin beneath her fingers, the blue and green plaid shirt he wore over it, hung open. He looked hot; the layers doing nothing to disguise the hard planes of his chest and stomach underneath the fine, close-fitting cotton material, nor the broad shoulders. The two women gazed at him in dazzled silence, and I wondered if Ryan was even aware of it, though it was quite obvious to the rest of the world. It was sort of silly, and I made a mental note not to allow myself to act like an idiot around him. I took slow steps toward him to make sure he saw me, not wanting to interrupt the conversation with his friends.

He bent slightly to listen to something the woman touching him said, but his eyes continued their search for me. My heart stopped when his gaze finally landed on mine, and his lips lifted in the start of a small smile. He was so breathtakingly handsome. This was a chance just to look at him. He put up his hand and spoke to the group around him. Excusing himself, he walked toward me with his backpack slung over his right shoulder. The two girls turned to watch him walk away, disappointment and curiosity in their eyes as they looked me over thoroughly.

"Hey." His soft voice washed over me warmly as he flashed a quick smile.

He was several inches taller than me, and I had to look up into his face. I wanted to bite my lip, hardly able to contain the grin that was trying to break out across my mouth. "Hey," I returned. "How was class?"

"Boring as hell. I can't wait until all of this basic shit is out of the way. Want to find a place to sit, and then I can get us something to eat?"

"Yeah. Did you want to invite your friends to join us?"

Ryan smiled again and shook his head. "Nah."

He motioned toward an empty booth in the corner and I preceded him to it, flung my backpack in, and shoved it closer to the wall as I slid in. Ryan did the same across from me. I watched him run a hand through his hair.

"Did you get the psych assignment read?" he asked.

"Ugh," I rolled my eyes, and Ryan chuckled. "It was so bad I couldn't concentrate. I think I'll have to read it out loud to get through it."

"That's what I'm afraid of. Maybe we can take turns then just fill each other in."

I smiled, leaning back against the booth, pleased at the prospect of studying together. It meant I'd be seeing more of him and I wanted nothing more. "Okay."

We started talking and time flew. We talked about my parents' divorce, his life growing up in Chicago, how his family adopted his best friend when they were ten and my father's latest criminal case, both of us leaning in toward each other intently. I ate up his words and he was equally engaged; truly interested in all I was telling him. We fell into a rhythm that was easy, yet made my heart thud inside my chest. I'd forgotten I was hungry until my stomach rumbled loudly and Ryan chuckled.

My eyes widened. "Wow. That's embarrassing."

"It's my fault! I promised you lunch and I've completely failed." He looked around at the clock on the wall. It was ten minutes to three. "The grill closes soon so we'd better order. What would you like?"

"I'm not picky. Grilled chicken sandwich and tea?"

"I'll be back." I watched him walk away, and couldn't help but admire the easy grace with which he moved or the eyes that followed his every move. I wondered about the young woman he was speaking to before. Surely she wasn't his girlfriend or she would have joined us for lunch. In no time, I had the sandwich, green tea and a pile of fries in front of me. Ryan had a burger, onion rings, and a Coke. He shoved the rings toward me. "I wasn't sure if you wanted fries or rings, so…"

I pushed my fries in the middle of the table, too. "How 'bout we share?"

Ryan smiled and grabbed an onion ring. "I hoped you'd say that." He dipped it in the ketchup I squirted alongside and took a big bite. "How come I haven't seen you around before?"

I lifted my right shoulder in a half-shrug. "Not sure. I don't socialize much. First semester, I was worried about my grades so

I kept to the books. Wasn't sure what to expect, you know?" My eyes flashed up, and he was intently studying my face. I reluctantly reached for my sandwich. "Plus, you're in arts and science and I'm business admin. It isn't likely we'd share many classes."

Ryan nodded. "Yeah, that sucks. So, business," he said, using it as if it were my name, "What are you going to declare?"

I swallowed the food in my mouth before I answered. "Well, I'm having trouble deciding, because, really, I'd like to double in marketing and art, but it crosses the schools, so they won't allow it."

"So, you're an artist, then?"

"I feel weird saying that." I shrugged a little, despite loving it and being told by teachers, friends, and family that I was talented, I still hesitated to allow myself the luxury of the label. "I've always been artistic, and I'd like to do something with it when I graduate, but my dad doesn't think there is much of a financial future in it. So, the best I can do is take as many art electives as possible. I'll also take extra classes during the summers so I can get the requirements in and, at least, mimic the major. Even if I can't say I have a degree, I'll have the knowledge."

"I see. That makes a lot of sense." The admiration on his face sent a small thrill through me. "It's sort of the same for me. Stanford doesn't offer a pre-med program per se, so I have to pick a science curriculum that I like best as a major that will still facilitate my getting into medical school." I watched him talk, how he moved his hands and the expressions that changed his features. "At this point, I'm leaning toward chem or bio."

"What kind of doctor do you want to be?"

"Hmmph!" He let out his breath with an amused laugh. "To be honest, I don't have a clue, but probably some sort of specialty, though. My dad is a brain surgeon," Ryan said so nonchalantly, it had to be true.

"Are you serious?" My eyes widened as I tried to picture Ryan's home life. Was his dad a stuffed shirt who was gone all the time and his mother a suburban princess? If so, it certainly wasn't evident in their son. He was so down to earth and genuine.

"Yes. No pressure there," he smirked. "He's sort of brilliant. He's a very giving man, but he can be tough as nails at the same time." Ryan laughed and continued to talk about his parents. It was obvious he loved them very much, and his words refuted my original mental impression of them. He was animated and enthusiastic; his mood was infectious. "Tell me about you."

"Not much more to tell, really. I mean, when my parents divorced, I moved to Kansas City with my mom. Since I was eight, I've spent every summer in California with my father. I think he felt guilty he wasn't around more, but I liked my life with my mom. She's cool; way cooler than most of my friends' moms. We like the same music and share clothes. I can talk to her about anything."

"Is it weird for you, though? Being in the middle of your parents? I can't imagine it since mine have always been together."

"No. They stayed friends and always parented together. Well, most of the time."

He stopped eating and leaned back, his eyes coming back to mine. "I can't imagine trying to be friends with someone I was in love with. I don't know if I could do it."

A little shiver ran through me at his words, and I wondered if anyone had ever been lucky enough to have him in love with them. "It wasn't always easy, but I don't think they split due to lack of love. My mom resented my dad's long hours, and she didn't know many people out west. She got lonely and wanted to be closer to family. He was just starting out and working very hard. He wanted to be a prosecuting attorney, and it required long hours in the D.A.'s office. He wasn't willing to give up his dream. Looking back, I know he was only doing it for us, but at the time, he just wasn't there. I know he was very angry when they first split." I wiped my fingers on the paper napkin in my lap. "But after we moved, Mom was happier, and then, so was I."

Ryan nodded in understanding.

"Do you live on campus?" I asked, wondering if he'd be heading my way and not wanting to end the afternoon, and knowing the answer since that girl, Rita had asked him in the lecture hall.

"No. My parents argued about it. It's cheaper to rent a place for Aaron and me than to pay room and board, and anyway, the food sucks ass and Aaron would've died of starvation." Ryan had an easy laugh that was disarming. "Eventually my mom gave in to my dad's logic, but she still worries we'll party too much." A gorgeous grin split across his face and amusement danced in his bright blue eyes.

I laughed and nodded. "And? Do you?"

Ryan joined in with a chuckle. "No. Sure, there are parties. Aaron's rushing Phi Kappa Nu, so some are inevitable."

"Not you, though?"

"No. I don't want someone picking my friends. At least, that's how I see it. You? Any sorority?"

I shook my head with a small laugh. "No. I'm of your way of thinking."

He smirked at me. "There are worst things."

"Agreed." I nodded, still smiling.

We got up, gathered our things, and began making our way toward the door. Ryan's hand closed around the strap of the backpack hanging off my shoulder to carry it for me. His fingers brushed against my shirt, and I could feel his warmth through the material. I tried not to let him see the small tremor his touch caused. No other guy had ever offered to carry my books before. He was amazing, and I could barely stop myself from staring in rapt adoration like the girls he'd been talking to earlier.

"I'm jealous about the food. I have to be careful not to pack on the freshman fifteen. The food is awful in the cafeteria."

"Ah. So you're on campus."

I sighed. "Unfortunately, but it's all good. That's how I met Ellie. She's my roommate."

We walked across campus toward my dorm and I started to shiver. The wind was cold, and I regretted my lack of jacket and realized Ryan didn't have one either. "Is your car this way?" I asked, indicating the direction I needed to go. "If not, you don't have to walk me. It's sort of chilly."

"Julia." My name rolled off his tongue for the first time. "I'm happy to suffer for you."

My mouth clamped shut as I tried to figure out what he was thinking. I glanced at him then straight ahead. "Thank you for lunch. My turn next time?" I was trying to gauge the nature of our relationship. Were we going to be friends or dating?

"Um…" Ryan began hesitantly, and I wondered if maybe he didn't want to have lunch again. "Sure. I've had a good time talking to you…"

"Me, too. But?"

"But, I don't let girls buy my meals."

I inhaled slowly, wondering if that meant this was a date, or we were just friends. I really enjoyed spending time with him, so in whatever way that would happen, I'd take.

"That asinine class might even be tolerable now." His shoulder lightly nudged mine as we walked and it sent a jolt of something right through me. I could feel my face grow hot as I looked down at the pavement moving underneath my feet and I smiled, returning the nudge ever so slightly.

"I'm glad I met you, Ryan."

"Yeah. Me, too. Can I get your number? We can text Wednesday and meet before class so we can sit together. Cool?"

My heart thumped hard in my chest. "Cool."

Ryan ~

I was laying on the couch, my foot propped up on the back of it, rhythmically throwing a basketball against the wall over and over. Aaron was in the shower, and I was waiting for my turn. We'd just come from a two-on-two basketball game with two guys who lived next door, and despite the cool weather, we were both dripping sweat. My hair was damp with it and stuck to my forehead. We kicked their asses but not without a serious work-out. I knew I reeked, and Aaron was worse. I thumped the ball against the wall again, catching it casually as my thoughts wandered to Julia.

It had been a month since we'd met and I was into her in ways I'd never been into a girl before. I found myself looking forward to seeing her and every time her name flashed on my phone, I smiled so hard my face hurt; and not because she was hot. She was, and it kept me up at night, but that wasn't the only reason. I huffed at the irony of it.

I wanted to take her out on dates. To kiss her, and yes, I wanted her. It sucked because it didn't take long to discover she was the person I wanted to spend time with more than anyone else. I didn't want to lose that. What if we dated, then it tanked? I'd miss her. I always missed her when she wasn't around. It didn't matter what I was doing. If something happened, good or bad, she was the first person I wanted to share it with. I was confused as hell and struggling.

We made a study date for Sunday since our first exam in psych was Monday, but it was Saturday morning, and I found myself racking my brain for a reason to see her today. I'd almost asked her to come to the basketball game just to watch us play, but that was lame and something a guy's girlfriend does. I didn't know what we were. If she did want me to ask her out or make a move, she was probably thinking I was a first class asshole for not doing so.

I was in an uncomfortable position. I didn't know what I wanted for the first time ever in reference to a woman. I liked her. More than liked her, but I wasn't sure what the fuck I was doing about it. My stomach tightened and I threw the ball against the wall again, this time a little harder. I'd tried to work out why I hesitated to ask her out but the answers didn't sit well. I couldn't figure out a way to guarantee the outcome would be what I wanted.

Thump. Thump. Thump. I threw the ball over and over.

"Ryan. I'm out of the shower," Aaron called as he walked out of the bathroom and into his bedroom with a towel around his waist.

Thump. Thump. Thump. I didn't move, lost in my thoughts.

Five minutes later, Aaron came out of his room, pulling a gray T-shirt over his head and sliding his arms into it. "Ryan?"

"Yeah." I clasped the ball between my hands and sat up, putting my feet on the floor. I glanced at him. When he met her two weeks earlier, he'd hammered me about why I wasn't trying to date her because she was so beautiful. How could I make him understand when I didn't know myself? He hadn't stopped until I'd shouted at him to shut the fuck up and that it was none of his goddamned business.

"Okay. I'm going." I was distracted, but stood and passed the ball to him. I started toward my room to gather clean clothes but stopped when he called my name.

"Ryan, there is that party tonight at the frat house, remember? Are you coming?"

I raised a shoulder in a shrug. "I don't know. Maybe? Who's going to be there?"

"A lot of people. Can you call Julia and make sure she'll go?"

"What? Why?" I turned fully around to face him. Heat started to rush under the skin of my face. Maybe he thought if I wasn't going to date her, he would. I didn't think I could take watching it.

"David Kessler wants to meet her. He was with me the other day when I was waiting for you in the commons, and he saw her with you. He thinks she's hot, and he's president of my frat. I'd like to introduce them. It will give me an in and for sure, I'll make the frat."

Heat turned to fire, quickly licking its way up over my face and down my chest. "Um..." I began not sure what to say, but my chest felt tight at the thought.

"You don't have a problem with it, right?" He sat down and started to shove his feet into his shoes.

"Yeah, we're just friends." I rubbed the back of my neck. It was the truth, Julia and I were just friends, but it felt odd saying it. "But," I struggled to find something to say that would dismiss the subject. "She's not really into frat guys. She thinks all that social who's who is a load of bullshit."

Aaron looked up at me, skepticism filling his expression. "Really?"

I shrugged. "Sorry, dude." I began to turn away, but Aaron wasn't ready to let it go.

"Are you planning to date her? Because if you're not, David has serious interest."

I stopped again. "I'm not sure what I'm planning... I'm not really planning. Just going with the flow."

"But you don't want her to see anyone else? That shit will not fly for long. Guys are into her, and eventually someone will land her. A chick that hot won't be content to hang out with her *friend*."

Exasperation welled inside my chest, and I wanted to punch him. "I don't know. She's cool. I like being with her, talking to her. I feel easy with her, and she doesn't put all that annoying shit on me like most girls do. I mean, she's not all superficial and clingy."

"But, she's super hot. I mean... spending time with her, how do you not go for it?"

"It's not easy sometimes. I'm not blind. But I like her more than I want to get into her pants. I never end up friends with girls I have sex with and Julia isn't a girl you bang on a Saturday night for fun."

He looked at me as if my head had twirled around on top of my shoulders. "So, you're not moving on her. If that's true, and if you two are just friends, what's the problem if Dave asks her out?"

I sighed. I really couldn't argue with him, but I wanted the subject dropped. I couldn't have it both ways, and I couldn't continue this conversation without it exposing how I really felt... Hell, I didn't really know how I felt at this point, so how could I explain it to Aaron, even if I wanted to? I wanted her, more than I'd probably wanted any other girl before, but she was quickly becoming important in ways that were new and unfamiliar to me. I was like a fish out of water, trying to get my bearings. Heat began to seep up my neck and into my face; that burning kind you get that makes you feel like the floor is about to drop out from beneath you. I didn't want Aaron to see my discomfort.

"Okay, I'll see what she's doing. But, I'm going to tell her about that guy. I don't want her to feel set-up." I didn't know how Julia interpreted what was between us, anyway. Maybe we *were* only friends. If so, that word held more meaning than it ever had before. "If she doesn't want to go, she doesn't want to go, and I'll expect you to drop it."

"This is weird, Ryan. If you're not into this girl like that, what's your problem?"

"Aaron, I said I'd ask her. So shut the fuck up about it, okay?"

He sat back on the coach and watched me fidget. "You *are* into her."

"I said I like her, but spending time with her is most important."

He whistled and smiled wryly. "Never thought I'd see you confused over a chick."

I huffed and went off toward my room, muttering. "That isn't a word I use to describe her. Julia is no chick."

*****

"Hey, you." Julia's voice was soft and a little raspy when she answered the phone. "What are you doing?"

It had become common to call each other every day, to know what and where the other was at all times. It wasn't weird for her to ask me. I might have resented it if it was anyone else, but it was how we were with each other. How I wanted it.

"Trying to get Aaron off my ass. He wants me to go to this party tonight. Some frat thing." I groaned, hoping she'd get how unenthused I was about going.

"I think Ellie is planning on something like that. Which house?"

"Kappa Nu. Aaron's frat."

"Oh. I see. Are you going?"

"No. I don't know. Look, I told Aaron I'd ask you to come."

"Aaron?" Her voice sounded hesitant.

"Yeah. Some asshole he wants to impress saw you with us, and wants to meet you." My stomach felt sick when I said the words out loud.

"Hmmph," Julia huffed. I couldn't tell if she was amused or pissed until she spoke. "Well, if he's an asshole, bring him on. Sounds just like my type," she teased.

The fact is, we hadn't talked about her type, or mine for that matter. I hadn't asked another girl out since I'd met her, and she hadn't dated either.

I rubbed the back of my neck with my left hand as the fingers of my right gripped tightly around the phone. "Look, I told him you probably wouldn't want to go."

"Who's the guy?"

I was taken aback that she asked, but what did I expect her to do? I had no right to be pissed or even feel upset. I hadn't asked her on a real date. "Um..." I struggled to find the name in my mind. "David something or other. He's the president of Aaron's fraternity." I filled up my lungs and tried to let the air out without Julia hearing it over the phone.

"Should I go?"

"I didn't... I mean, I don't know," I stammered then paused.

"Are you going?" she asked again.

"I didn't make plans. Do you want me to? I can go with you, er, if you want. Make sure you're okay."

"I don't want to usurp your plans, Ryan."

I sat down on my bed and swiped my hand through my hair. Julia used words like usurp when so many didn't even know that the hell it meant. I needed air. My lungs wanted to fill up into a huge sigh, but she'd hear it and know the conversation was weird for me.

"I didn't really have any plans." *Other than call you and see what you were doing*, I thought. I was pissing myself off right now. *Why the fuck did I even ask her about that stupid party in the first place?*

"I'm not feeling the greatest. My throat is scratchy and my nose is stuffy. I think I'm coming down with something, so I wasn't really planning on going anywhere tonight. Anyway, I'm sure I look like crap."

I sat up a little, not happy she was sick, but ecstatic I didn't have to go to that damn party and watch some prick hit on her all night. I sighed in relief. "Want me to bring you some soup? Do you need medicine?"

"I had one of those instant noodle things." She cleared her throat and let out a small cough.

I hated the thought of her sick and all alone, and found myself wanting to take care of her.

"Jules… why don't I come get you? Aaron will be out all night tonight. He's chasing a new girl, and with that party, I doubt he'll come home until morning. I'll stop on the way and pick up some Nyquil, Kleenex, and stuff."

"That's sweet, Ryan, but you have better things to do than listen to me blow my nose. I don't want you to get sick."

"I won't. I'll be over in an hour."

"Ry—" she began, but I interrupted.

"Don't argue, Julia. I'll get some movies and lots of junk food, too. Lots of salty stuff to help your throat."

I hung up without giving her a chance to protest, and an hour later I was waiting for her in the lobby of her dorm. When the elevator opened, and she came out in gray sweatpants and a dark purple parka, carrying her pillow and a box of tissues, my heart did flip-flops. Her hair was tied up in a knot on top of her head, she was pale, and her nose was unnaturally red. It was easy to see she felt like hell, but I couldn't help the small smile that came to my mouth as she walked toward me.

"What are you smiling at? Don't look at me," Julia muttered, wiping her nose.

I wrapped an arm around her shoulders and started walking toward the doors that would take us out to my car. "You look fine. For a *sicky*." I gave her a squeeze and laughed softly, happier than hell at the prospect of spending the evening with her, despite the state of her health.

Her little fist came out and punched me hard in the ribs, but my coat provided enough padding to keep it from hurting.

"Is that all you got?"

"No. I'm gonna breathe on you and spit in your mouth," she teased miserably. "Just wait."

I laughed out loud and piled her into the waiting car to drive the short distance to the apartment Aaron and I shared. It was in an old turn of the century house that had been converted into four apartments. It was nice but not very big. I'd rushed around and picked the place up, but it still wasn't as clean as I'd wanted for the first time Julia came over. She walked in ahead of me when I pushed the door open, slowly glancing around. There was an old couch and a large TV in the living room, with two mismatched chairs, and the kitchen was small; off to one side, the table, that looked left over from some fifties sitcom, was cluttered with books and legal pads.

"I bought you Diet Coke, Cheetos and one of those veggie sandwiches you like from Ike's," I murmured, setting the bag, paper cups filled with pop, and the videos on one end of the counter. I pulled off my coat and hung it over the back of one of the kitchen chairs.

"Thanks." She wrapped her arms around herself, still clad in her coat. "What'd you get?"

"Roast beef. I thought we could share, if you wanted."

"Yeah." She nodded and went to sink down on the couch, setting her pillow down.

"Do you have the chills? You look cold."

"A little."

I went to my room and pulled the comforter from my bed, and in less than a minute, I had her shoes and coat off and the covers tucked all around her as she lay on the couch. My hands shoved the covers under her legs and feet. Her green eyes locked onto mine.

"You look like a cannoli."

"My throat hurts. Do you have ice cream?"

I rolled my eyes. "It doesn't matter. You can't have it, anyway. It'll make mucus and you're already a snotty bitch."

Her laugh followed me to the kitchen as I went to retrieve the bag of food I'd gotten from the sandwich shop, the sodas, and the bag of cold medicine I'd picked up at Walgreens. Soon, it turned into a raspy coughing jag.

"Dickhead," she managed finally when she'd gotten it under control.

My lips quirked in amusement at her jibe, even though I felt guilty for making her laugh in the first place. I unwrapped the food, set her sandwich on the coffee table in front of her alongside mine, and then flipped on the TV.

Julia coughed again, covering her mouth with a tissue. "Ryan," she said between coughs, "this is a bad idea. I never get sick, so this must be a bad bug. I seriously don't want you to catch it." She snuggled down deeper into the blanket, curling on her side, and closing her eyes. I could have taken the chair at the end of the couch, but I sat down next to her and lifted her legs so they rested across my lap. I grabbed the remote and half of my sandwich, my arm resting across her legs. I watched her face for her reaction, to see if I was overstepping the bounds of friendship, but she just sighed.

"Not hungry right now?"

She shook her head. "Maybe in a bit." She breathed in, her eyes still closed. "This smells like you."

I flushed. Should I have gotten a clean blanket out of the closet instead? "Do you want a different one?" I started to take a bite.

"No. I like it. It's like you're wrapped all around me. It feels good."

My heart stopped. I still didn't know how the fuck to classify our relationship, or what we were to each other. But one thing was for sure, I liked the way that sounded. To say we were friends was the fucking understatement of the century.

"Thank you, Ryan."

"For what?"

"Getting sick with me," she said sleepily. Yeah, I probably would get sick as a dog and in that moment, I didn't give a rat's ass.

I smiled. As long as anything was with Julia, whatever it was, I was in. *All* in.

~2~

Uncomfortably Close

Julia ~

"Julia, are you coming?" Ellie asked, impatience growing on her face.

"Er..." I hesitated. I didn't know what I was doing. I hadn't heard from Ryan this afternoon. We'd talked about going to see the new Spiderman movie and grabbing some curry at the tandoori restaurant near the theater. "I'm not sure."

"Well, we're leaving in thirty minutes!" Ellie seemed exasperated. "Chris is picking us up. I thought you wanted to go? We have to get in line early if we expect to get a table near the dance floor." She stared at my state of dress, and her face twisted in disdain. "You can't go like that! Why haven't you changed?"

Ellie, and a couple of her other friends, were going to a new dance bar. Supposedly, it would be the hottest thing in the Stanford club circuit, with the added hook of free Wi-Fi. It had been heavily promoted since the beginning of the semester in the Stanford News, and signs were tacked up all over campus, so we'd talked about it a lot and were both excited for it to open. Tonight was the official grand opening.

"I'm not sure I'm going." I cringed as I waited for her to blow a gasket. I was sitting on her bed while she was in the bathroom. Ellie paused putting on her mascara and looked around the corner, still holding the black tube in her hand.

"What? Why?" Her brow wrinkled into a displeased frown.

Afraid she would be pissed with my answer, I plowed forward. "Ryan and I might do something."

She stared at me with wide eyes; her expression hardening further and her lips pursing. "Ryan?"

"Yeah." My shoulders lifted in a small shrug and I cast her a brief glance, unable to meet her eyes.

"But, we planned on this!" she huffed. "What? Are you guys dating now? I thought you were just friends."

One leg was curled in front of me and the other foot was flat on the mattress as I leaned one elbow on my bent knee and one hand played with a strand of hair. I sighed. "We are."

"You'd blow off the grand opening of HotSpot for a guy who's just *a friend*?" She stared hard at me and waited for me to answer. "A *friend*, who, let me remind you, is the hottest guy either of us knows," she said knowingly. I still couldn't meet her eyes. "Super-hot *friend*, Ryan."

She made quote symbols with two fingers of each hand lost her grip on the mascara in her right hand. "Shit!" she said as it went tumbling to clatter on the linoleum floor of her bathroom. "Why don't you just bring him along?" She bent to pick it up and threw it in the sink, muttering obscenities.

"We haven't really had much time to talk this week and he wanted to see that new Spiderman movie."

"How much talking can you get done in a movie?"

"Yeah, we've thought of that. We're going to the midnight movie so we can have a late dinner first."

"Does it have to be tonight, Julia? We planned this for almost two months," Ellie lamented.

She was right, but my heart sank. I wasn't being a great friend, and I hadn't heard from Ryan, in any case. He did tell me he had a study group for his chem lab, so maybe it was running late. My phone was sitting on the bed next to me, and I looked at the screen. Blank. He hadn't texted or called.

"Maybe Ryan and I can go out tomorrow night," I admitted. I wanted to tell Ellie I needed to text Ryan before I committed, but that would sound silly. I was already committed to going with her, and I should have told Ryan so this afternoon, instead of making plans with him.

Was I really almost ditching plans with one best friend for another? Especially when they weren't even set? I wasn't sure if I'd forgotten about going with Ellie, or time with Ryan was just beginning to take priority over everything else.

Ever since I'd been sick last month, and I'd spent the entire weekend at his apartment, we'd seen each other practically every day. I kept telling myself we were just friends, because I had no indication from him that he wanted to be more, but he was amazing and sweet. I'd have to be a blind idiot not to realize how wonderful he was. That said, I couldn't become one of the gaggle of women on campus who swooned whenever he walked into a room or gazed adoringly at him like insipid morons. I inwardly cringed at the thought. I was certain a big part of the reason he liked to hang out with me was because I didn't fawn all over him.

He hadn't even tried to hold my hand, kiss me or made even a single move that indicated he thought of me as anything other than a friend, but the casual way he draped his arm over my shoulder sometimes, or when our hands would accidentally touch, was affecting me in ways I didn't want to analyze. In the weeks after I first met him, I had serious insecurities about my abilities to attract him, given the platonic state of our relationship. So, I told myself I couldn't let myself get wrapped up in romantic dreams of Ryan. Too many women wanted him, anyway, and I didn't want to compete.

I cleared my throat and looked up at her. "You're right, El. I'll get ready in a flash!" I jumped up from the bed and ran into my bedroom to get ready. I pulled a black dress from the closet and threw it on the bed. Picking up my phone, I began to type out a text to Ryan. Regret surged and tightened my heart, but I tried to push it down. I'd looked forward to this club opening for a long time, and it would be fun. I'd *make it fun* or die trying. I need to stop acting like an idiot. It was one night.

One night… without Ryan.

*****

Ryan ~

I glanced at the clock on the wall. 10 PM.

Fuck!

I was agitated. I felt claustrophobic and couldn't wait to get the hell out of the lab. My lab partner, Nathan, kept yammering on, asking me to give him tips on landing some girl he was hot for. I grimaced. What the fuck gave him the idea I could help him? I'd rather he just focus on the assignment so I could get the hell out of there. I hadn't had a chance to message Julia, and I felt bad about it. I promised I'd get back to her before seven, and it was already ten. My chest expanded as I set up the vacuum flask and aspirator. I was sure she'd be pissed by now, so our plans were probably flushed.

Nathan stopped talking and watched what I was doing. He'd dropped the first flask, and we'd had to start over from the beginning. It pissed me off, considering I was planning on the movie with Julia, but I did my best not to let it show.

"Dude, that's not right. We're supposed to grow the crystals out of the solution. So, what are you doing?"

"This isn't the first time I've synthesized acetylsalicylic acid, Nate. Trust me. My brother Aaron and I did this stuff all the time. We didn't get science kits for Christmas, but we did experiments all the time. We both wanted to be doctors, like my dad, and he taught us stuff like this on a regular basis. Doing it this way is quicker."

"What are you doing, exactly?"

"I'm creating a vacuum to separate the liquid from the solid, but it will still be too slow. I don't want to be here all night."

"Won't we get in trouble for not following instructions?"

I grunted, sarcasm my only acknowledgment of what he'd asked. "Can you get that filter paper and weigh it, please? Do it twice to make sure it's accurate. And, no, we won't get in trouble. We should get an extra credit for knowing how to do it more than one way; but we don't even need to tell Dr. Johnson. All we need is the correct weight of solid from the solution and we'll ace it."

Nate took the paper to the scale and calibrated it, before writing down the weight and handing it back to me. I had the solution flask chilling in an ice water bath as I rigged up the makeshift vacuum, securing a Buchner funnel to the top of the vacuum flask and placing the piece of coffee filter that Nate had weighed into it. It would collect the solids from the saturated solution. We would then weigh it again, subtract the weight of the filter paper, and we'd have our finished weight of the acid solids.

After the solution was poured into the funnel, the aspirator began to suck the liquid into the flask at a snail's pace, drop by frustrating drop. *Ugh!* I pulled the phone out and looked at the screen, and I had three messages. I scrolled through them and landed on the one from Julia.

Since I didn't hear from you, I went to HotSpot with Ellie. I promised her months ago anyway. It's the grand opening and

I'd forgotten. Sorry! Hope your experiment turns out. Maybe
we can do the movie tomorrow night?

Disappointment, and a new rush of anger at Nathan, surged
through me. I couldn't go the following night because some girl
in my trig class invited me to a keg party her sorority was
throwing at their house off campus. When Aaron found out,
there was no getting out of going. He was all about meeting new
girls. I considered that I could invite Julia and Ellie to come
along, but the woman who'd invited me had done it because she
wanted to get to know me, and it would be rude to invite other
women. Especially Julia. I'd be talking to her all night, and
besides, she might think bringing her would be a fucked up thing
to do. I was royally screwed.

I glanced impatiently at Nate. He was washing the crystals
by putting more distilled water through the aspirator. The
substance had to be as pure as we could possibly make it to get
to the correct weight. Any overage would lower our grade. It had
to be exact.

I ran a hand over the stubble on my jaw, scratched along its
edge before turning my back to Nate and typed out my reply to
Julia.

I got hung up at the lab making aspirin with Nate.
Tomorrow night won't work, but how about Sunday? I'm really
sorry about tonight.

If the girls were at a club, I knew there was no way Julia
would get back to me tonight. Part of me wanted to finish up at
the lab then wait outside her dorm or go to the club. I sighed. I'd
look like an idiot if I did that.

I realized I was missing her, and it was unsettling. She was
becoming the best friend I'd ever had. I didn't know if it was
because I could talk to her about things I couldn't discuss with
Aaron, or the attraction I felt that made me want to spend every

waking moment with her. Admittedly, she was easier on the eyes, smelled better, and, maybe best of all, she fed me.

There was no way in hell I was going to chase her down. That was just weird, and it might send the wrong message, though I was unclear what message I wanted to send. She was beautiful and sexy, and I couldn't get her out of my head.

I checked the connection between the flask and the rubber tube that helped create the suction.

Nate was bent over his phone, but suddenly popped up, excited. "Dude, this girl I'm dating asked me to come over to her apartment right now because her roommate isn't home. I think I'm gonna get laid. Do you mind if I bail?"

Sure, I thought. *Fucking leave me with finishing the experiment, and then cleanup alone. Why the hell not? Your clumsy ass has already ruined my night.* My mouth thinned as I pressed my lips into a line. "Really?" I asked in exasperation.

"Dude, *come on*," he pleaded with me. "I've been trying to get into this girl's pants since the beginning of the year."

"Okay." I nodded toward the door, silently telling him to get the fuck out. "But you owe me."

"You got it. Thanks!"

Nate left, and I turned back to the flask to check the progress of the experiment. Drip. Drip. *Fucking drip.*

*****

I rolled over in my bed, burying my face in the pillow, and threw an arm over my head. The sun was shining in through the window—the blinds were bent almost to the point of being destroyed. *I'll ask mom to get new ones over Thanksgiving*, I thought. The morning sun leaked through into the room and landed right in my face. I groaned in protest. There were noises coming from Aaron's room. The apartment we shared was in an old house, not far from campus.

The night before, I'd come home from the lab to an empty apartment, grabbed a beer, turned on the TV, and ordered pizza. Granted, I was under age and shouldn't have been drinking, but one of Aaron's older frat brothers left them in our fridge, so whatever. I was bored, feeling agitated, and needed to take the edge off. I hoped one or two beers might make me sleepy.

I'd gnawed on the pizza at the same time as watching the lame movie that was playing on HBO. Anxious irritation with myself for checking my phone every ten minutes, looking for a text from Julia nagged at me. It never came in, and the hours ticked by at a crawl. Three beers later, my eyes finally started to get heavy. I'd pushed up from the couch and somehow ended up sans clothes and flopped across my bed.

The sound of a woman giggling nudged me awake. I raised my head so I could glance over my shoulder, my eyes opened to a squint. The giggle wasn't one I recognized, so who in the hell was it? I tried to focus on the form in the doorway. Her hair was unnaturally red, to the point of being obnoxious, and she was wearing bright pink panties but nothing else.

"Nice ass, Ryan. Maybe I was in bed with the wrong Matthews."

The door to my room was open, so apparently my ass was on display. I didn't recognize the girl, and I reached down to pull the sheet over me. "What the hell? Do you mind?" My hand held the sheet together around my waist, and I pushed up off the bed to take three steps and yell down the hall at Aaron. "Yo! Dude! Can you keep your toys in your own room, please?"

I frowned at the nameless girl who was looking me up and down and preening in front of me. She ran her fingers through one side of her long hair and made no move to cover her bare tits from my view. Her skin was ruddy and covered in freckles, and her nipples brownish. Instead of turning me on as she intended, it just pissed me off.

"If you'll excuse me," I said. My free hand grabbed the edge of the door and I flung it shut with a slam. Seriously, it wasn't like me to be so rude, but I was feeling pensive. If she didn't have any fucking manners then I didn't need them either.

I fell back onto my bed and the springs squeaked. My parents' idea of roughing it at college went a little far in my estimation. When my phone chimed a few seconds later, I rolled over to retrieve it off of the floor. Finally! A text from Julia.

I just saw your text, sorry. I didn't get home until after two. What's going on tonight? Hot date?

Damn the party tonight, and damn how shitty I felt having to tell her. I wasn't sure why I felt like I wanted to lie and say it was some boys' night out instead of what it really was. I closed my eyes briefly, considering what to say before opening them to type out my response.

Not sure how hot it is, or even if it's a date. I was invited to a sorority party.

I crawled from the bed, buck-naked and walked into the bathroom, carrying my phone with me. The one saving grace of this shitty apartment was that each bedroom had its own bathroom, albeit a small one. I glanced in the mirror. I looked like hell. My hair was standing up all over my head and I had a thick growth of beard on my jaw. I scratched at it absently and glanced down at my silent phone. *Shit!* I reached in and turned on the shower, not bothering to adjust the temperature of the water.

Her response came in as I climbed under the hot spray. It was too hot and burned my chest. I jumped back, cussing at myself, and fumbled with the faucet. I leaned out to look at Julia's text, without picking up the phone.

Oh, okay. Well, have fun. I'll just talk to you tomorrow.

I grimaced at the trite response. At least it *seemed* trite. Maybe she didn't even mean it that way, and maybe it was all in my head. I got back in the shower, arguing with myself. We'd met less than two months ago, but since last month when she stayed the weekend, it had become a habit to see each other, or at least talk, every day. We'd fallen into being friends after an uncomfortable few weeks where my dick rebelled against my brain. Who was I kidding? It still rebelled just about every time I saw her, but I liked being around her, despite the constant fight with my libido. She was funny, and smart, and it was easy being with her. I could be myself.

We weren't dating, so what the fuck was my problem? I wasn't even sure I wanted to date Julia because it might damage the amazing friendship we shared. Yet, it felt strangely uncomfortable telling her I couldn't see her because I would be out with someone else. It was stupid! If I'd gotten that text from Aaron, Nate, or even any other woman I knew, I wouldn't have given it a second thought. I would have taken it at face value, end of story.

I was overthinking. *Way* overthinking. Sexually, I wanted her, so that had to be the reason for my confusion. Did I want more than friendship? Was I afraid to hurt her feelings? Whatever the hell it was, I had to figure it out and fast. We were friends, and that was that. She wasn't giving me anything specific that hinted she wanted anything beyond what it was, so why was I analyzing the shit out of it? I rinsed the shampoo from my hair and turned off the water. Dripping wet, I grabbed my phone and typed out a quick response.

Okay, I'll call you when I get up.

*****

So, all day Saturday, I could have studied but I wasn't motivated beyond a couple hours with the books. Thanksgiving break was coming up, and classes the coming week would be weak, at best. Stanford would only be in session on Monday and Tuesday, so the week would be short. I went for a run in the cold, late fall air and puttered around the apartment watching sports and doing laundry for the rest of the day.

I didn't hear from Julia at all, and though I didn't really expect to, I was still thinking about her. She had a paper due in her business writing class, and she'd no doubt be working on it. I was dying to ask how her night went, but I didn't really want to talk about the party I was obligated to go later that night. Maybe the lack of communication was best, even if it didn't sit well. I just wanted this night to be done and over with. Tomorrow, Julia wouldn't ask me about it, and we'd hang out as we planned. It probably bothered me more than it did her. I shook my head, wishing my thoughts would stop.

Aaron was screwing off the entire day with some of his fraternity brothers; which made it easy for me to stay in the apartment to study. The math assignment I was working on blurred, as my thoughts wandered again. The ringing of my phone startled me out of it, and I quickly reached for it. I knew it would be my mother because she called every Saturday around the same time.

"Hey, Mom," I answered.

"How's my baby?"

"Mom, please." I rolled my eyes, got up, and walked into the kitchen. It was small and littered with remnants of my late night pizza delivery. Beer bottles were scattered around the counter and on the coffee table in the living room. The pizza had been terrible, but it was the only pizza place that delivered late at night. Julia referred to it as The Cardboard Palace. "Are you ever going to stop calling me your baby?"

"You'll always be my baby. Is Aaron home?"

I shook my head out of habit, even though she couldn't see me. "No, but I'm meeting him for dinner in a bit, and then later, he's dragging me to a party."

"Funny, I spoke to him earlier, and he said you were the one invited by one of the sorority sisters."

"That's a technicality. He's the one who wants to go." I opened the refrigerator and pulled out a carton of juice, opened it up, and took a pull directly from the container.

"It will be fun, won't it? Tell me about the girl. Is she pretty?"

I cringed internally at my lack of facts. I hardly knew anything about her but tried to remember the details of her face so I could at least not sound like a total prick to my mom. "I don't know her that well, but yeah, she's pretty." I was holding the phone between my shoulder and ear so I could close the juice and place it back in the fridge.

"You don't sound overly enthused, honey."

"You should be glad I'm not. It's a kegger. Loud music, lots of people drunk off of their asses and half of them puking by the driveway. And probably weed. I can always smell it in the air at these things." I grinned at her audible gasp. "Um, except not Aaron and me, Mom. We just go to watch the girls." I couldn't help teasing. My mother was sort of refined, and rowdy college antics might not have occurred to her unless I planted the seed. She'd attended private schools her entire life.

"Sure you do, Ryan. I wasn't born last night."

I laughed. "Sure, it should be fun. I guess."

"About Thanksgiving; I have your flights arranged for Tuesday evening. I thought we'd get to spend a long weekend together and you boys wouldn't be so tired. Dad is really looking forward to having you both home."

"Me, too. Aaron has a new girl he's into, so he might not be so keen to come to Chicago."

"Well, that's too bad. We haven't seen you two since August."

"I know, but you know how it is, Mom."

"Honestly, Ryan, I thought it would be you who would be reluctant to come home, for the same reason."

"Naw. I miss home. Do you think Dad can get tickets to the Blackhawks?"

"I'm sure he'd love that!"

The call ended with me writing down the airline information and making note of the time we had to be at the airport. It was almost six, and Aaron would be on my ass to meet him out for dinner before the party, so I pulled a clean pair of jeans and boxer briefs from the dresser and blue button-down from the closet before heading into the bathroom to shower.

*****

The next morning, I woke up in bed with the girl who invited me to the party. Her body strung over me, and she was sleeping soundly, the dead weight making it hard to move. I lifted my head and looked around. It was bright from the mid-morning sunlight streaming in. I squinted and searched for a clock, finding a digital alarm type sitting on an old crate next to her bed. My clothes had to be somewhere, but I could only see one of my socks. It was the second morning in a row that I awoke to be blinded by the fucking sun. My head was pounding like a mother; a reminder of how much alcohol I'd consumed the night before.

The night was a blur of loud music, flirting, and beer. I'd lost count how many beers I'd downed, but it was definitely more than usual. I remembered checking my phone for Julia's text between each round, only to be disappointed and getting more and more pissed off as the hours wore on, so when Annie, the girl who'd invited me, convinced me to dance, I did. The music changed to a slow song, she started kissing me, and pushing her tits into my chest, and I went with it.

Aaron disappeared with a pretty buxom blonde he'd introduced to me briefly, and I was left with a woman I barely knew. She was nice and attentive. I relaxed more as the evening wore on and a few more beers later, when she invited me up to her room, the party was in full swing. I went, thinking it would be easier to talk. I wasn't drunk, but I'd been feeling good. Her roommate was still out, and she got me another beer from the small refrigerator, which stood beneath the window. It was quieter, and the beer was better than the keg beer they were serving. She plugged in her iPod and we just sat and talked for a while, and almost the entire time I was comparing her to Julia. I hated myself. When she kissed me, I closed my eyes and allowed myself to imagine green eyes and long, dark hair. I knew what I was doing. Part of me felt like hell doing it, and another part of me wanted the fantasy. I'd never have Julia, so I closed my eyes and let my mind convince me I wasn't with this obscure girl who was now laying on top of me, yet meant nothing.

I had no clue what to do next. She was nice, but this is as far as this would go. I was a dick for having sex with her, but I wasn't going to compound it by leading her on, and I itched to make my escape. Panic seized my chest momentarily until I saw the empty foil packet on the nightstand. Thank God, I wasn't so drunk off my ass that I forgot to be safe.

I gently pushed her sleeping form off my chest and scooted closer to the edge of the bed. My phone chimed from the floor. It had fallen from the back pocket of my jeans and some sixth sense told me that was Julia texting. I wanted to talk to her, but obviously I couldn't do it here. I scouted the room and found my clothes strewn across the floor, mixed with Annie's in a pile between her bed and her roommate's empty one. In two minutes flat, I was dressed, out the door and in my CRV. I ran a hand through my hair. My mouth was dry, and I wanted to brush my teeth, shower and shave, as if doing so would erase the events of the prior evening.

I shoved the key in the ignition. It was cold, my breath clearly visible in the November air. I was shivering, and I didn't want Julia to ask questions so I couldn't call her as I wanted. I reached out, flipping on the heat full blast, but only frigid air rushed from the vents. I threw my phone on the passenger seat and shoved the car in gear. The sooner I got home, the better I'd feel. I only hoped Aaron was otherwise occupied so I could get inside without his knowledge. The last thing I needed was him running his mouth about my walk of shame in front of Julia. Technically, I'd done nothing wrong, aside from casual sex, but something in my gut said Julia did not need to know.

*****

Julia ~

It was 11 AM on Sunday morning and I hadn't heard from Ryan. In two months, this was probably the first Sunday we weren't already on the phone or meeting up somewhere by this time. I tried to shrug it off. I'd slept in a little longer than usual after my night out with Ellie, and maybe Ryan was still sleeping as well.

My stomach rumbled slightly. I hadn't eaten last night because I planned on eating with Ryan, and after we hit the club, I'd forgotten about it. I hated living in the dorms because it meant I couldn't eat without showering and getting dressed first. Ellie was already MIA, and I wondered if she was still in the shower or already gone.

Walking down the hall to the shower carting my towel and the bucket that contained my shampoo, conditioner and shower gel. I was reminded why Ellie already left. There were two shower rooms on our floor—one on each end—and when I opened the one closest to my room, I was faced with the screeching voice of Amy Jefferson. I cringed and leaned against the wall. I had a writing class with her and her personality was grating. She had bright red hair cropped short, almost like a man's, except for the longer bit on top, and her face was covered with a bad case of acne. I would have felt sorry for her, except for her narcissistic tendency. She had aspirations of being an opera star, thinking she had the greatest voice ever, and went around making comparisons of her voice to Sarah Brightman and dissing Barbara Streisand. It was all I could do not to tell her off or roll my eyes right in her face when she started that crap. She was in flat-out belting mode, and I debated leaving and making the walk to the other showers on the other end.

"Amy, who sings this song?" someone asked from a stall on the end, her voice loud enough to shout over the singing and the sound of three running showers.

"Celine Dion!" Amy stopped singing long enough to answer happily.

"How about we keep it that way?" the unknown voice retorted dryly.

I couldn't help giggling. Most of the dorms on campus were large and I didn't know all of the girls personally. I didn't recognize the voice, but she was funnier than hell.

"That's rude!" Amy said angrily.

"You're rude! My ears are bleeding from that shit. Stop torturing us, already," the anonymous girl retorted.

I couldn't stifle the full-out laugh that burst out, and so I darted into a stall, pulling the curtain shut behind me. The last thing I needed was for Amy to know I was laughing, even though I wasn't the only one.

"Well said, Jen!" Ellie's voice interjected. "Enough, already."

My eyes widened. Ellie was so soft-spoken and kind, it wasn't like her to add her support to any type of criticism. I shed my flannel pajama pants and T-shirt and was in and out of the shower in just a few minutes. Ellie was dressed and towel drying her short hair by the time I got back to our room.

"Can you believe that ding-dong, Amy?" Ellie asked incredulously.

"Yeah, she's delusional. Who was that other girl? Jen, I think you called her?"

"I don't know her that well, but she's cool. She's in one of my liberal arts classes."

"She's funny."

Ellie nodded, picking up the blow dryer. "Ryan called," she said.

My heart leapt a little in my chest. "He did?"

"Sorry. I answered it when I saw who it was. He wants you to call him back. Did you see him last night?"

"No. He had a date, I think."

I could feel her eyes follow my movements. "Do you think he was mad that you didn't meet him the other night?"

"I doubt it." I went to pick out a pair of jeans and a purple V-neck T-shirt. The black leather portfolio that my mother had given me for my last birthday was tucked between the foot of my bed and the closet. It had been empty since I'd come to school, but last night, after a night spent alone drawing, it now had its first occupant. I flushed a little.

Our room was small, so privacy was limited while we were both there. I was thankful she'd been out on a date of her own when my stupid emotions got the better of me. I was shaken by how Ryan going on a date affected me. I got all choked up and sad that he was with some faceless woman I didn't know. I'd come to rely on his presence, and I wasn't prepared for how miserable the prospect of losing time with him made me feel. I felt ridiculously wounded, but I had no right to feel that way.

I cleared my throat, the memory of it all feeling fresh and new. The last thing I needed was to relive it.

Ellie finished drying her hair, and I took my turn in front of the mirror to dry mine, pull it back, and put on a little make-up. I stared at my reflection, mentally comparing my green eyes, pale complexion, and dark hair to the imaginary beauty I'd conjured in my head. What if he got serious about some girl and we couldn't hang out any more? I didn't want to think about it.

"When do you leave for Kansas City, Julia?"

"Wednesday morning. I'm sort of looking forward to it." I wanted some perspective, and I hoped distance away from Ryan was the one, sure way to get it. I sat down on the bed and pulled on some thick socks.

Ellie was sitting on her own bed, which was across from mine. Both of them were twin beds in the small dorm room. She grabbed one of her textbooks from the shelf over her desk and opened it. "Aren't you going to call Ryan back?"

I shrugged. I should. I had no right to feel indignant about his date, but I still felt fragile and I didn't know how to handle it. I wasn't sure if I was capable of hiding my feelings from him.

"Probably. I want to go over my paper once more before I email it to my professor. I think I'll take my laptop to the library."

The truth was, I had a lot left to do on it. The night before I'd felt too crappy to concentrate and self-medicated the whole evening away, taking a hot shower, then spending the rest of the night drawing a portrait of Ryan. It was the first I'd done of him, and I spent hours on it, wanting to get every nuance of his face perfect. Somehow, it helped ease the ache because in drawing him, he was with me.

"Okay." I could sense she had questions, but she didn't press me.

I was in serious danger of getting my heart crushed. I'd known it for weeks, but it didn't stop me from spending time with him. If I were honest, my time with Ryan was the best part of my day.

I threw a heavy sweater on over my T-shirt, my leftover melancholy not diminishing by Ryan's attempt to get in touch with me. In the process of packing my computer and notes into my backpack, my phone jingled. I knew who it was before I picked it up and rather than being thrilled, I was apprehensive. Still, I read his text.

Jules, are you around? I called. Did Ellie tell you?

I quickly typed out an answer before sliding my arms into my coat and grabbing my backpack.

Yes. I'm on my way to the library to finish my paper.

His response was immediate.

Oh. I hoped you were done so we could hang out today.

My heart swelled with relief. Whatever happened on that date, it wasn't enough to preoccupy Ryan today.

I'd like to, but I should study at least a couple of hours.

Can you meet me for coffee later? Maybe 3 or 4?

4 will be better. The Student Union?

Cool. If you're finished by then, maybe we can hit the movie tonight?

Yes. :)

Great. See you then.

Suddenly, everything was right with my world.

~3~

Christmas in Chicago

Ryan ~

I was bored shitless; lying on the floor of my room at my parents' house with my lower legs flung on top of the bed. I didn't know what to fucking do with myself. I'd been home two days, and I was going stir crazy.

I tossed the baseball against the wall opposite me. My dad caught it from a pop fly on opening day two years before when Aramis Ramirez was at bat. I threw it again, remembering how pissed Aaron had been that I'd won the coin toss and, in turn, this ball. In retrospect, I realized I probably could have just let him have it. I rolled it around in my hand, admiring the smooth, almost-new leather before I resumed the mindless activity. Thump, thump, thump... The noise and the motion of it providing the white noise I needed.

At the last minute, Aaron had decided to stay behind at college with Jenna. We'd both come home for Thanksgiving, but he refused to spend two weeks away from his girlfriend. I would have joined him, but my mother would have been completely crushed having both of us bail on Christmas at home.

Now I was stuck in this rotten cold weather without a damn thing to do. My dad was called in for emergency surgery, so he wasn't even in the house. Thump, thump, thump... I threw it harder in my frustration.

The door to my room burst open, and my mother stuck her head in. "Ryan! What is all that banging? What are you doing in here?"

I flushed guiltily. "Oh, sorry," I mumbled, holding up the ball in explanation.

Her features softened. She was always so elegant, dressed to perfection, her shoulder-length hair, the same color as mine, was never out of place, even at home. We were a study in opposites, now, however, as I laid around like a slob in baggy gray sweatpants, white crew socks and an old Nine Inch Nails T-shirt. I scratched my head then my stomach. I definitely needed a shower.

"I know you're bored, honey. Can you call some of your high school friends?"

I sat up and shrugged. "Maybe." I'd only been at school a few months, but now, the thought of my old friends didn't excite me. Earlier, I'd thought about trying to get together a game of ice hockey at the local rink but reconsidered. No doubt, the ice time would be monopolized by local league tournaments over the holidays.

"I'm going downtown shopping later. Do you want to come?"

"Maybe," I mumbled again, my lack of enthusiasm tangible. I hated shopping. Period. Especially shopping downtown. I hated the traffic; I hated the slushy streets, I hated hauling bags and sweating in stores because I was wearing a coat. I stood up and went to my desk to fire-up the laptop. "I guess I do need to buy a few presents. I'm not good at buying stuff for girls and I need to get Julia something. I could use your help."

Mom came into the room and sat on the edge of the bed. My room was pretty much unchanged from the day I left for Stanford. My high school football and basketball jerseys were stuck to the walls with pushpins among posters of Milla Jovovich and Megan Fox, sports trophies, concert tickets and a bunch of pictures.

"What does she like?"

"Everything. She's cool." I could get her a couple of tickets to the San Francisco 49ers or the Oakland A's and she'd be happy with it. Jules was unassuming and easy going.

"Is she the tomboy-type?"

I huffed in amusement as I looked through my email. "Hardly. Why would you assume that?"

"I don't know. She hangs out with my son but she's not his girlfriend? That's my first clue. You never spend any time with girls you aren't dating, that I recall."

Something inside me stopped. "Yeah, well, Jules is different. She has a brain, and we can talk about stuff. We relate on many levels. She's just cool," I said again, searching for the right words to describe Julia without making it sound like I had a crush on her.

"Ryan! Are you insinuating that most women are mindless?" Her eyebrow shot up in disapproval.

"No, it's just..." I paused, searching for the right words. "Julia doesn't yap on and on about clothes and make-up and meaningless crap. She isn't always batting her eyelashes and acting dumb."

"Ryan." My mother cautioned. "Girls bat their eyelashes? Nice exaggeration."

"Come on, Mom!" I lamented. "You know what I mean. She's the first girl who I've ever respected like that." She shot me another reprimanding look. "Besides you, I mean." I flashed a full-on grin, and she smiled in return.

"Girls like bath oil, shower gel, and lotions. You could get her a gift basket or gift card."

"Ugh! Seriously? That shit's lame. It's what you get your kindergarten teacher or old Aunt Hester. Besides, I heard Jenna dissing another guy who gave some girl one of those things for her birthday. There isn't thought in something like that. It's too generic."

Mom chuckled. "If you like Julia that much, why aren't you dating her?"

I stopped playing with my computer as I contemplated the question. I half-assed shrugged and shook my head. It wasn't as if I hadn't asked myself the same question. "We're good friends. It might get weird if we dated."

"Is she pretty?"

"Yeah," I answered without thinking. "Super hot. Aaron thinks my dick's broken."

"Ryan!"

Shit! Did I just say that to my mom? I flushed guiltily then grinned. "What?" I asked incredulously. "He's the one who said it, not me!"

My mother rolled her eyes and smiled despite her motherly chagrin. "I'll have to have a talk with your brother. So, she is pretty."

"She's, er… amazing."

"Amazing, huh?"

"Yeah, but amazing goes way beyond looks. She's smart and funny. She's fun to hang out with."

"Do you think if you spend so much time together, you should get her something a little personal for Christmas?"

"Probably, but I don't know what."

My computer dinged and an IM came up from Julia. I looked guiltily at my mom, hoping she'd take the hint and exit my room.

"Okay, we'll figure it out. After I'm done putting a roast in the crock pot, I'll have a few hours, and we can go out."

"Sure." My computer dinged again and still I waited until my mother left.

Ryan? You there?

Yes. Bored as hell. You?

Same. My dad is working on some big murder case, and he's never here. This house feels like a tomb when it's empty. I wish I'd stayed at Stanford.

Funny, I had the same idea.

How's the weather, there? :-/

It was obvious she knew it was like an iceberg. California might be cool, but Chicago was colder than hell.

Frigid, I typed back.

I don't want to hear about your last one-nighter. LOL

I laughed out loud at her teasing remark.

Ha ha. *Shut up. It's nice here. Wanna come over?* :)

I wish I could! I typed furiously on the remote keyboard, wishing I could hop an early plane back to California. *My mom would kill me, though. She has this big shindig planned for Christmas Eve and Christmas Day.*

My dad's living at his office. I've seen him for 2 hours in the 2 days I've been here, so it looks like it's turkey burger-ville and rented movies for Christmas.

You know there are all kinds of bird parts in that nasty shit! Beaks, skin.... Gross! Can you get on Skype? I hated the thought of her all alone on Christmas and I wanted to see her face.

Yeah. Give me a minute.

I sat, impatiently tapping my foot, my knee bouncing obnoxiously, as I waited for Julia to log on. I knew I looked like hell, but she wouldn't care. I ran my hand through my hair and shoved my Cubs hat on my head, pushing the hair around the edge beneath it.

It wasn't long before her call came in, and I opened the window. She wore a dark pink hoodie with a Nike swoosh in navy blue across the front, and her hair was down and flow-y. She didn't have on make-up, but she still looked beautiful in a natural, unpretentious sort of way.

"Hey," she said. "I thought I was gonna get a break from your unbearable presence for a couple of weeks, Matthews."

I grinned and leaned back in my chair. "You know you miss me, but I won't make you say it." Julia looked at me through the computer, her brows furrowed and mouth pursed. I could tell she was doing her best not to smile.

"Whatever. As if you could. I can see your ego hasn't taken a hiatus," she deadpanned.

I burst out laughing at her joke. It was just like her to goad me. "It's gonna snow tomorrow so the lake effect will probably have me stranded in the house. Yay."

"It's pretty cool here, but I don't think we'll get snow."

"So, will your dad be around at all on Christmas?"

"One of his partners has this big to-do on Christmas Eve and he wants me to go with him. It's a bunch of stuffed shirts, so I don't think I'm going."

I shifted in my chair, not loving how uncomfortable I felt at the thought of her canoodling at a party without me. I knew only too well what happened in situations like that.

"Why? Is there some hot law student he wants you to meet?"

"I'm not interested in law students. They're almost as unbearable as doctor wannabes." She smiled big at me through the screen.

I laughed at her teasing. "That's what I hear. You could always come here," I suggested sheepishly, deep down hoping to hell she'd agree and hop on the first flight out. I never got nervous with girls, and this was my closest friend, so it was annoying that I felt nervous asking.

"To Chicago?"

"Yeah."

"Seriously?"

"Yeah," I said again. "But you gotta get here before the storm hits, so we can be snowed in together."

Julia inhaled and shook her head slightly. "You're serious."

"Yes!" I quickly opened Expedia.com and began looking for flights. "The best deal will probably be out of San Francisco International."

"Ryan, slow down. I have to speak to my dad, and don't you have to ask your parents if it's okay?"

"Nah. Aaron's room is open." I probably should ask them, but I'd rather beg forgiveness than ask permission if it meant Julia would be here in a few hours' time.

"Ew. Really, you want me to sleep in Aaron's room? Dude, that's weird. It probably smells like a sweaty jock."

A smile split across my face as I kept up my flight search. "We have two other rooms, but one is my dad's study, and Mom is remodeling the other, so you can have my room, if you'd rather." I winced a little, thinking Julia would find my room juvenile. For sure she'd make fun of the girly posters.

"I don't want to inconvenience anyone."

"Julia! Shut up and call your old man, will ya? I'm booking the ticket right now." I found a ticket out that afternoon and then yanked out the printout of my own return itinerary, and booked another seat on the same flight. Her seat wouldn't be next to mine, but I'd deal with that later.

"Ryan, wait! I can't afford this, and I don't want to ask my dad."

"I said: *I'm* booking the ticket. Consider it my Christmas gift to you. I've been struggling with what to get you anyway, so this is perfect!" My blood was racing with excitement and anticipation. Suddenly, the break didn't seem so mundane after all.

I ran across the room to the jeans lying in a pile of dirty clothes and began to rummage through the pockets for my wallet and debit card.

"Ryan, will you wait?" Julia shouted over the computer.

I bit my lip over a smile as I sat back down at the computer and began to type in the card information. "Better hurry, your flight leaves in three hours."

"You're impossible! I should let you lose your money and stew in your own juice!" She was moving around her room and I could hear a big thump from what was surely her closet. "Ouch!"

"What happened?"

"My hiking boots just fell off a shelf and hit me in the head! I don't know what to bring? Do you get dressed up on Christmas? I don't have gifts for your parents! I'll feel like an idiot."

"I'll see you in a few hours. The flight is direct, United 1489 to O'Hare. I'll be waiting just beyond the gates."

"You're crazy!"

"This will be great!" I was so excited I could hardly sit still. She said something else while she rummaged through her closet, but I couldn't catch it.

"Just stop your mumbling and get your little ass on that plane." At the sound of Julia's tinkling laughter, I raced out of my room and down the stairs to inform my mother that my best friend would be with us for the remainder of Christmas break.

Julia ~

The jet bridge was filled with the sounds of people talking, laughing and the grating whiz of the wheels of the many carry-on cases being carted up to the terminal. Butterflies filled my stomach.

I had to admit when Ryan suggested I fly to Chicago for Christmas, I was thrilled and filled with excited anticipation. I'd never seen Chicago in the winter, but it was the fact Ryan insisted I come, that was responsible for the nervous adrenaline pumping through my veins. This was Ryan, my best friend. My gorgeous best friend, true, but still, he was like my other half, the calm in my storm, the cream in my coffee. I told myself it was the prospect of meeting his parents that had my stomach all tied up in knots.

I'd shoved a few changes of clothes and the bare necessities into a carry-on and grabbed a cab to the airport. The fare was fifty dollars, and I charged it on the credit card my dad had given me for emergencies when I started college. I inwardly shrugged.

This *was* an emergency. I was dying of boredom at my dad's and seriously missing the easy camaraderie that Ryan and I shared. It was really the first time we'd been separated since we'd met, beyond a long weekend, and I'd been seriously unprepared for how much I'd miss him. I looked down at my Nike-clad feet and my stomach dropped. I hadn't had time to shower or change and still wore the tattered jeans and hoodie I'd thrown on that morning. The purple coat that was shoved under my left arm was the first one I could grab as I'd rushed from my father's house. The first impression with Ryan's family certainly would not be what I wanted. The butterflies did somersaults in my stomach again, and I swallowed hard, wishing I had a soda or bottle of water with me. There were plenty of places to stop and pick one up, but my anxiousness to get to Ryan overshadowed the need. My iPhone blipped in the front pocket of my sweatshirt, and my hand plunged in to retrieve it, a smile already plastered on my face. Typical impatience from Ryan, only this time, I mirrored the feeling.

Jules? You here?

I furiously typed my answer one-handed as I pulled my luggage behind me and made my way past the security checkpoint where out-going passengers were being screened. The lines were insane and I was thankful I didn't have to fight that mess.

Yeah. Walking into the main terminal.

The airport was huge, and the walk seemed endless, but when I saw the glass windows at the front of the terminal come into view, my eyes began the search for Ryan. He was leaning up against one of the large pillars, nonchalantly scanning the crowd, his hands shoved unceremoniously into the front pockets of his jeans, a black leather jacket covering his broad shoulders. My heart did the little flip it always did when I saw him, and as usual, I pushed it away. He was so gorgeous. I did have breasts and a vagina, so I wasn't sure why I expected to be immune to the incredible pull he held over women. Even Brian, an openly gay student who was a member of my philosophy discussion group, would gape and drool. Every time Ryan would come pick me up after one of our study sessions at the campus library, the guy would make it ridiculously obvious he was attracted. Ryan's discomfort on such occasions was palpable and I thought, hilarious.

"Brian is no different than the hordes of women fawning all over you constantly. That doesn't seem to bother you, Matthews!"

I'd mumbled under my breath. "And, he's prettier than some of them."

He'd had the grace to blush and shot me a look that could kill, his eyes warning me to stop my goading. "Shut up or I'll punish you," he warned with a quirk of his lips. "His dick would be the difference." Later, he'd held me down in my dorm room and tickled me furiously until I was screaming with laughter and begging him to stop the torture. He didn't let me go until I promised I'd never tease him about Brian again.

Ryan's face lit up with a brilliant smile when he caught sight of me. He quickly came forward and wrapped me in a tight bear hug. The scent of his cologne engulfed me as his arms tightened around my shoulders. I inhaled as deeply as I could, closing my eyes as my cheek pressed into the soft material of his sweatshirt over the solid muscles of his chest and my arms wound around his waist. I was keen on memorizing how he smelled and how it felt to be held in his strong arms. My coat dropped to the floor and the handle of my carry-on clanked against the tile as it dropped. Ryan had hugged me before. He'd given me numerous piggyback rides and slung his arm around my shoulders on countless occasions, but this hug had me plastered against every inch of his body, my softness smashed to the hard contours of his male form, my breasts crushed against his chest. It felt amazing, and I was in heaven. I felt flustered and unsettled as I moved back to glance up into his face. His blue eyes sparkled with excitement.

"I'm so glad you're here," he said. His voice oozed over me as his hands grabbed my shoulders. "My mom is circling the terminals and should be around to pick us up in a couple of minutes."

"I didn't have time to get ready. I look a mess. Thanks for that."

Ryan chuckled and bent to pick up my bag and coat. He pushed the handle down and easily slung the bag over his shoulder before handing the coat back with a sardonic grimace. "You'll look like The Giant Purple People Eater," he teased, "or, a bloated grape."

"Thanks," I retorted shortly. "Again, it's your fault, dickhead. I didn't even look at what I grabbed out of the closet!"

"Did you wear that when you were five?" His shoulder nudged into mine and I couldn't help but smile. "I don't think I can take you downtown in that. I may have to buy you a new one."

"It's fine."

"No, it's not. It's hideous!"

"Some of us aren't as vain as others," I shot back as we started to walk toward the large revolving doors that would take us out to the curb, silently dreading wearing the horrible thing. "You said it was going to be a blizzard here. I didn't think we'd do much beyond making a snowman in your backyard."

"Well, I certainly wouldn't lose you in that, even in a whiteout. Here comes my mom."

A sleek silver Lexus stopped and Ryan went around the back to deposit my bag in the trunk as a slender woman in a long black cashmere coat and black leather gloves emerged from behind the wheel. I didn't find similarities in their features, but her blue eyes and sandy hair were identical to her son's. She was impeccably groomed, which only made my unkempt appearance more annoying.

"Julia, it's so nice to meet you! I'm Ryan's mother, Elyse." She embraced me warmly as the cold Chicago wind whipped around us and blew my long hair across my face. It felt like I was being stabbed with icicles. I began to shiver and my teeth started chattering. I tried to smile through it all, hesitating to put on the ugly coat.

"Thank you, Mrs. Matthews. Sorry for the short notice."

She whisked my objection away with a casual wave of her hand. "It's no trouble at all, and you must call me Elyse. Ryan, you drive, darling. I want to get acquainted with your friend." She tossed Ryan the keys before he handed me my coat then held open the back passenger-side door and ushered me inside.

The drive and shopping trip proved to be a lot of fun, and I found an easy camaraderie with Ryan's mom. She was warm, easygoing, and very welcoming. She chatted on about Ryan and Aaron, the tree house they built in the backyard with their dad when they were ten, and how Ryan broke his arm when he fell out of it the following spring. Overall, there weren't many embarrassing things I'd be able to tease Ryan with when the need arose to blackmail him, but things changed that night at dinner.

"Ryan, have you bought any whores yet?" his father asked with a laugh.

I gasped and some of the roast beef I'd been eating got sucked into my lungs. I began coughing uncontrollably, covering my mouth with the fine linen napkin that had been resting in my lap. My eyes began to tear as my chest convulsed painfully.

"Jesus, Dad!" Ryan admonished, pushing back his chair and pounding on my back. "Sorry, Jules, it's a joke."

Elyse rose from her chair and rounded the table toward the two of us, the tears in my eyes increasing as I struggled to regain my breath between coughing spurts. She picked up the glass of ice water next to my plate and offered it to me. I coughed again, wiped my tears and reached for it. I was acutely conscious of Ryan's hand rubbing back and forth over my back between my shoulder blades.

"I'm so sorry, Julia. I often tease Ryan about his whores." The handsome face, so similar to his son's, flashed a full grin as I finally took my seat again. I raised my eyebrow at Ryan who ran his hand through his hair. His agitation was clear.

"Gabe, explain to the poor girl," Elyse insisted.

Ryan rolled his eyes. "Or not," he insisted forcefully.

"No, I'd like to hear this," I said with a laugh, then flushed when Ryan shot me a warning look. I guess he didn't think it was funny, but I sure as hell did.

His father burst out laughing. "I like this girl, son. She's smart."

"Smart *ass*, you mean."

"Ryan and Aaron went to summer camp for two weeks every summer from the age of seven. It had horseback riding, canoeing and a lot of other fun stuff. Ryan particularly liked the horses and he'd write home telling us he'd like to buy a horse, only he spelled it H O R E S, so it's been an ongoing joke. Ryan and his *whores*."

"Oh, my God!" I laughed out loud. "Awww!" I reached out and pushed against his arm roughly. "I guess not much has changed, huh?" I asked my friend.

"Nice, Julia." Ryan looked annoyed.

"Well?" I teased.

"Jealous?"

"In your dreams."

Four eyes bore into me as they waited for an explanation. "Um, well, it's just that Ryan dates a bunch, um… uh, a lot of girls like him."

Elyse rescued me from embarrassing myself further. "He's always had a bevy of girlfriends, but we've yet to meet anyone he's serious about. Only one he dated more than a month. Ryan, do you still keep in touch with Jennifer?"

"Mom!"

"What?" she asked, setting down her wine glass. "Surely it's nothing your best friend wouldn't already know."

"Can we just *not*... talk about that stuff? Please?" Ryan begged. He shifted uncomfortably in his chair, his face taking on a reddish-pink hue.

The truth was, I was feeling the pain as well. We never seemed to get around to talking about the past much, not when it came to relationships. We always focused on the present, but this particular conversation put me in a weird place. Of course, my subconscious knew he'd had at least one major girlfriend in his past. He was funny, smart and gorgeous. I wasn't stupid, but somehow I'd managed to keep the thought buried in the back of my mind. I glanced in Ryan's direction out of the corner of my eye. He was staring down at his plate.

After dinner, Ryan and I helped with the dishes without a lot of conversation and I started to wonder if maybe coming to Chicago was a bad idea. He stacked the last of the plates into the dishwasher after I'd rinsed them, then nodded in the direction of the stairs and I followed him to his room.

"Don't make fun of me," he said with a slight smile and went into his room ahead of me. He turned on a bedside lamp and the television on the wall opposite the double bed.

"What are *best friends* for?" I asked. I always thought of Ryan as my best friend, but it's never something we'd said to each other, nor had I ever heard him refer to me as such, but apparently he'd said it to his mother and I wanted him to know I caught it.

He flopped down on his bed as I glanced around his room. I could see his eyes follow me as I checked out the trophies and the photographs. I saw one of Ryan in a black tux with a blonde girl in a bright pink, sequined dress and guessed that must be the infamous Jennifer. He looked so handsome, and the girl gazed up into his face adoringly as Ryan looked at the camera. Thank God, he wasn't wearing some ridiculous bright pink tie and cummerbund but had chosen classic all the way. He looked perfect and I could barely rip my eyes away from the photo.

I sensed his hesitation; my face burned and my lungs felt on fire. I inhaled, trying to ease the heat and calm the weird emotions racing through me. He studied me intently.

"What?" I asked, the bed giving softly beneath my weight as I finally sat down next to him.

"Is that okay?" His jaw stiffened slightly and my eyes skittered over the shadow of whiskers shading it. My heart thumped unexpectedly in my chest. I knew what he wanted to know.

"Yeah. You are my best friend. Duh."

"Yeah. Good."

I wanted to put him at ease. "I told your mom I'd help her cook Christmas dinner. Do you have any traditions?"

"Sure. We have to suffer my dad's Aunt Mabel's fruitcake. It's so disgusting! Dad takes it and practically drowns it in rum to try to make it palatable and it still sucks ass. Don't eat it, whatever you do."

I laughed and grabbed the remote out of his hand. He let me take it without protest. "Doesn't your mother make your favorite dessert?"

"No. She said it's not holiday-ish."

"Hmmm. I always make my dad cake and prime rib for Christmas."

He watched me with sparkling eyes. "I like strawberry cheesecake, but that sounds delicious, too. What is it?"

I flipped from channel to channel and shrugged.

"Chocolate cake soaked with cherry liqueur, filled with cherries, whipped cream and chocolate shavings. It's a lot of work, but it's super yummy."

"Sounds good."

"Yeah, I know. It is." Tongue in cheek I waited for him to ask. He would ask. I would make him ask. The seconds ticked by, both of us staring at the T.V. without speaking. Finally, he caved.

"Will you make them and save me from the gross fruitcake?"

"I don't know. Your mom's right. Cheesecake isn't Christmas-y. Strawberries are out of season." I said, training my eyes on the T.V. and waiting, baiting Ryan more as I rattled off reasons not to make his beloved cheesecake.

Ryan huffed and laid down on his bed, finally leaning over and stealing the remote out of my hand. "Fine!" he muttered.

"Moody much?" My lips crept up at the corners.

"You tease me with that shit and then renege. Just remember, payback's a bitch."

I bit my lip to stop a laugh. "Fuck you. You called me a bloated grape! So what was it you were saying about payback?"

"Your ticket was $636 dollars and change. I take cash or check." His elbow nudged my arm as he shifted again then leaned into me as the channel settled onto HBO. The Bill Murray version of "A Christmas Carol" was just starting.

"Okay, I'll make it if you'll stop pouting already. But, you have to go to the store and buy the stuff."

"What?" he asked incredulously, a beautiful smile lighting up his face. "The fucking thing already cost me $636!"

A laugh erupted from my chest, and Ryan joined me. "It'll be worth every cent."

"It already is."

Ryan ~

Christmas break sped by after Julia came to Chicago. I actually regretted that it was over. We stayed up most of the night playing video games and watching old movies. I'd considered that spending so much time together, day-in and day-out, we might get sick of each other. Didn't happen.

Now we were at O'Hare and my mother was dropping us off at the curb. Julia was wrapped in my leather jacket because I'd thrown that purple atrocity in the trash the second day after she arrived. We'd been dumped on by a foot and a half of lake effect snow and stayed in practically the entire time. Except when we went snowmobiling on Sunday.

Julia stood there in quiet acquiescence as I pulled two of my sweaters over her head, one after the other, and gave her a pair of my old sweats to wear over her jeans for added warmth. The spare ski gloves I found were way too big for her small hands, but they, along with the layers, my mother's parka, and a cashmere scarf my grandmother brought back for me from Germany, kept her warm enough. Her green eyes peeking out of the scarf that was securely wrapped around her head and over her mouth, rolled at me.

"I look like the Stay Puff marshmallow man. Only in color," she'd mumbled through the fine wool.

"And cuter."

"Whatever, Matthews."

I hugged my mom goodbye, leaving her to gush over Julia while I retrieved our luggage from the trunk. "Come back and see us again, sweetheart. We loved having you, and Gabe won't stop raving about your cooking."

"Thank you, ma'am. I really appreciated being with your family."

"Next time I see you, I don't want to hear any of that ma'am stuff. Got it?"

Julia smiled. My mother cupped my cheek and stood on tiptoe to kiss me one last time. "Take care, son. Have Aaron call me."

"I will. Don't get a ticket." I nodded at the policeman on the sidewalk. He was walking two cars down from where I'd parked the car.

She nodded and opened her door. "Have a safe flight and—"

"—Call when we get down. I know." Julia stood with her arms crossed over her chest, trying not to shiver, so I tried to hurry. "Bye," I said and turned with Julia to go through the sliding glass doors into the terminal.

"Ryan, that bag dude was waiting." Julia looked up at me as she walked by my side, unraveling the scarf from around her head. Her hair was full of static electricity and many of the long, dark strands stood out from her head.

I screwed up my face. "So? We need to check in at the counter."

"Why?" She half-stopped, turned and pointed back in the direction we came.

"Just... come on."

I had both of our bags and she followed two feet behind me as I looked at my options. I picked out a particularly pretty and young-looking woman checking bags at one end of the United counter and got in her line.

"Ryan, that line is shorter." Julia indicated another as I passed it.

"Just... shh." I grinned. She was looking at me like I was mental.

When it was our turn, I turned over my driver's license. "Do you have bags to check?" She was pretty, with bright pink cheeks, and shoulder-length hair that bobbed when she moved or talked.

"No. It's a carry-on. But, I'm traveling with my friend, and we booked our tickets at different times." I laid a smooth smile on her. "We'd really like to sit together, if possible. Could you reassign our seats?"

She began typing quickly. "May I see the young lady's ID?"

Julia handed it over, glancing at me through hooded eyes.

"Most of the seats are full, sir."

"Please?" I asked. "I have a nut allergy, and planes have nuts and she knows how to administer epinephrine, in case I have an attack."

The woman stopped typing and looked me straight in the eye, her own narrowing just a bit.

"Ryan," Julia began, and I squeezed her hand to cut her off.

"Yes, sir. It seems I do have two in first class. But that's it."

"Okay." I whipped out my wallet. "How much more is it?"

"I'll go ahead and just upgrade you. Since it's a medical emergency." She shot me a small wink.

"Unbelievable," Julia snorted.

The desk attendant printed off two boarding passes and soon we were on the way to the gate.

"You're welcome," I gloated, a smug smile playing on my lips.

"There's no room for me in first class with you and your ego!"

When we got to security, I kicked off my shoes and dumped them in one of those gray bins. We both had laptop computers and had to take them out of the bags and place them in two of their own tubs. I tossed both bags up and pushed them toward the conveyor, watching Julia go through the security X-ray machine. She collected her things, stowed her laptop again, and was already putting her shoes back on by the time I got through and grabbed my bag.

I looked at the sour look on her face. "Why are you pissed? Now we can sit together."

"You're a shitty liar, Ryan." She put her bag on the chair next to the one I was sitting on as I tied my shoes. She used her thumb and index finger on one hand to grab the tip of her tongue.

"I hav ah nu allery," she mocked a swollen tongue, and again rolled her big green eyes. "As if batting your eyes like Shirley Temple wasn't enough." She referenced the little girl from a movie we fell asleep to the night before.

I burst out laughing, as did the two people sitting next to me on the opposite side.

"Who's Shirley Temple, again?" I asked in fake innocence, still chuckling. I dug my boarding pass out of my back pocket and checked our gate.

"It's sickening. It's like you have some sort of poison love potion that wafts around you and works on anyone with a vag."

I couldn't stop smiling. I loved that she thought I had some magical power over women. It made me puff up like a peacock.

"Why doesn't it work on you, then?" I leaned down and blew on the side of her face.

Julia huffed playfully. "Immunity from repetitive small dose exposure over time... Geez. Some doctor you're gonna be!"

I laughed and nudged her shoulder as our gate finally came into view. "Shut up. I don't want to put up with your whining for three hours."

She was smiling when we found two chairs by a window and sat down. I went to get us drinks and by the time I returned, she was looking through the Stanford spring semester course catalogue. A guy sitting across from her was checking her out, but Julia was completely immersed in figuring out her schedule. Registrations were due by Monday at noon.

I twisted the bottle cap off of the green tea I'd purchased for her and took a swig before handing it over. Her hand took the bottle and she drank from it without looking up. I took the chair next to her, leaning in, shoulders touching, to see what she was looking at. I tossed a hooded glance at the guy across the aisle as I opened my own drink.

"Is there anything in there we can take together?"

Julia looked up and turned her face toward me. She held her bottle close to her chest, her arm curled in, the neck of the bottle resting on her lower lip. "Really?" she asked softly, almost as if she didn't think I was serious.

"Yeah. I'll miss seeing you in psych."

A little crinkle appeared above her nose as she frowned. "We see each other all the time, Ryan."

"I know. But I'm sort of used to you now, and this might be the last semester we'll be able to have a class together. Once electives and base recs are done."

"Afraid my immunity will wear off?"

My lips twitched and one corner lifted in half smile. "Something like that."

"Well, I think we should see what time we both have open then look for something in that time slot."

"Sounds good." I had a heavy math and science load in front of me for the next three years, and beyond six hours of electives and the basic liberal arts stuff, it was pretty much mapped out. But I wanted a class with her. Even if I had to take more hours than I needed.

It wasn't long before we both had our schedules lined up, with an English lit class together at 11 AM on Mondays, Wednesdays, and Fridays.

"Reading and writing. I can handle that," I teased. They began boarding our flight and Julia stuffed it all back in her bag. We settled into our first class seats, both tired from the night before, and I began to drift, my eyes heavy. Her perfume was familiar and comforting and it wasn't long before I felt her head drop onto my shoulder.

~4~

Valentine's Between Friends

Ryan ~

Fucking Valentine's Day! I hated everything about it and always had. Ever since I'd hit puberty, there was always at least one girl expecting something I wasn't willing to give; batting their doe eyes in expectation then angry or crying when I didn't fulfill their sugarplum visions. It was uncomfortable as hell and I really didn't get it. I rolled my eyes in disgust. I had a feeling this year would be worse than ever.

Aaron wasn't the romantic type at *all*! In fact, I'd call him the actions-speak-louder-than-words sort of guy; as long as the actions included the humpty dance, that is. *His words,* not mine.

Me? I had more finesse. Women wanted me and I knew it, but my delivery was much more refined. Admittedly, most of the time I was more interested in physical release than making a mental connection, but I tried not to abuse it and seriously, it was because I hadn't found anyone I wanted to talk to more than have sex with. Other than Julia and I couldn't even think about taking my relationship with her to that level, so I had to make do with the options I had. I balked a little at the thought. Was it my fault if they threw themselves at me? I'm only human. I huffed then smirked because I seriously found it amusing.

The only thing that redeemed me was that Aaron was worse. However, this year, he was stumbling all over himself to show his new girlfriend, Jenna, he was a one-woman man. I couldn't tell if he wanted more than sex with her, since he went on and on about how mind-blowing it was, but his actions gave me hope. I had to stop and make sure I wasn't imagining it, but my brother was pacing back and forth, going over what to write on the card. You'd think he was going to his execution instead of a dinner date. He was so stressed out it was ridiculous!

What the hell, I may not have anyone I wanted to fawn over, but the least I could do was help him out. "Aaron. Chill, dude. Stop fidgeting, for Christ's sake! You'll scare the shit out of her."

"Shut up! It's only because you're never invested in your relationships that you can be so cool about women. I actually care about this girl."

"You're right. I'm not the fawning type." He looked at me in confusion. "I don't fawn. I bask in the fawning." I explained simply, grinning.

Aaron frowned and stared at me blankly. "What the hell are you talking about?"

"You! You're a mess. Get your balls back, man!"

"Well, some of us have to work at it, pretty boy."

"Yeah, Ryan, you have it easy! I mean, look at that mug!" Julia huffed at me. "It's not as if you've ever had to work for it, so cut Aaron a break!"

My eyes darted to my best friend, sitting on the chair at the other end of the sofa in the small apartment I shared with my brother. She was concentrating on her calculus assignment, and wasn't looking at me, so I let my eyes roam over her.

Her fine brows were knitted together as she worked out a problem, glancing between her notes and textbook, once in a while grimacing and taking her eraser to the page. The long, flowing dark brunette hair falling almost to her waist in waves, draped over her face at one point and she impatiently shoved it behind her ear. Her small, rose-colored bow of a mouth looked so soft. Not to mention her firm little body, with the lush curves I'd imagined naked a hundred times, just lying in wait to be discovered. I inhaled, filling my chest to capacity before blowing it out and running my hand through my hair. Once again, I had to remind myself who she was, and what we were.

She was so beautiful, but off limits. Off. Fucking. Limits. I tried to convince myself she wasn't a woman and treat her only as my best friend. It shouldn't have been that difficult because she was unlike most of the women I knew. The few months since we'd met, felt like a lifetime. I liked her mind, she was funny and she didn't take my shit… I had serious respect for her. She was the best of both worlds; I could be myself around her, goof around or tell her absolutely anything. She was the first person I wanted to talk to in the morning, and the last person I wanted to see at night. She got me. And I got her. Now, if only I could convince my dick, but it was a constant struggle. My lips thinned in determination.

"Shut up, Abbott. You've probably got gaggles of poor assholes just waiting in line with hearts and flowers today. What happened to that sap making googly eyes at you in the library, yesterday? Poor bastard!" I scoffed.

Her eyes lifted from her assignment, and she scowled at me. "Martin Frank? You've got to be kidding me!"

One side of my mouth lifted in a lopsided smirk. The dude had it bad for her, but he was a first class nerd. No way in hell she'd ever be interested in a worm like him. "Yeah, you guys could probably use the grease in his hair for lube." I continued to goad, fighting hard not to laugh out loud, but couldn't stop myself.

She smiled and bit her lip, trying not to join my laughter but when her eyes locked with mine she grinned wide, and one eyebrow shot up. She was so beautiful. If only I could forget how beautiful she was.

"Um, not all women *need* lube you know, Matthews. Maybe you aren't motivating enough." Amusement danced over her face and her large green orbs, sparkled. "Just sayin'."

"Humph!" I snorted in disgust and dared her with my eyes. "That's not why they need it," I suggested wryly. I loved teasing her, and more than that, I loved how this particular subject made her squirm.

"Ugh," she moaned, blushing slightly. I loved it when she blushed. It was ninety percent of the reason I teased her so mercilessly, the other ten percent was to keep myself from touching her. "Whatever. Your ego knows no bounds."

"It's part of my charm."

"I'd love to stay and bask in your greatness, but as it happens, *I* do have a date. Not with Martin Frank, however." She shoved her books into her backpack and rose from the chair. "It is Valentine's Day, and he's no worm."

I sat up, my interest more than piqued as my mind sorted through the possibilities. The tightening in my gut almost hurt. "Really," I mocked. "If he's so wonderful, why is this the first I've heard of him?"

Out of the corner of my eye, I registered that Aaron picked up the bouquet of roses and the card he'd just finished signing. He took it with him toward the hall to get his jacket. He shrugged into it, awkwardly juggling the flowers from one hand to the other in the process.

Nonplussed, Julia continued her task of closing her backpack. "Good luck, Aaron. Have fun."

"We will. We'll be at The Mill later. You going there with your date?" He smiled at Julia and I sat back, annoyed. *What the fuck?* They were making plans that didn't include me. I wasn't so selfish that I always had to be included, but I was bothered.

"Maybe." She half-shrugged. "He's making the plans."

"And, who is *he*?" I interrupted.

To my chagrin, Aaron shook his head knowingly and chuckled. "Later, bro. You should meet us, too."

I followed Julia into the small kitchen after she picked up the plates from the cheese quesadillas Aaron and I had wolfed down an hour earlier. Aaron hovered by the door waiting for my reply.

Julia eyed me warily, and I frowned.

"Do I know him?"

"Jesus, Ryan!" She rinsed the plates and stacked them by the sink. "It's not a big deal! He's a guy from my econ class. He's nice. It's a flipping date."

My interest in Julia's date was more than I wanted it to be, but I told myself she was my friend, and I wanted to make sure she was okay. "Okay, then tell me who it is, Jules."

"Bryan Kelly."

My eyes widened slightly before I could stop them, but I quickly masked my expression to one of mild interest. Bryan Kelly was an upperclassman and one of the big wigs in the Phi Psi fraternity; they kept the university's focus away from their womanizing ways with their high GPAs. They were slick, good looking, and smart as hell. They'd recruited me hard first semester, but I decided not to rush. If Harvard was even going to be a possibility, I had to focus on academics as much as possible. Didn't mean I didn't have fun, but my inner circle was small and close-knit.

My skin prickled with agitation and an unfamiliar emotion I couldn't label. I tried not to let it show, casually leaning against the counter with my hip; I crossed my arms nonchalantly, watching her. The scent that was Julia, a subtle mixture of her perfume and something else uniquely her, wafted up to my nostrils. I recognized the perfume. I'd given it to her for her birthday. She pushed the sleeves of her dark blue sweater halfway up her arms and started running water in the sink to wash the dishes.

"Yeah, I heard of him," I said as blandly as I could manage, my eyes darted between her hands in the soapy water to the curve of her face. Suddenly, I wasn't sure I wanted her to meet my eyes. "He's not as nice as you think."

"Relax, Ryan" Aaron said. "Let her have some fun without you hovering."

My cool control broke. "Don't you have somewhere to be? I'm not hovering, but I don't trust the guy! You know what I'm talking about, Aaron!"

Julia rolled her eyes again and walked to get the dirty sheet pan that was resting on top of the stove. Before she reached it, she patted Aaron on the stomach. "It's okay. I can handle Ryan and his moody ass. Go have fun with Jenna. Text later and I'll see where we are."

Julia knew Jenna because they were in the same dorm, and she was a good friend of Ellie's. It was sort of fate it worked out that way, and our little group was a lock-in.

I shifted until my back was to the counter and folded my arms. Aaron's gaze met mine, and mine narrowed in silent communication. I knew he'd let me know where Julia and her date landed once she'd texted him. Aaron knew why I was worried. We'd both heard the dude bragging about his latest conquests on more than one occasion. Normally, I wouldn't give a rat's ass if the girls were too silly to realize what the asshole was about, but this was Julia. Aaron left without another word, and Julia brought the pan to the sink to wash it. Our apartment was too old and run down to have a dishwasher, but before I met Julia, we lived on take-out food and frozen pizza, so we never missed one. Now, Aaron and I begged her to cook whenever she came over.

My eyes bored into her. She had to feel it. "I'm not being moody. The guy only wants to get in your pants."

She stopped and looked up at me then burst out laughing. "Wow. Really? Amazing deduction, Sherlock. Doesn't mean I'm stupid enough to fall for it. But, you know what? Maybe I want in *his*. Ever think of that?"

I sat back and looked hard at her. I'd never considered that *she'd* just want to get laid, just for the sake of it. I shook my head in astonishment. "No. You're not like that."

"Like what? The kind of girls you date? Like them? Like you? You have no problem hitting it when you need it. So how is Bryan worse than you? And why shouldn't I? It might be fun."

She was right. Why shouldn't she? She was gorgeous, and a lot of dudes wanted her. I'd seen it over and over. But I didn't want it to be that asshole. I struggled with how to answer, because really, could I stomach Julia being with anyone? I wasn't sure.

"I actually like the girls I date. I don't prey on women for sex."

She shook her head and looked hurt. "I like Bryan. He's been sweet. And, you don't have to prey, Ryan! Girls will drop their panties if you snap your fingers!"

"I'm not like him. He targets women."

"Yeah, he couldn't possibly like me, right? That is what you're saying, isn't it?"

I had the grace to flush. "No! That's not what I meant, and you know it."

She glared at me. "You think a guy can't want to get to know me and be more than my friend? That he can't want my brain and not just my body? Just because you feel that way about me, doesn't mean Bryan does. One doesn't have to be mutually exclusive of the other!"

I'd just royally fucked myself. Obviously, I couldn't tell her I also wanted her in my bed, but I didn't want her to feel I didn't see her as a beautiful and desirable woman.

"Julia—" I began.

She turned and angrily wiped her hand on a dishtowel before throwing it down. "Thanks for trying to ruin my night, dickhead!"

I stepped forward and grabbed her arm, feeling duly subjugated. I was acting like a jealous prick and I had no right. If I didn't want to take a risk at a romantic relationship with her, then she deserved to have one with someone else. I knew it, but it killed me.

"Julia, I'm not trying to ruin anything. I'm worried about you. I don't want you getting hurt. And I especially don't want you getting used." I felt the words rising up and couldn't stop them. "I care about you."

Her head cocked to one side, and the anger left her features. Julia sighed, her deep green eyes looking right through me, seeing everything I didn't want to see myself. "Ryan, I'm a big girl."

My head moved in the negative, just one short movement, and I swear I could feel my face drop into a pout. I cared about her. "No, you're not!" I protested a little too strongly, and she shot me a warning look. "You're soft and fragile and too sweet for someone like him. He's a snake. I've seen him in action. You need to trust me on this."

Her shoulder nudged my arm as Julia leaned against the counter next to me. "I appreciate your concern, but I'm going, Ryan. I'm not some bimbo with wide eyes and nothing between my ears, or some prudish, goody two-shoes. Besides, won't you be too busy tonight to care?"

I couldn't stand the hurt look on her face. Halfway through another sigh, I realized and stopped myself. The skin on my face started to get hot when I didn't like her answer, so I took on some bravado, hoping I could distract her from my discomfort. "No. I don't give anyone delusions with stupid hearts and flowers. I was hoping we'd hang out."

She reached out, and slid her fingers down my arm. "You should have told me sooner. Sorry."

"Where are you going?"

She shook her head, continuing to clean up the kitchen. "Uh uh. If you show up, Bryan will feel like a third wheel. Remember when we did that double date at the arcade with Kevin Armister and Maria... um..."

I remembered. It was a night from hell, sitting across from Julia and watching some loser fall all over himself, trying to impress her. It was damn embarrassing to watch, and I was so preoccupied, I wasn't able to focus on my date at all.

Her face crinkled up, and she looked at the ceiling as she pretended not to remember my date's last name, and my lips lifted in a small smile. She was so sweet. I had to fight the urge to crush her to me and kiss her silly. "What was her last name again?" She smiled wide, and my heart flip-flopped inside my chest.

By the end of the night, we were side-by-side with both our dates completely pissed off. "Williams," I said and leaned in enough so our shoulders were touching. "They were both boring as hell anyway."

"Yeah. Did you know they're dating now?"

"No shit? Match made in heaven." I smiled, but my face sobered soon after. "So where did you say you were going?"

Julia launched away from the counter and turned to face me. "Ugh! Ryan! I can't have a date with you lurking in the background."

"Okay, I concede. But, you can tell me where that dickhead is taking you. Or... you can call and cancel, and then we can go to a movie or maybe that arcade again. We had a great time last time, didn't we?"

She bit her lip and looked at me, her eyes locking with mine. I could see my struggle mirrored in her eyes. I was going to win this one.

"Come on, Abbott. You know you'd rather hang with me."

"That doesn't mean it's what I should do."

Again, she was right. It was unfair that I tried to keep her from dating, from possibly finding a boyfriend, but it just didn't sit right. "I know." I shrugged. "So?"

"So..." Julia's face mirrored her inner struggle. "Hand me my phone."

Julia ~

I couldn't believe I was actually cancelling a date with a hot guy who fifty other girls would kill to have a date with. On Valentine's Day, no less! The thing was, I was cancelling to spend time with one whom ten times that many women would kill to be with. I sighed. I couldn't decide if Ryan was just being over-protective or if Bryan really was the huge predator as he claimed. It was hard to tell with Ryan sometimes.

All the time we spent together made us close. He was my best friend, the best friend I'd ever had; but I knew I loved him. If I didn't, it wouldn't kill me so much when he dated. I tried to act nonchalantly, as if it didn't matter. But it mattered more than anything; especially, since Christmas.

By now, my portfolio had two dozen portraits of Ryan in it, and Ellie was getting suspicious whenever I chose to stay in instead of going out with the group on nights Ryan wasn't with us. I couldn't help it. My face was expressive, and I had to work so hard to hide how I really felt. It was exhausting, and on those nights, when I was so miserable, it was impossible. Plus, it helped my misery to play music and recreate his face by candlelight. It was like he was with me. I was still hurting, but it got me through it.

"I'm just going to go in the other room to make the call." I began to walk down the hall to his room.

Ryan nodded and flopped down on the couch, grabbing the remote from the floor in front of it. "Sure. Should we just leave from here, then?"

I turned, looking down at my jeans and sweater. My clothes were perfectly fine for a friend night out, but it was Valentine's Day, and everywhere we went, people might be more dressed up for their dates. "Um, I would like to freshen up a little, if that's okay?"

"Sure," he threw over his shoulder, now fully ensconced in whatever was on the screen. It sounded like some sporting event from where I stood. I hovered in the hall, rethinking my decision. I wanted to be with Ryan, no question, but I would bleed eventually. It wasn't a gradual realization. It hit me hard and fast about ten minutes after I'd met him, and I couldn't stop it... I couldn't stay away.

I walked the rest of the way into Ryan's room and closed the door behind me. It smelled like him; a mixture of cologne and just him. It was nice. I sank down on his bed, inhaling deeply. Looking around, it was clear he was a serious musician, and his intelligence was on the verge of brilliance. There were a few classic novels and a very old copy of *Gray's Anatomy*, his keyboard, some concert tickets pinned to a bulletin board and loads of CDs. He had a stereo, not just an iPod dock like a lot of people.

"Julia? Did you call?" Ryan called from down the hall and I fumbled around almost dropping the phone in my haste to get it started.

Crap.

Bryan answered the phone on the first ring.

"Hi!" His voice was exuberant and I cringed because of what I was about to say. Should I lie? I couldn't be honest without sounding like a bitch or idiot.

"Hi. Listen, I know it's short notice." I shifted on the bed and Ryan pushed the door open a smidge and peeked in. I flushed. "I'm not feeling great. I think I'm coming down with the flu."

Ryan threw himself down on the bed, lying down behind me. I could feel his eyes boring into me, though my back was turned, and the back of my ears started to burn, realizing he was listening to the call.

"Really? You sound fine."

"Ye-yah," I stammered. "It's not a cold. It's the stomach flu."

"Shit. I'm sorry."

"Yes, me, too."

"Can we reschedule?"

"Sure. I'd like that. I'm really sorry."

"Okay. I'll call you in a couple of days?" Bryan asked.

"Sure. Sounds good."

"So do you need me to bring you anything? I can come over."

Ryan was quiet but shifted on the bed, and I felt it move beneath his weight.

"No, I'm... I mean, I don't want you to see this."

"Okay."

"I'm sorry about the short notice. I hope you can find someone to spend the evening with."

"I'm not sure. My roommate is having a party at our house. It's probably because he doesn't have a date."

I smiled, my head bent, and I pulled a stray tendril behind my ear. "Probably."

"If you feel better, call me and I'll come get you."

"Sure. Thanks." I said the words, knowing I wouldn't. I felt bad. Bryan seemed nice, which was a huge contradiction to Ryan's description of him, and he was good looking. Any number of girls would love to spend time with him. "Have a good night."

"You, too. I hope you feel better."

"Thank you. Bye."

"Bye."

I ended the call and did a half-twist to look at Ryan, to find his intense blue eyes trained on my face. "What?" I asked. He was relaxed but staring at me. His face could stop my breath.

"Did he take it okay?"

I half-shrugged. "I guess. What's he going to say?"

He sat up and pressed a hand to his chest with a grin. "Julia, you can puke on me any day." He was mocking Bryan.

"Hey, I feel sorry for the guy. I shouldn't have lied."

"So why did you?" Ryan scooted around me and I could almost feel the heat radiating between us as he got up from the bed and walked to his closet, peering inside and starting to push through a few of his button-downs.

"Because, I like him. I want to see him again."

He stopped and looked at me, a frown dropping his brows.

"Look, Julia, if you want to go with him, you should go."

"Shut up, Ryan." I put a hand to my forehead. "It's done."

He pulled a shirt from his closet. It was a light aquamarine with a fine vertical stripe running through it, and he threw it on the bed, hanger and all, before pulling his T-shirt over his head and tossing it on the floor.

My eyes widened. I couldn't help but stare. The muscles on his chest, abs, and arms were defined and solid. Not huge, but definitely powerful. His jeans were low on his hips, leaving the V and happy trail visible. I could see the top of his underwear. I swallowed. It wasn't the first time I'd seen men dressed this way, and I'd seen hundreds of guys wearing their pants loose enough to show part of their underwear. Some, their entire ass showed at times, but this was Ryan. I felt the skin of my face and on the back of my neck infuse with heat and I turned away, discretely. It was a waste of effort as he moved around the room and back into my sightline.

He acted like I wasn't even in the room, as he grabbed deodorant and used it, before removing the shirt from the hanger and shrugging it onto his broad shoulders. I tried not to look at the way the muscles of his back moved.

"Good. Where do you want to go? Better make sure your boyfriend doesn't show or we're busted."

I tried to tear my gaze away from all that bare skin. I knew my mouth was hanging open and at the sound of his voice, I looked down quickly. "Um, doesn't matter." We could go to a movie so I could be closer to him, lean into him, close my eyes and breathe him in and he wouldn't know. We could go out for dinner, and we could talk for hours. We could go to the arcade we liked, spend the night playing games and laughing. We could stay here, I could make Pad Thai, rent a movie, and make popcorn. I truly didn't care.

Any of it would be fine, as long as it was with Ryan. I rubbed my cheek quickly, hoping the heat would diffuse and I wouldn't turn red at the train of my thoughts.

He ran a comb through his unruly mop of hair, without a mirror. He tossed the comb on his desk, and it landed with a clatter before he turned to look at me and began to button his shirt. I was still feeling embarrassed at my feelings and found it hard to look at him. He was standing beside the bed and I was sitting on the end, trembling like a leaf.

"Jules. Seriously. Whatever you want to do is fine with me."

I couldn't let him see my discomfort, so I clasped my hands in my lap and smiled up at him. "Okay, how about a drive-through and movie? Let's go somewhere dark."

His eyebrow rose, and he bent to gather a pair of black dress shoes from the bottom of his closet and shoved his feet into them. He was wearing jeans, but they were made of dark denim and new, and they looked great with his shirt. He looked hot.

"Really? Want to take advantage of me?" he teased with a smile. "Is that it?"

If only he knew. The truth was, my feelings were too close to the surface and I wasn't sure I could hide them if he was looking right at me all night.

"Yeah, sure. Like I could," I said sarcastically.

"You could." He almost sounded serious.

My heart stopped then started hammering against my ribs. How should I answer that? How could I answer? I'd look like an idiot if I called him on it and he was kidding. "Me and half the planet."

"Whatever, Abbott." Ryan dismissed my comment, and though he'd been cocky earlier about the opposite sex, now I sensed he was pissed. "You ready?" He grabbed his leather jacket in his right hand and waited for me to precede him out of the room.

I wondered how he'd react if I pranced around in front of him half-dressed. Probably as cool as a cucumber, that's how. He had naked women around a lot, and I hadn't even been with a guy once. It was humiliating in a way. He waited while I put my coat on then followed me out of his apartment and the old house it was in.

As we walked to Ryan's car, I glanced at his face. He wasn't talking and I didn't want him upset or mad at me. Maybe I should come up with some sort of reason, even if it wasn't the truth. "The truth is, it's less likely Bryan will see us out at a movie. His roommate is having a party, and he'll probably be there, but who knows? I just don't want to run into him and have to explain."

"Fuck him," Ryan muttered as he unlocked my door and held it open for me. I had to pass him.

"Ryan, come on," I reasoned as I climbed into his SUV. It was an older model Honda CRV, but he kept it clean and nice. "You'd be pissed if a girl canceled on you then you saw her out with another guy."

He shut my door and walked around the front end. I couldn't take my eyes off him. His jaw was pushed out and his expression tight.

"Right?" I pulled my knees up and turned in my seat toward him.

"Buckle your seat belt," was all he said as he pulled his down around him and clicked it into place. I hadn't buckled mine, and he glared at me until I secured it around me.

"What's your problem? Did you get your period?"

"Ha ha," he said flatly.

"Seriously, Ryan. Why are you in such a pissy mood?" My mouth curled up in amusement. If I didn't know better, I'd say he was jealous. The thought sent a thrill all the way down to my toes.

"If you care so much about that prick, then you should have gone out with him."

"I didn't say that. I said I didn't need to be a bitch and hurt his feelings. It's bad enough I lied about it."

He revved the engine, peeled away from the curb, and made a jerky right turn in the direction of campus.

I sat back in my seat and looked out the window, my mind racing with this change in him. When I glanced at him, the muscle in his jaw was working overtime. *What the fuck?*

"Ryan—" I began incredulously, shaking my head. "Why are you mad at me? I thought we were going to have fun tonight. Don't make me regret that I changed my plans."

His fingers were tight around the steering wheel and he visibly relaxed, his grip loosening. He pulled in a deep sigh and let it out with equal strength. So deep I could hear it, not just see the rise and fall of his chest.

"Sorry."

"It's okay. I just don't get it."

He parked in the lot next to my dorm and shut off the car. It was cold out and February snow dusted the ground outside the car. It wouldn't be long and the heat from our breath would be steaming up the windows. "I don't want to feel like I'm keeping you if you'd rather be on your date."

"I don't." I shook my head, my eyes imploring him. This was the first time Ryan had been angry with me, and it didn't sit well. I wanted to ask him to explain but wasn't sure even he knew. It was better just to move beyond it and get back to our evening. "Do you want to wait out here or come in?"

"I can't wait in your room if you're changing your clothes." His voice was quiet and resigned. I studied his profile, wanting desperately for happy Ryan to return.

"You can come up. I can change in the bathroom, or you can turn around or keep your eyes closed. I'm sure Ellie is already out."

Ryan looked at me with apologetic blue eyes, his expression gentle. "Sure?"

I nodded. I wanted so badly to touch him and I couldn't help it. My hand reached out and wrapped around his forearm. He wasn't wearing his coat and the sleeves of his shirt were rolled up to expose the hard flesh and smooth skin. My fingers couldn't reach completely around it, but the connection stunned me as always. "Yes." I nodded toward the building.

He stared at me for a good minute, looking as if he wanted to say something but couldn't. I didn't want it to get awkward. The way we were together, ninety-nine percent of the time; that's the way I wanted it. "I can wait in the lobby."

"Pfft! Come on, Dr. Jekyll, but leave Mr. Hyde here, okay?"

A slow smile slid across his handsome face. "Okay, Jules, I'm—"

I put a hand up to stop him. "Nope! One sorry is enough. Aren't you cold? Get your coat on."

He pulled it from the back seat where he'd tossed it and pushed his arms into the sleeves. In less than a minute, he was around to the passenger side and hauling me up into a piggyback ride.

"Hey! People will stare at us, Ryan," I protested, even as I was thrilled at the prospect and gave a little hop to assist the process.

Ryan ignored me. It wasn't long before my arms were wrapped around his shoulders, his arms hooked under my knees, and he was walking across the street from the parking lot and onto the Stanford campus toward my dorm "Screw them."

I smiled, my face pressed into the curve of his neck. He smelled nice. It felt good being this close to him and I prayed he couldn't feel my heart hammering against this back. I'd be the envy of every woman who saw this then subjected to a bevy of questions if we ran into anyone I knew inside the lobby.

"Okay, but you have to let me down when we get close to my building."

"Why?" he asked and kept on walking, taking my weight easily.

"I don't want my eyes scratched out. I need them." *To look at you*, I added silently, but he only chuckled.

I held on to Ryan—and my heart—for dear life.

Ryan ~

I studied Julia all through dinner, wondering what it was about her that had me so tied up. It felt easy with her. The more time we were together, the easier—and harder—it got. I could look at her for hours and never get tired of it. Watching her talk, she was animated, enthralling, and funny. And, she was beautiful. Many times, I found myself breathless or struggling for words. That never happened to me before.

I enjoyed the time with her more than any other woman I'd ever met, and I was hornier than hell. If I went out and screwed someone, it was only because I was in physical pain. I felt sleazy doing it, but besides beating off in the shower three times a day, or throwing Julia down on sight, it was necessary. The only other solution was not to see her as much and that wasn't happening. Being close to her, smelling her perfume or shampoo, it was bad. *Like now.*

Thank God, the movie was almost over because it was all I could do not to reach over and take her hand. I had to settle for our shoulders touching on occasion as we both leaned into each other. I sighed and glanced to my right. Julia wasn't looking at me, her profile open to my scrutiny, even in the dark. I loved the curve of her face; her small, perfect nose and how she bit her lower lip in concentration, watching the scene up on the screen. She grabbed her soda and brought it to her mouth without taking her eyes off of the movie. It was the end of the second Spiderman movie, and though I'd wanted to see it for a few months, we'd never gotten around to it. It was playing at a discount theater we often frequented. College students are poor bastards, even when your dad is a neurosurgeon. He was adamant that Aaron and I learn to manage money, so that meant roughing it.

I set the half-full popcorn bucket on the floor, just as the credits began to roll.

Julia looked at me. "That was so sad!"

The corner of my mouth twitched. I'd have to take her word for it since I stopped paying attention after the chick cracked her head on the floor. You never knew in these movies. People were always coming back from the dead. Hell, movies were made and remade with different shit all the time. "Maybe she isn't really dead," I said as I stood up and helped her with her coat.

She shot me a wry glance and began to walk down the aisle in front of me and I followed her out and down the stairs, and out of the theater auditorium.

She looked up at me and gave those big green eyes a roll. "Ryan, he went to the funeral. She's dead."

I shrugged. "Okay."

"Didn't you like the movie? You picked it!" We filed out of the main doors, just part of the crowd. It was smaller than usual, probably due to the holiday.

"It was okay."

It was cold and the car was parked a few blocks down the street. The theater was an old time style, on a regular street without the huge parking lot and patrons had to find parking on the streets around it. It was dark, and starting to flurry, so the light from the streetlamps reflected off the flakes.

I watched Julia's breath come out in a frosty huff. Soon she would be shivering. "Come on! You'll freeze your little ass off." I grabbed her hand and pulled her along toward the car.

"Quit it, Matthews! You're my friend, so stop looking at my ass. It's weird." She said the words but she was laughing, as was I.

"Shut up, Abbott! I've been staring at your ass for months now."

She didn't say anything about my comment or about where we were. I'd taken her back to my apartment because, even though we'd spent practically the entire day together, I wasn't ready for the evening to end. Aaron had some beer in the refrigerator and it felt like we hadn't even eaten dinner.

I opened the door for her and waited for her to breeze past me into the living room. When we were peeling off our coats and kicking off our shoes, my stomach growled loudly. My eyes shot sheepishly to Julia's.

"Oh, God. Okay!" she lamented then went into the kitchen and started opening cupboards. "Whatcha got?" She opened the refrigerator that was conspicuously bare except for some milk and beer. Maybe there was some yogurt that Jen stashed inside, but other than that nothing but some moldy cheese and a few potatoes. Julia's nose crinkled in disgust as she pulled out the smelly cheddar that was beginning to turn all green and fuzzy. "Ugh! Ryan!"

I moved into the living room and flopped down on the couch, leaning forward to grab the remote off the table. The furnishings were eclectic: a mixture of stuff my mom was willing to part with and other shit we'd gotten at garage sales and through newspaper ads in the month before classes began two years earlier. The only thing we had that was worth anything was the flat screen. It looked obnoxiously out of place, but we had an Xbox 360 and cable TV. Those were our splurges. Aaron spent all his money on sports and war games before he met Jen.

Julia came in holding two potatoes. "Do you like potato soup? It won't be up to my usual standards because the cheese is moldy so I can't use it, and there isn't any bacon, but I'll try."

"Sure. Anything. I'm starving." The truth was, I wasn't a huge soup guy. Soup was for pussies, but it was too late to order pizza and if Julia made it, I'd eat it.

"I have no clue what you guys eat," she mumbled and left the room.

I stretched out and settled on old reruns of SNL. It was a mash-up of Jimmy Fallon and Will Ferrell skits Soon, I was laughing my ass off.

"Ryan, what are you watching?" Julia called from the kitchen.

"Old episodes of SNL on Comedy Central! The older casts were freaking hilarious."

"I'm almost done."

Five minutes later she was setting a bowl of steamy white soup in front of me on the coffee table along with a slice of buttered bread. She disappeared briefly, to return with a second bowl.

I'd grabbed two beers when we first arrived, so I cracked the second open and scooted it in front of her. "There's a skit coming up with JT and Fallon."

Julia settled onto the couch next to me. I picked up the spoon to taste the soup. It was surprisingly delicious. I looked at her, amazed that she could take an empty refrigerator and come up with this. She was concentrating on the TV and not really interested in her soup.

"Julia, this is really good."

"It would be better if you actually had *food*," she mocked. "Lucky I found part of an onion and a bit of butter or it would taste like crap, for sure."

"How'd you get it so creamy? My mom's potato soup is runny, almost like it's just hot, white water. It tastes like ass."

Julia laughed. "I made extra potatoes and mushed them up."

I really didn't care how she did it. I was too busy wolfing it down. "I didn't think I liked soup."

She smiled softly and leaned back on the couch, bringing her legs up and curling them beneath her.

When the episode came back on, it was a skit where Jimmy Fallon was Nick Lachey and Justin Timberlake played Jessica Simpson as a blonde ditz. It was funny as fuck. Soon, we were both laughing so hard I almost snorted soup out my nose, and Julia's head fell back and she held her stomach as wave after wave of laughter peeled out of her.

As much as I'd dreaded this night, it was turning out great. For the next hour, we watched the rest of the show, and I finished the rest of Julia's soup. My beer was gone, but she still had half of one, and she pushed it toward me after noticing I'd finished.

It was comfortable and natural. If I'd finished any other chick's beer, she'd probably twist it into a commitment of some kind when really, all it meant was I was thirsty. The thing was, with Jules, I wasn't certain what this was, exactly. Maybe I'd be okay if she assumed I was interested in her romantically, but Julia would never do that. I sighed as my thoughts smacked me upside my head. I was distracted, getting tired, or maybe the later skits weren't as funny, but we fell into a comfortable silence.

When the show was over and the soup gone, Julia yawned. "I should go clean up the kitchen."

I was flipping through the HD channels looking for a movie. "Nah. Leave it. I can clean it up in the morning."

She yawned again. "I'm really tired, Ryan. I should get going."

I got up, went to the window, and opened the blinds. It was snowing moderately, leaving a rare white blanket over the streets. "It's snowing." I glanced back at her, and she was half-lying down on the couch, cuddled up into a ball, her eyes closed. She looked so soft and alluring; my heart flopped around inside my chest. The feeling was uncomfortable and foreign. Literally, it skipped a beat, and I pressed on the wall of my chest with my hand in an unconscious effort to assuage it. "Why don't you stay here? I'll take the couch, and you can have my bed."

Her eyes opened halfway then closed again. "I don't want to take your bed," she murmured sleepily.

I glanced at the clock. It was almost 2 AM, and Aaron wasn't home, so he was surely cohabitating with Jenna in her dorm for the night, which meant all the sappy V-day shit worked for him.

"Julia, please. You'll be doing me a favor. I won't have to drive in the storm. It's cold out and neither one of us needs to go out in that."

"Okay, but can I just stay here on the couch? I'm so sleepy." Her eyes were closed and I could tell from her voice she was more than halfway gone.

I went into my room, peeled the comforter off my bed, and took it back to the living room. When I put it over her, she snuggled down in a similar way she had when she'd been sick a few months back. Now, like then, all I wanted to do was take her in my arms and hold her, to snuggle up next to her and feel her soft warmth against me.

Snuggling? Seriously? If anyone suggested that to me before, I would have beaten the living shit out of them or laughed in their face.

"Mmm...." Julia murmured and pulled the blanket closer around her. The sound went straight to my dick. *Good thing her eyes were closed*, I thought as I pulled on the crotch of my jeans. Jeans were not made for getting boners and it downright hurt. I undid my belt and pulled it from the waistband, then unbuttoned my pants so it would be less restricting.

I sighed as I looked down at her, my groin throbbing painfully. The TV was still on and was the only light in the room. It cast bluish-gray shadows on the stunning features of her face. I loved just watching her. Her eyelashes were ridiculous, fanning out on the smooth surface of her cheeks. She was gorgeous. I doubted I'd ever think another woman was this beautiful.

I picked up the remote and turned the volume down. *Probably, because I know how cool she is*, I reasoned. I sighed and meandered back to my room, to grab sweats and a T-shirt from my dresser, then headed back to the bathroom for a quick, and decidedly cold, shower. "Yeah. It's not her perfect body at all.

Nope. Not a bit. Keep telling yourself that, Matthews," I said softly as I turned on the spray. I peeled off my clothes and left them in a heap. "Maybe you'll convince yourself."

As I stepped under the spray, I had to ask myself if I wanted to keep torturing myself like this. The way I saw it, I had three options. One: keep getting a case of blue balls that required I beat off in the shower and dating various women who never seemed to measure up; two: give in and try to take it to a romantic place with Julia and risk fucking our friendship; or three: stop spending so much time with her so the friendship was bearable.

I closed my eyes and soaped up my body. I sighed, deep in my chest, leaning a bent arm on the side of the shower stall. The problem was, I didn't want to risk the friendship, but neither did I want to stop spending time with her. She made me happy, and when I was pissed or upset, she was the first person I wanted to talk to.

Somehow, I'd have to get the libido under control. Aaron, and any other guy I knew would just think about fucking her, but it wasn't so easy for me. Julia was important to my life, even as a friend. I didn't want to lose that.

Why did I have to think so goddamned much? It was the middle of the night and I was standing in the shower arguing with myself about whether I should try to get into my best friend's panties. I mean, what the fuck? Really, I had to get a handle on it. I had shit to do here, and while I cared about this girl, I couldn't lose focus. I had to keep my eye on the ball, and that ball was medical school. After this year it would get messier—harder classes, more labs, MCATS, less time for partying. There were a million assholes, just like me, competing to land a slot at Harvard Med, and I had to remember that.

No. I'd have to cool it with Julia. As much as I hated the realization, distance was the only way I was going to keep my head on straight. Maybe I'd see her just on Sundays. It would hurt her if I stopped seeing her altogether. And, I'd miss her.

I'd finished shampooing my hair and was rinsing it out when I got a sick feeling inside, mainly because we were great friends, and Julia was the last person on earth I wanted to hurt. My mind began racing with the question: should I tell her what I was doing or just distance myself? That was the typical "guy" thing to do. I'd done it many times. A girl got too clingy or needy and I'd just stop calling. I'd always found those situations uncomfortable to deal with, except Julia wasn't like one of those girls. She was just awesome, and the reason I couldn't see her had more to do with me than it did her.

I pushed back the shower curtain and grabbed a towel, briskly rubbing myself down. My dick was now blissfully re-laxed, but my gut strangely aching. I pulled on the sweats and T-shirt, and draped the damp towel around my neck, using it to rub the water from my hair with one hand as I walked back down the dimly lit hall toward where Julia lay on the couch, now fully asleep.

I stood there and looked at her for a good sixty seconds. Yes, tomorrow at coffee I'd talk to her. I threw the towel across the back of the couch then bent, sliding one arm under her knees. I was about to lift her into my arms and carry into my room when her eyes fluttered open.

"Ryan?" She lifted her head a little at being disturbed. "What's the matter?"

I shook my head and stood up with her in my arms. "Nothing. It's late and I'm putting you in my bed. Don't wake up."

Her body was slight, and I lifted her easily, still wrapped in my comforter. She was warm and soft as she snuggled into me. I wasn't sure if she even knew she was doing it. The beer would have made her sleep harder than usual. Julia rarely drank beer, though she only had a little it might affect her.

"You don't need to do that. I'm fine here." Sleep filled her voice and her head lolled on my shoulder. I made short work of the walk to my room and kicked open the bedroom door, being careful not to hit her head or feet on the frame as I angled through it, letting the glow from the television in the other room be the only light.

When I laid her down, she rolled onto her side and pulled the covers closer around her.

"Night, Jules. See you in the morning." I reached out, touched her hair then let the back of my knuckles graze her cheek. This would be even harder than I thought.

~5~

Up Close & Personal

Julia ~

I woke up a little disoriented. I sat up and blinked, glancing around then down at myself. I was in Ryan's room still fully clothed in the jeans and sweater I'd worn the night before when Ryan and I had gone to the movie. I put both hands to my head, and threaded my fingers through my hair. It was a snarled mess in the back.

"Ugh," I moaned as I tried to pull through the tangles with my fingers, to no avail. I didn't have any of my stuff, and I was sure my make-up was either smeared or completely worn off. I probably looked like total shit.

I pushed back the covers and climbed out of Ryan's bed. I couldn't help but wonder how many girls had spent the night in this bed. But *with* him. I shuddered as jealousy shot through me. Maybe there was something wrong with me. He didn't seem to have issues with girls. And even though I'd joked the night before, I caught him looking at me many times, and I could swear he was pissed by my "almost" date with Bryan. The mixed signals were confusing.

When I padded down the hall, I found Ryan on the couch, one arm thrown over his face and his feet dangling off one end. He looked uncomfortable, yet he was fast asleep, his strong jaw darkened by the shadow of stubble.

I didn't have a ride, but I didn't want to wake up Ryan. "Shit!" I whispered to myself. My coat and purse were on a hook by the door, and my boots were under the coffee table. I could see through the kitchen window that it had stopped snowing, but it was still overcast. Who knew how much snow had fallen, and I'd have to deal with that. Ryan and Aaron's apartment was within a mile of campus, but my dorm was on the opposite end. I wasn't looking forward to walking that far in the cold.

Ryan wasn't moving. It had been late when I'd fallen asleep and I flushed, remembering how he'd lifted me and carried me to his room. Too bad I was so out of it. It would have been nice to enjoy it more.

I sat down in the chair, crouching down to grab my boots and shove my feet inside. There was nothing else I could do if I didn't want to wake Ryan up or sit there and watch him sleep. I had no choice but to walk. I quietly shrugged into my coat, put my scarf around my face and neck, and took my purse and care-fully unlocked Ryan's doors. When the chain lock clanked a lit-tle, I grimaced and glanced in Ryan's direction. He was out cold. I'd text him later.

I didn't have gloves, so I shoved my hands into the deep pockets of the new wool coat Ryan's parents had given me for Christmas, but the icy wind hit me in the face like a million tiny needles. This was the coldest it had been this winter. I was used to Northern California, but the climate was usually more moderate then this freak snowstorm. I couldn't remember one ever being this bad. Ryan shrugged off the temperature here, used to the extreme highs and lows of the Midwest. I'd been shocked at the frigid temperatures in Chicago, and this wasn't close to that, but it was way below the norm.

My boots were more a fashion statement, but I was thankful I had them when I stepped onto the sidewalk. The snow was maybe six inches deep and my feet sank down to my ankles, walking would be impossible without them.

I had my head down against the wind as I walked, the wind whipping the snow around me as I hurried along.

"Julia?" Aaron's voice called from the street. I stopped and looked up to find him in a beat-up, beige Toyota Corolla that I didn't recognize. His window was rolled halfway down. "Is that you?"

"Ye-yes," I stuttered, my teeth now in a full chatter and my body shaking with shivers.

"Are you coming from our place?" When I nodded, he continued. "Want a ride home?"

I thought he'd never ask. Rather than answer I hurried around the front of his car and hopped into the passenger seat. "Thanks. Holy cow, it's cold!"

Aaron smiled as he pulled into the first driveway so he could turn around and head back in the direction he'd just come. "Nah. This is balmy."

I smiled as I huddled in my seat. Thankfully, he reached forward and pushed the heater on full blast.

"Thanks for stopping."

"You and Ryan have a late night?" he asked suggestively.

"We went to see a movie then just hung out. Did you get a new, old car?" I teased, wanting to get the focus off of Ryan and me.

"No. This is Jenna's."

"I know Jenna, but I didn't know she even drove anywhere. She lives in my dorm. On my floor, to be precise."

"Yes, I know." He grinned. Clearly, he'd just spent the night there.

"So, you're going to get kicked out of Stanford?" I asked. Cohabitation on campus property is against school rules. "How'd you get out of there? Guys aren't allowed on our floor until noon."

"Jenna snuck me down the stairwell."

"So are you guys an item now? I like her. She's a smartass."

"She is. I'm not sure yet, but I do like her a lot."

"I'm glad." I smiled softly. "She's in some classes with Ellie, and we have a mutual disdain for this obnoxious woman on our floor who sings opera in the showers."

"Maybe we can double date sometime."

I flushed at the implication. Ryan and I with him and Jenna? "Um... double date?"

"Yes. One of my fraternity brothers is always hounding me to introduce you two."

My heart fell. Of course, he didn't mean me and Ryan and I quickly hid my disappointment. "Really?"

"Yes. He's been after me since rush. Ryan doesn't like him, but he's a good guy. I'm a dude, so I can't say he's hot or anything, but girls seem to like him." Aaron chuckled.

He pulled up on the driveway that went directly in front of my dorm entrance from the street. Suddenly, the car felt like a matchbox, and I needed to make a hasty retreat. I ditched a date the night before to be with Ryan, but given the weird status of our relationship, I wasn't sure what was going on. "Um, okay. Text me the details? You can get my number from Ryan." My hand closed around the door handle, I pulled it, and pushed open the door. "Thanks for the ride."

I hopped out and was soon in the lobby of my dorm, waiting for the elevator. A dark haired girl I recognized from my litera-ture class gave me the once over. "Was that Ryan Matthews' brother?" I wanted to huff. Badly. True, Ryan was also in that lit class, but was there one woman on the fucking campus who didn't know him by name?

"Yes," I answered shortly, bowing my head a little and playing with one side of my hair. I pulled it down with my fingers, hoping if she couldn't see my eyes, she'd stop probing about Ryan.

"So, are you guys a thing?"

"We're friends," I admitted with an uncomfortable flush rushing to my cheeks.

"If you're not dating, can you hook me up? He makes me all fluttery."

How gratifying for you, my brain shouted. I wanted to gag. I stopped pulling on my hair as my head snapped up, and I glared at her. "Ryan doesn't need me to arrange his dates. If he wants to date you, I promise, he'll ask."

"Do you think he does?" she asked hopefully. *Oh, my God!* She was dense. "I mean, really?" Her eyes were wide and beseeching.

I shrugged. The elevator finally arrived and I charged in front of her, hoping to hell she wasn't going up as far as me. I pressed the ninth floor and she pressed the eleventh. *Crap.*

"Well?"

"Sorry, not my day to babysit his schedule."

Her lips turned into a pout. Her skin was almost as white as a sheet and her lips painted an obnoxious shade of red. At least on a nineteen year-old girl it seemed obnoxious.

"Geez, Julia. He's so cute, and the Sadie Hawkins dance is coming up."

I felt fairly certain Ryan wasn't the Sadie Hawkins type. Hell, I wasn't the Sadie Hawkins type. My eyes trained on the lighted numbers above my head as the elevator climbed, silently willing it to get there already. "It is?" I asked blankly.

"Yes. Can't you help a girl out?"

The doors opened, and I stepped through then turned back to her, holding the door open with one hand. "I don't tell him who to ask out. Ryan's cool, but it would be weird if I tried to set him up." If it wasn't weird for Ryan, it definitely was for me.

She frowned at my words. Clearly, that wasn't the answer she wanted to hear. "Would it kill you to drop a little hint?"

"Probably, yeah." I took my hand away and let the doors close in her face.

I was feeling waspish. I was hot, my coat an annoyance, and I whipped the scarf off from around my neck on the way to my room. I pulled the key out of my pocket and shoved it in the door. Once inside the small space, the coat, scarf, and my boots were quickly discarded and shoved, unceremoniously, into the closet. Ellie was sitting on her bed doing something on her laptop when I threw myself face down on mine. Maybe I was feeling bitchy because I hadn't gotten that much sleep.

"Rough night?" she asked.

I rolled over and stared at the ceiling, not sure I even wanted to talk at all. The ceiling had that white corkboard tile in rows. The overhead light was off, and other than that, we each had a lamp under the bookshelves that lined the walls above our beds. Ellie's was on.

"No." My eyes didn't move from the ceiling. I sighed, feeling every ounce of air as it filled my lungs then rushed out.

"Did you finally sleep with Ryan?"

My head snapped over and I scowled at her. "Why is every woman, even *you*, on this fucking campus always thinking about Ryan in the sack? And why don't you give it a rest, Ellie!" I felt my eyes begin to well with frustrated tears, and my throat started to ache.

"You mean—you don't? Think about him like that?"

"No," I lied and turned my back on her, pulling the extra blanket at the foot of my bed up and over me. "I need to sleep for a couple of hours."

"Because you didn't sleep?" The innuendo was back in her voice.

I closed my eyes in annoyance because she wouldn't drop the subject.

"I slept. We stayed up late watching old SNL episodes, and I'm tired. Besides, it's cold and gray; it's sleeping weather."

"Julia, it's just... you guys are always together," Ellie persisted. "You cancel dates to be with him. I mean, what is that, if you aren't interested in him?"

She was right. If Ryan was giving me mixed signals, probably, I was doing the same to him. "It's us being good friends," I answered, annoyed, and still with my back to her.

"How many students attend Stanford undergrad, Julia? Eight thousand? He's probably one of the nicest, smartest, most beautiful guys on campus."

"Then *why* don't you date him?"

"Because my best friend would hate my guts, that's why! But it's probably the only reason."

What could I say to that? I was thankful she didn't go after him because I wasn't sure how I'd handle it. She knew how I felt about Ryan without my admitting it, but I just hoped I wasn't as transparent to Ryan. I couldn't talk about it with anyone, even Ellie, because then it became more real. For now, it was tucked away inside my mind, heart, and portfolio.

My phone vibrated in my back pocket, and I'd forgotten I'd shoved it there before I'd left Ryan and Aaron's apartment. I willed myself to ignore it but my hand was already reaching for it. I knew it would be from Ryan.

Aaron told me he dropped you off. Sorry I didn't wake up.

I quickly typed out a response with both thumbs.

No problem. I'm going to crash for a few hours. I'm wiped.

Too much SNL?

Maybe.

I have some homework to do first, but coffee later?

Say no, Julia. Just say no, my mind screamed. I held the phone in my hand, and as I fought with myself, another message from Ryan came through.

I want to talk to you about something.

Why didn't you talk to me last night?

I'll explain when I see you.

Is everything okay?

Yeah. I'll call you in a few hours. K?

To say I was anxious and worried was an understatement. I wish he'd just tell me and get it over with. I mean, nothing like dumping shit in my lap and making me wonder for hours. Ugh! *Whatever*, I thought in frustration.

K.

I texted back and shut my phone off. I had calculus and a résumé assignment for my business writing course that needed to be finished, but I was so flipping tired. Maybe I should sleep then be too busy for the coffee date. I silently chastised myself for even thinking the word "date." We spent time together, but we didn't date. If we were dating, or if he even had the desire to do so, I was sure Ryan would have made a move by now.

I slammed my fist into the pillow next to my head. What the fuck was I doing? The sooner I stopped mooning over Ryan, the better. That wasn't going to happen if I canceled dates with guys I knew did have that kind of interest in me to be with my best "buddy." I felt disgusted with myself.

"What was that about?" Ellie asked, surprised by the sound of my pillow punch.

I sat up, threw my legs over the side of my bed, and stood up abruptly. "Nothing. I have too much to do to sleep." I walked to the closet that was at the foot of my bed and grabbed the white towel I had hanging on a hook behind the curtain that served as the makeshift door. Each side of the room was a mirror image of the other, the twin beds along the sides, shelving above each of them, with a built-in desk at the head of each bed, and a closet at the end. There was a sink near the door, and a little refrigerator underneath the window that was between the desks.

I felt her eyes watching me as I reached under the sink for my shampoo, conditioner and shower gel. "Um, okay," she said uncertainly. "I thought I'd go to the library for a while, but want to meet back here at six? We can go to the Union for dinner. Wanna?"

"Sure." My hand closed around the doorknob and I yanked open the door so I could head to the shower room down the hall. "See you at six."

*****

I watched from a small table by the window as Ryan got our coffee. The Beanery was more crowded than usual, and though we liked to take a seat near the fireplace on the couches and plush chairs that rested there, today they were in use. The crisp chill outside made the fire inside and the warm drinks all the more inviting. Many of the students filling the establishment were reading, others had their laptops open and were studying or typing. Probably most were on social media. I tried hard not to fall into that trap, though I barely missed it. I had a small circle of friends who I spent all of my time with, and we kept in touch via text and phone calls, so I didn't really need it for anything other than the groups some of the professors set up for my various classes.

Because I was unobserved by him, I stared at Ryan's tall frame. His back was to me, and I noted he needed a haircut. His golden blond locks were well below the collar of his dark blue and black shirt. I couldn't help notice how warm and snuggly the flannel looked and wondered what it would feel like to be held close to him. I closed my eyes and wanted to beat myself over the head with my textbook.

He'd dumped his leather jacket on the chair across from me before he went to get the coffee. When he came back to the table and set a steaming drink in front of me, he pushed his coat unceremoniously to the floor before taking his seat. The coat was expensive. Everything about Ryan was perfect in an expensive, effortless sort of way. Even when his shirt was rumpled as if he'd slept in it all night, and his hair messy, he was still really sexy and somehow seemed put together.

I noticed two girls at a table next to us blatantly eyeing him then whispering loudly to each other. Bile rose up in my throat. Could they be more obvious? I wanted to scream at them. *Sluts.*

Ryan didn't speak right away, and though he seemed oblivious to the girls ogling, he was also uneasy as he removed the lid of his cup and set it down on the table. Clearly, he was hedging.

"What's going on?" I asked, tired of the dance between us. Something was clearly wrong. "Just say it, Ryan. You're acting weird. Just get it out."

He glanced up at me, flushing when his eyes met mine. His right hand reached up and rubbed the back of his neck warily.

I could see him visibly take a deep breath. "Nothing like getting straight to the point, Julia."

"Well? You had me worrying about it all afternoon and that was mean. So just tell me."

"I'm sorry. I wasn't trying to be mean," he said gently, sitting back in his chair. He waited for a beat, and I gave him my *"well?"* expression with a shake of my head. "I just—" He stopped and just looked at me.

"What?" I said, my voice raising. Panic rose in my chest and made it harder to breath and tears began to sting the back of my eyes. "Are you sick or something?"

He shook his head, his hand coming up to stop me. "No. Julia, I'm not sick."

I visibly relaxed, sagged back in my chair and raised a hand over my eyes as I blinked away the telltale tears.

"I've been thinking about all the time I spend not studying and my last test in chem was barely an A. That's not going to get me where I want to go. I need a 4.0. I feel I should be focusing more."

My panic was replaced by other emotions. I felt hurt. He *almost didn't get an A*? What the hell? "Are you saying I'm keeping you from hitting the books?" My eyebrows rose in question. My throat started to ache. "Just me? It's my fault?"

"No. But I do spend the majority of my time with you. So, if I'm not as available, I didn't want you to be mad or upset. I'm not blaming you. It's my responsibility, and I let myself get sidetracked." His blue eyes implored me to understand, but I felt embarrassed. My face began to flush. "You know how important getting into Harvard is to me. My father reminded me that out of the 6500 students that apply only 165 are sent offers of acceptance every year. I only have a small chance as it is, and I just can't screw it up. Also, Aaron needs my help, too. I'd feel like an asshole if I made it and he didn't."

At some point, I had retreated from him, sitting back in my chair and crossing my arms over my chest as my defenses had gone up like a solid steel gate. Ryan was now leaning on the table toward me and speaking in soft, coaxing tones.

"Okay," I said simply. "I'm not sure what you want me to do." I shrugged. "So, why didn't you stay in and study last night and let me go on my date?" I was starting to get pissed off. I scowled at him, even though my brain knew he was right. He had to keep his mind on school; but I wasn't the only one in whatever this was between us. We were both equally guilty of blowing shit off to spend time together.

"I—" he began, but I interrupted.

"You said your dad reminded you. When?"

"Last week."

I nodded, my chin jutting out. "Okay, so you knew this yesterday. I mean, last night. You *knew*. Why do I feel like you're blaming me for your 'almost B'? I blow shit off for you, too."

His nod turned into a shake of his head. "Yeah, I know. We shouldn't do that."

"*Really?*" I mocked incredulously.

Ryan's mouth pressed into a line. "Look, I'm not sure why you're mad at me. I'm trying to be honest. I didn't want you thinking I wasn't your friend anymore or was blowing you off!" His voice became harder. "I care about you, but I have to be serious here."

"Then stop asking me to blow off other guys! Especially the day before you tell me you can't hang out anymore. That's not fair!" I felt like crying. I blinked to stop my eyes from tearing up and prayed my emotions weren't all over my face or in my voice. But, I knew I was an open book where Ryan was concerned. He did this to me, but I had to get a grip. He weaseled his way into my life, became the center of every thought I had, and now he didn't want to see me. Maybe school was just an excuse for something else. Maybe he had a girlfriend who couldn't handle us being friends. My chest constricted further.

Ryan's face softened. "You're right. I shouldn't do that. It's selfish."

"You think?" All I could do was agree. I felt if I opened my mouth, I'd start bawling all over the place. I tried to concentrate on breathing through my nose so a sob wouldn't break from my chest.

"I'm sorry. It won't happen again." It was difficult, but I kept my voice fairly steady.

We both sat there, staring at the other until I had to look away. My throat was aching and any second, the floodgate of tears would open. I had to get out of there. Now. "Okay. I'm gonna go."

"Julia." Ryan reached for my hand across the table, and I pulled it away abruptly. If he touched me, I'd lose it. I couldn't look at him as I shoved my arms in my coat. I didn't want this to matter so much. Why the fuck did it matter so much? Why did it hurt like someone set my soul on fire? We were friends; most likely, we'd stay friends, just not so up close and personal. It wasn't like he was breaking up with me. So, why did it feel that way?

"Um, so I'll just talk to you when I talk to you then." I dismissed him. "Or, see you in lit?" I hadn't touched my coffee and it didn't matter he'd just paid five dollars for it. This was the shortest time we'd ever spent in the coffee shop. Usually, it was at least two hours.

"Jules this doesn't mean I don't want to see you at all."

"I know." I swallowed and stopped, turning back to look at him, my backpack laden with books weighing me down. "I have to meet up with Ellie." I shoved my hands in the pockets of my coat. "It's just the way this has happened. It's really abrupt and you make me feel like it's all my fault. Like, I don't care about your goals or something, and somehow lured you astray. But you know that isn't true at all."

"I know. Will you sit back down, just for a minute?"

I glanced around the coffee shop and several people were looking in our direction. Those two girls were eyeing me up and down, and I wanted to punch something. Or scream. "Why?"

"Because. It's not your fault. It's mine. And, because I still..." he stammered. "We're still friends. If I have time for anyone, it's you, okay?"

I sat back down and met his eyes, salvation nudging me gently at his words. Still, I wouldn't let him humiliate me. There had to be rules. "Why are you doing this? You were finishing strong, now your flailing around like a wimp. You don't get to have it both ways. My schedule isn't hanging open for you just when you have time. I won't rearrange shit for you, and you can't ask me to. If it works out, great, but if not, then that's tough. And you're going to stop dumping on every guy that's interested in me."

It was a good five seconds before he answered, his eyes boring into mine. "That's fair. But—" He stopped.

"But?"

"Let's still plan on coffee every Sunday at 4. We'll meet here every week at the same time to catch up with each other."

I sucked in my breath, the pain in my chest easing slightly. It was something, and at least, it meant he wasn't trying to ditch me altogether. I wasn't sure which one of us was sucked back in.

"Yeah?" he asked, when I didn't answer right away.

I shrugged; noncommittal. I wanted to see him, but I felt like my heart was broken. It was stupid and I felt like an idiot. "Like I said, if it works out."

I picked up my cup and left him sitting in the coffee shop with those two women looking him over and inwardly cheering at our falling out.

As I walked out into the cold and began my trek across campus, I tried to tell myself this would be better for me, too. I was already more than half in love with him and I had to get it out of my system. It would be a change not seeing him every day, but I'd deal. I'd deal, and... I'd draw.

~6~

Smoke & Mirrors

Ryan ~

I'd fucked myself.

It had been two weeks since I'd seen Julia other than in literature class and she always sat with someone else. As I sat there, my eyes watching the door like I was starving, waiting for her to walk through the one place I was certain to see her, I couldn't decide if I was more pissed at her or me.

Even if I was a dumbass in my reasoning, didn't she know me better than that? So what if I'd said that stupid shit two weeks before? She had to know this was harder than hell for me. It was worse not seeing her. I couldn't focus on school because my mind was always wondering what she was doing. I was moody and snapping at Aaron and Jenna whenever she was over, but she snapped right back, which effectively ruined any chance I had of asking her to tell me what was up with Julia. I felt like an idiot; like my dog just died, or worse, that I'd lost my best friend. Well, it was ridiculous to feel like I'd just chopped off my right fucking arm, when all I had to do was talk to her. Didn't I? This was our first fight, to speak of. We'd been inseparable, and of course, it would hurt her feelings when I tried to shut it off like a faucet, but I truly believed it was better than being in pain whenever we were in the same room. I still had a gnawing ache, it just moved about two and half feet further north.

I leaned back in my chair, my movement abrupt and jerky enough to draw attention from a girl sitting next to me. She always came in after me, and sat in the conspicuously vacant chair to my right. She was pretty in a hard, angular sort of way. Her hair was almost pitch black, she had pale white skin and lips painted crimson. Besides her over-skinny frame, she had huge gray eyes that looked out of place around her thin, almost pointed nose and overly pronounced cheekbones.

She was talking, but I wasn't listening. My eyes still searching for Julia's softer curves and long, flowing dark brown hair, silently hoping she'd make eye contact. When she came through the door with the dude who had now become like a parasite, attached to her at the hip, I tensed. Her eyes met mine briefly. I could see the same sadness I felt before her gaze ricocheted away in a brief instant. She was carrying her coat, lopped over and through the straps of her backpack, and had on a dark green sweater I was particularly fond of over a dark pair of jeans. I couldn't see her eyes, but I knew the color of the sweater made them even more brilliant. My heart, that sped up at the sight of her, fell at the rebuff.

I opened my notebook, blocking out the babbling of the woman next to me. The professor came in and started to lecture and engage a discussion about *Great Expectations*, but I was too busy watching the way the guy next to Julia was leaning into her and trying to make her laugh.

I felt sick when she smiled at him before directing her attention back to taking notes and listening as the instructor spoke.

"So, Ryan... Julia mentioned she'd talk to you about me. She said you might be interested in going out together?"

My brain registered nothing other than Julia's name, but it was enough to make my head turn toward the gaunt girl beside me. "Wha—?" I said, distracted. "Hmm?"

"Your friend. She said, well, this is weird because I was hoping she'd introduce us. But Julia said you might like to take me out?"

Anger settled in my chest as well as confusion. It didn't seem like Julia to set me up with someone, especially given she knew I had recently rearranged my priorities. I frowned and blinked at the girl. "She did?"

"Yeah. Um, I'm in her dorm, and she mentioned it one day in the elevator. I was wondering if you two were a couple, and she set me straight."

My jaw shot out, and my mouth clamped into a line. My eyes went back to Julia who was glancing over her shoulder, right at me, and this girl whose name I didn't even know.

"I'm sorry," I rested my chin on my fist and fell in a half-assed lean over the desk in her direction as I made the pretense of taking notes, my eyes still returning to land on Julia's back several rows in front and to my left. "What was your name?" I asked quietly then wrote it down when she answered. *Jessica.* "Sorry, Jessica. Maybe she forgot, but she didn't mention you to me, but then we haven't been hanging out as much lately."

The gray eyes widened and a bright smile slid across her features. "Oh, well, that's okay."

The class was ending, the professor was dismissing the class and I rushed to shove the novel and notebook back into my black backpack as quickly as possible. I wanted to catch up with Julia before she split with that asshole.

"Will you call me?" Jessica pressed.

"Um, sure. I'm in a hurry right now, but I'll grab your number on Friday." I said words I didn't mean then left her standing there. "See ya," I threw over my shoulder. Julia was a good twenty yards in front of me by now, at the end of the hallway and turning to go down the stairs that would take her to the building entrance a floor below. The guy talking to her didn't seem to want to let her go, and I lengthened my stride to shorten the distance separating us. My purpose was singular, and all the others milling through the hallways, into and out of classrooms, slowed down my progress because I had to wait for someone slower in front of me, or when someone would merge into the hall at my right. "Julia!"

At the sound of my voice, she stopped, turned, and looked at me. The boy-man beside her stopped with her, waiting to see what she was doing. She said something to him, leaning in so he'd hear her over the din of voices. When he moved toward me, I focused on Julia and when he passed, I was still moving in her direction. She, however, had turned away and was walking quickly away from me. "Julia, stop!" I called again.

I was holding my coat, folded in my hand and my backpack banged into someone as I passed. "Oh, sorry," I muttered, finally catching up to Julia. She burst through the doors out into the March air. There wasn't snow on the ground but it was still chilly and she'd need the coat she was holding against her front, as it draped over her arm. I caught up with her and she kept walking, glancing up to glare at me.

"Leave me alone, Ryan."

"No." I wasn't sure what else to say; I only knew I wasn't leaving her alone until we talked.

"Better not get too close, you might flunk out of school." Her words were hard and laced with bitterness. It didn't suit her at all. It didn't matter, though they pissed me off even more.

"Yeah, well thanks for getting Miley's creepy, gothic twin in my face. I don't need you lining up my social calendar." I glowered at her. "I thought I made it clear I needed to concentrate on my classes."

She huffed and threw me a disgusted look. "As if! She practically stalks me, begging for me to introduce you to her silly ass. Bet you wouldn't say 'no' if you thought her bones wouldn't puncture your lung when you climbed on top of her."

Did she really think this was about that girl? Could she really think I'd be interested in someone like that? "Stop it, Julia," I commanded as she continued her powerwalk next to me. "You're being a complete bitch."

We were getting closer to the Student Union, and up until two weeks ago, we would have met there for lunch. "Fuck off, Ryan."

I reached out and wrapped a hand around her arm, stopping her mid-step and pulling her around. "Just a goddamned minute, Julia! I want to talk to you."

"Oh, well, you don't always get what you want," she said sweetly, but her expression was full of disgust. "I want world peace and zero unemployment. You see how that fucking turned out!"

I ran a hand through my hair as we stood face to face in front of the union, other students passing us to get in or out, some of them pausing to gawk at us. Her chest heaved as she glowered at me.

"*What?* What do you want, Ryan?"

I sighed heavily. I hated fighting with her, and I hated the hurt look on her beautiful face, the crinkle appearing above her nose as she frowned; her green eyes glassy.

"I told you, I want to talk to you." My voice softened.

"The last time we talked didn't turn out so great for me, so I think I'll pass."

She turned and began walking toward the building. I hesitated a beat, still arguing with myself. If she was going to be so dumb, why did I give a shit how she felt? I should just let her stomp off into her happy place and think I didn't give a rat's ass one way or the other.

Yeah, that wasn't happening.

"Damn it!" I muttered and stormed after her.

She went to the booth we sat in the day we met, threw her backpack and coat toward the wall on the opposite end and slid in, unaware I followed. She sat there for maybe five seconds while I stood watching from a mere six feet away. She sucked in a painful breath as her face crumpled, and she covered it with her hands. My heart fell. She wasn't just angry; she was hurt.

I didn't ask permission, and I wasn't even sure if she knew I was there, but I slid in across from her, laying my stuff on the seat next to me. I waited for her to calm down, and she snuffled, a sure sign she was crying. It made me feel like hell. I wasn't even sure what I was doing, but I knew something had to give.

She wiped under each eye with one finger, and she was startled when, opening them both, she found me sitting across from her. Her cheeks flushed a bright pink. She sighed and met my eyes. Tears still clung to her lashes making them a spikey black frame around her vibrant eyes. Her make-up was smudged, but it didn't matter to me at all. Julia wiped the end of her nose with a napkin and waited. Waited... for me to say something. Now that I had the chance, I found myself tongue-tied for the first time ever with her. I opened my mouth then shut it.

"What do you want, Ryan?" she asked again, defeated.

"I'm not sure," I began. *But I miss you,* my thoughts clamored.

"I don't understand you. You wanted distance. I gave it to you, so why are you chasing me across campus like a lunatic?"

"Yes, you gave me space. But you were supposed to meet for coffee. You didn't even call or text to tell me you weren't coming."

"You're such a spoiled brat! I'm sorry! I'm mad!" Her voice rose slightly. "You hurt my feelings, and I just didn't feel like having coffee with you! I'm not sure if I even want to be friends anymore."

A small gasp escaped my chest. I'd never considered that she might not want to be my friend, but it was a frightening prospect.

"Wow. I'm not sure what to say."

Julia's eyes got liquid again, her chin trembled almost imperceptibly, and then she looked away and cleared her throat at the same time, blinking rapidly. "Ughhhhmmm. You don't get to have it both ways. I just—" She wiped at her eyes then looked at me. "I just don't know how to be your 'sort of' friend. It's too much work. I have to stop myself from calling you and looking for you on campus. I'm deliberately avoiding places I think you'll be. It makes me feel like shit, and it sucks!"

I couldn't take my eyes off hers as tears filled her eyes and tumbled from first one, then the other. Again, she wiped at the offending wetness with her hand. "I don't want to worry about getting the blame if something you do isn't perfect. I don't... ughhh." She cleared her throat again. "I don't like how unhappy I am now."

I nodded and swallowed at the tight lump in my throat. I knew what she meant. Exactly what she meant. "I know. I am, too." Another tear fell, and I wanted to reach out and catch it with the tip of my finger.

"Guess you should have thought of that, huh?" Her little shoulders lifted in a half-shrug and half-sob. "I don't understand what this is now."

Julia represented extremes to me. Happy, miserable, horny, pissed off or hurt, there was no halfway with her. I couldn't stand to see her cry. Especially, because of me. Whatever emotions she evoked inside me, it was a full on assault. That was what I was trying to avoid. It was dangerous.

Had anything changed in the time between our talk two weeks earlier, and now? Not one damn thing. Maybe it was even worse than it was before. This fight and the distance I'd put between us only reiterated how significant she actually was to my life. I'd wanted to make things easier, but I'd only succeeded in hurting her and making myself more miserable than I'd ever been. It was almost as if I couldn't breathe. Especially when she was mad at me. When she said she didn't want to be friends anymore, I was done.

I shook my head and looked away, running an exasperated hand through my mop of hair as I did so. "I don't either, Jules. I'm sorry. I fucked up how I handled it, but this isn't how I want it. I wasn't trying to stop being friends. I just wanted to explain why I wouldn't be around as much."

I couldn't look away from her sad, tear-stained, beautiful face, and it seemed she couldn't break away either. Most girls would be freaking out that they were crying and looking hideous in the middle of four hundred people, but not Julia. She didn't even seem to notice.

"I'd never do anything to intentionally hurt your chances at Harvard," she said softly. "You should know that."

I was pissed at myself that I'd ever said that to her. Really, the whole fucking thing was about my own weakness and nothing she had done.

"I know. I'm a giant asshole. It came out completely wrong."

I couldn't tell her my real reasons because, again, it put it on her, and it would make those feelings harder to fight if she knew. Especially if there was a chance she felt any bit of it, too. "The truth is, I'd rather spend time hanging out with you than studying, but I can't let that happen. I figured it would be easier this way, but I was an idiot to think distancing from you would help keep my head in the books. I've been worried about you, and honestly, I couldn't stand it if you hated me." I leaned forward, aching to take her hand, but I resisted.

Julia met my gaze. "I don't hate you, but you hurt me. I felt like you blamed me for something that didn't even happen. You got an A on that test."

"Yes, but it was close. My window of opportunity is so tight, and a couple more points could have killed everything. That said; I miss just talking to you."

That was it. My dick would just have to deal with the temptation she presented, because the rest of me was miserable without her. It would be difficult, but not as difficult as fighting to stay away from her. I really would fuck up school then.

Julia closed her eyes tightly and nodded. I was certain more tears seeped out from the corners of her eyes. "Me, too. I've been so sad." Her voice was thick with emotion and snot.

I reached over and handed her a napkin so she could blow her nose. She did, and it was loud; loud enough to garner attention from some other students walking by. I grinned at the sound and her snuffley laugh that followed.

"Gross, Abbott," I tried to tease, but my expression was serious. My heart was full. I hated that I'd made her cry, but happy we were finally talking. The past two weeks had felt like a fucking year.

Julia wiped her eyes with another napkin. Her face was puffy and red from crying. "Now what do we do?"

"Well, for starters you stop ignoring me in English lit."

"It was either that or punch you in the face."

I could make a joke about the guy she was with, but this needed to be cleared up, not just brushed off. "So, will you come to coffee on Sundays and stop avoiding me in class?"

"Yes." Julia's tears had stopped and she'd become contemplative. "This is hard, Ryan."

"Yes. It's sort of a bitch. I've never had a friend like you, Julia. You're—" I stopped, not really knowing how to frame it. "I've had a lot of friends who were fun to be around, but with you, it's your words and opinion that mean the most. You're the voice in my head."

"If that is a nice way of saying I'm a drag, thanks a lot."

I nodded, wryly. "Yes. Huge drag." I smiled, and I waited until the corner of her mouth lifted in a slight grin before I continued. "No, I mean, your support is important. The past two weeks without you around felt like hell. It was weird not being able to call you." I was being careful with my words; that in itself felt foreign with Julia. There was a fine line between us and I didn't want to do anything to revert to that abyss we'd just squashed.

"Spring break is coming up, and that should give you time to catch up on classwork."

"Yes. Are you leaving campus?"

"Ellie wants to go to Cabo, but it's sort of last minute and expensive. My dad probably won't go for it. Are you going to Chicago?"

"No, but Aaron is. He's taking his new girlfriend home to meet the folks."

"Yes, Jenna, right?"

I nodded, somewhat surprised she knew about it, given our lack of contact for the past weeks. But then it occurred to me Aaron had an opportunity to tell her when he drove her home the day after Valentine's Day.

"You don't want to go to Mexico with Ellie? You sound less than enthusiastic."

Her right shoulder lifted in a half-shrug. "Yes, I guess. It helps that we're not fighting."

"Our first fight. Won't be our last, I'm sure."

"Next time you're such a giant dick, I *will* punch you."

I huffed out a laugh. "Funny to be happy about the prospect of being punched."

Julia sobered, her finger tracing patterns on the top of the worn wooden table, clearly the unspoken implication hung between us. It was worn from years and years of others sitting here, studying and making memories. This was the place we got to know about each other, and it was apparent the impact of it would resonate far into my future.

"How about this? I'll help you. I promise, I'll kick your ass if you don't get in to Harvard."

My lips quirked at the same time as my stomach growled. Just like that all of the crap between us was over. "Sounds like a plan. Wanna eat? Suddenly, I'm starving." The dark cloud of Julia's absence was now lifted and things would go back to normal, but with a little more awareness of what needed to be done and resistance of getting lost in her. But... she'd be around.

"Me, too. So hungry." She nodded, enthusiastically.

I stood to walk to the snack bar and ordered our lunch, knowing Julia would be happy with whatever I purchased for us to share. It was just that easy with her. Without her, it was so fucking hard; it was ridiculous.

~7~

From Here

Ryan ~

The week of spring break came and though Aaron took Jen to
Chicago, I didn't feel like making the trip. Needless to say, my
parents were bummed, but I told them I was using the time to
study, and that seemed to placate them well enough.

I used my thumb and first two fingers to rub both of my
tired eyes at once. Aside from homework, which was tedious, the
weekend had been boring. My mom called on Saturday morning
and Julia came over to make dinner. I'd been surprised and
slightly annoyed when two other guys from one of her marketing
classes showed up just minutes after she had. She didn't have
time to tell me once I'd gotten home, and I was chagrined she
hadn't texted to ask if I minded or to at least let me know in ad-
vance. Not that it would have changed anything, and after a few
minutes in, I relaxed; making small talk with them and taking
turns playing games on the Xbox while Julia prepared the food.

I realized, as I sat in the other room with the two dudes, the
one she'd introduced as Ted Watson was following her around
with his eyes. He stared at her as if she was the rising sun, his
mouth gaping open like a panting dog.

Poor schmuck, I thought, grunting and grabbing the game
control. I let myself get immersed in the game and tried to ignore
his obvious obsession. The reason I was pissed off wasn't because she'd invited them to my place without telling me; it was

because they were guys and it wasn't just going to be her and I. Ted was a total dweeb, and the other, Barry something-or-other, was gay. Julia wouldn't be interested in the nerdy one, and the other wasn't interested in her. In fact, it became a private joke between us during dinner. She'd put the baked chicken and mashed potatoes on the table and the two of them were in the living room watching TV while I helped her with the rest of the meal.

I nudged her a little too hard with my shoulder. "Ted wants to be *fed*," I said, amusement thick in my tone. I could barely keep from laughing my ass off. I didn't need to elaborate further. Julia knew me well enough to know what I meant.

"Quiet, jackass." Julia shot me an exasperated look and pushed past me to place the rolls, fresh from the oven, and butter on the table. Her eyebrow shot up as she met my eyes on her way back in my direction.

"What?" I asked incredulously with a small laugh. "He *does*. I bet he's *never* had a meal. He was shaking and drooling like he had rabies."

"Be nice. They didn't have anywhere to go. Both of them were alone for break."

"That doesn't change the fact that he's hot for you, Jules."

"That works out, then, because Barry about came in his pants when I told him I was making dinner at your place tonight."

The thought made me wince and I did when Julia poked me in the ribs. "He's not my type."

"So what? You're *his* type," she almost whispered, a smirk lingering on her face. "He wants your ass. Literally." She chuckled as she got the salad out of the refrigerator.

"Ha ha," I retorted and poked her back in a spot I knew was particularly ticklish. She squealed and the lettuce in the bowl she was holding went flying. We both burst out laughing, though trying to keep it quiet so the two in the other room didn't hear us.

"Stop, Ryan!" Julia squealed, and I had this unnerving urge to hug her.

For the remainder of the evening, every time Ted or Barry would be obvious in their adoration, we'd nudge each other or give each other teasing looks. It was a lot of fun, if I was honest, and later in the evening we made some excuse that we had to be somewhere so both of them would split, and we could hang out and just watch a movie together. It was almost three in the morning when I'd taken her back to her dorm.

When I'd asked her what she was doing tonight, she'd mentioned a party but didn't ask me to come along. It didn't feel right. She was going with people I didn't know. Logically, I argued with myself I didn't need to be with her constantly, and I shouldn't expect to be included in everything she did. In fact, I was making an effort to create a little distance between us, so I had no right to get all bent out of shape if she had other things going on. But it felt weird and I didn't have to like it.

I didn't want to think about her as much as I did. I'd admitted to myself that I had to hang out with Julia some of the time. To try not to, when it made us both miserable was just asinine, but I struggled to find the balance. What she did when we weren't together shouldn't matter to me. I kept hammering it into my brain, again and again. Julia and I were just friends. *Friends. Friends. Friends.* "Ugh!" I huffed.

I inhaled deeply as I pushed my laptop away and slid it back on the desk. I went to the refrigerator and took out the leftover plate Julia had made for me, removed the foil and popped it in the microwave. I didn't know what the hell to do with myself, so I went back and got a beer, opened it, and took a long pull, leaning up against the counter, waiting for the food to finish heating.

It smelled good, and my stomach rumbled, but I found myself wishing that I wasn't eating all by myself.

Maybe I was more bored than bothered. I stood there plucking my lip as I the thought rambled around in my head. If it was bothering me: I sure as shit didn't want it to.

I took my plate to the table, pulled some silverware out of the drawer, sat down and pushed the plastic cover off the Tupperware plate filled with leftovers.

My phone screamed at me from its position across the table. I forked up a bite of food and ate it. I managed to hold off grabbing the phone until I'd finished eating, rinsing the plate and silverware and stacking them in the dish drain.

My phone finally in hand, I headed down the short hall to my room. I decided to shower then find something to do and someone to do it with. If nothing else, I could hit a movie. Glancing down the screen was conspicuously lacking a text from Julia.

After I'd showered and dressed in clean jeans and a light blue button-down, my hair still damp but combed, my phone finally jingled and I reached for it. It was from her.

"Did you eat?"

I couldn't help the small rush I got when I knew she was thinking about me.

"Yes."

Are you studying hard?

I'm done. Bored.

Oh. Sorry, I'm trying not to distract you.

Is that why you didn't ask me to go out with you tonight? Being supportive?

That was a reason, at least, and despite all of my debating with myself, I still needed one.

Yes and No. It's a party at the Sigma Nu house. The only men allowed are the brothers.

Nice way to make the women exclusive, I thought derisively. My fingers flew as I typed out a response. That was Aaron's frat, and I'd feel a hell of a lot better if he was going to be there. All I could think was that the odds were David Kessler would be there.

Greedy bastards.

Do you wish you'd rushed?

Fuck, no.

I grunted as I typed.

They ban the rest of the male population by not allowing them at their parties, and the women have no choice but to talk to them. That's weak ass shit.

I wondered what she was thinking.

Are you going out?

Probably.

I knew I'd regret it, but I was going to ask even though I hated myself for it.

Is Kessler there?

Not sure. Ellie and I just got here. Have fun.

Disappointment and frustration filled me.

You, too.

I scrolled through my contacts. Shawn Williams, one of my friends from Organic Chemistry was staying in town over the break, too. Maybe he'd want to meet at Oasis for a beer and some pool. After a quick call, I was on my way out.

*****

Julia ~

The fraternity house was crowded, and music was blasting so loud the walls shook. Students were milling up and down the stairs, most of them carrying one of those plastic bar cups filled with beer; some of them were already falling-down drunk, but most were just having a good time. There was a keg in the backyard, in the basement, and on the main floor.

"Do you want beer?" Ellie was almost yelling so I could hear her above the din. Beer wasn't my bag but I nodded. If nothing else, I'd just carry it around. My eyes skirted the crowd and I saw David Kessler talking to a few people. They were all around him, gazing at him in rapt attention. His eyes lifted and met mine. He was attractive, no question. His hair was almost black as night and his skin was a warm bronze; he was tall and built, but not overly large. His build reminded me of Ryan.

Quit it! I chastised myself. "Okay," I said absently. Dave was disengaging from the group and moving toward me.

Ellie took note and nudged me. "I'll be right back."

"Sure," I managed, just before Dave approached. He was smiling brilliantly, and it reached all the way to his eyes.

"Finally! I'm so happy to see you!" He slid a hand down my back and let it rest on the back of my waist.

"Hey. Looks like the party's hopping!" I felt awkward. I knew he was interested in me and I wanted to be interested in him, but another set of blue eyes nagged at the back of my mind.

He shrugged. "Not as much as usual. Tons of people are gone for break."

"Wow! I can't imagine how it is normally!" I tried hard to make small talk. His light blue eyes roamed over me. I'd worn jeans and a burgundy cashmere sweater, and Ellie and I left our coats in her car.

"Yeah!" he said loudly. "Want a beer?"

"Ellie just went to get us one. She's my roommate," I explained, awkwardly.

Dave nodded and shoved the hand not holding his glass in the front pocket of his jeans. He was wearing a Sigma Nu sweatshirt.

"You look great! I've been pestering Aaron to give me your number."

"He didn't?" I smiled up at him.

"Not yet."

Ellie came back with two cups of beer and handed one to me. I took a drink and nodded to David. "Thanks, El. Do you know Dave?"

"Yes, we had accounting together. Hi," she said, and nodded to Dave.

"Hey."

"Dave!" A skinny guy was calling to him from the stairs. "The beer out back is empty. Help me put the last keg out?"

"Yeah!" He reached out and took my hand. "I'm sorry, duty calls for a minute. I'll be back later?" His eyebrows shot up. He seemed sincere, and a contradiction from everything Ryan had said.

"Sure."

"Okay, see you later. Nice to see you, Ellie."

"Bye!" Ellie said happily. When Dave was on his way up the stairs Ellie, who had been watching him go, turned toward me. "He's fine, Julia."

I took another drink of the bitter liquid. They charged a five-dollar cover charge to pay for the kegs, though the beer itself was not the best. I grimaced at the mouthful of beer before I swallowed it. "Yeah. He is."

"He *is!*" She gave me an incredulous look at my obvious lack of enthusiasm.

I gave a small shrug. "I know."

"Did you see all those girls sizing you up when he was talking to you? They looked like they wanted to scratch your eyes out."

I shrugged again. I was used to venomous looks from women. It happened a lot when I was with Ryan. I sighed, inwardly kicking myself again. "Sure. Whatever."

Ellie rolled her eyes. "What am I going to do with you, Julia?"

"What?"

"The guy is obviously interested and I remember you telling me about him last semester. So, what's the problem?"

I shook my head and took another sip from my glass. "Nothing. No problem!"

Her eyes shot to the heavens and she shook her head in disbelief. "Okay. It's stuffy in here. Wanna go out back?"

She'd told me about a guy from her statistics class who was a member of the frat, and I knew she was on the hunt for him. "Sure."

"Unless you want to wait here for Dave to come back? Which is what you should do, in my opinion." Her look said I was an idiot if I didn't jump on the chance to get to know Dave Kessler in a much more thorough way. I should. I knew it, but it didn't feel right.

"I'm good. Let's go." I nodded toward the stairs.

Ellie sighed. "Julia!" Obviously she was disgusted by my lack of enthusiasm, and I could only hope she wouldn't press me for more of an explanation. She might already know, but I wasn't going to deny or confirm her suspicions. "Ryan isn't sitting home tonight, you know."

Yep, she knew, but I wasn't going to feed into it. "I know."

It was a little chilly outside but not horrible with all the bodies crammed together as they were. I could smell marijuana in the air outside, and the music was blaring from a speaker mounted in one of the upstairs bedroom windows.

"Excuse me," I murmured as I squeezed between two groups of people. I brushed up against a guy to my right, my shoulder brushing his arm. "Sorry," I glanced up with an apologetic smile. He looked vaguely familiar.

"Hey." His hand reached out to stop me with a brief touch to my arm. "Julia, right?"

I looked at him, trying to place his face. Ellie stopped next to me. "Yes?"

"I'm Nate. We met that time at Ryan and Aaron's apartment?"

I racked my brain but I couldn't place him. I faked it, though, because I didn't want to make him feel bad. "Oh, sure. This is my roommate, Ellie."

He laughed. "It's okay if you don't remember me. I've had a couple classes with Ryan, and Aaron rushed with me freshman year."

"Oh, yeah. Sorry."

There were several picnic tables in the backyard, and Nate motioned to one of them. "Wanna have a seat?" He was looking at Ellie and I smiled, relieved. Maybe if Nate occupied her time, she'd have less time to pester me about my less than gasping reaction to David Kessler.

"Love to!" she said happily and we walked to one of the tables on the opposite side of the yard. The beer line extended the entire length of the backyard, and we had to navigate around it.

I spent the next two hours listening to Ellie and Nate talk. He was cute and seemed totally smitten with her. I watched the interaction between people, glancing around the party. I went all night without getting another beer despite Nate's offers to get one for me when he went to refill his and Ellie's glasses. I could tell she was getting a little tipsy.

Pretty late in the evening, Dave Kessler made his way down the back steps and through the throng of students to plant himself next to me. He straddled the bench, and scooted really close to me. I could smell his cologne and beer on him.

"I lost you inside!"

"Yes, Ellie wanted to come out here."

"So you know Nate?" He nodded across the table at his fraternity brother.

"He's in a couple classes with a friend of mine. We met one time."

I was leaning an elbow on the table, and Dave reached out and ran his fingers along the wrist I had dangling over the edge of the picnic table. When he reached my hand he took it in his, pulling it forward until our hands rested on his leg, his eyes never leaving my face. He smiled and I wondered if he was drunk.

"You are very pretty." His smile widened, but I felt embarrassed under his intense stare. My cheeks felt hot. His thumb started to rub the inside of my palm, and his eyes fell to the small amount of cleavage that was visible at the top of my sweater. "Verrrry pretty," he said when his eyes met mine again. I looked away and across the table at Ellie, nervously. He seemed intense and though I wouldn't mind getting to know him, I wondered if he was already making plans for a hot and heavy make-out session. Or more. Ryan's warning rambled around in my head.

"Thank you."

"So, help me remember. How does Aaron Matthews know you?"

"He's my best friend's brother."

"Oh, right. Is Ryan gay?" Dave smirked at me.

I huffed in amusement, my expression clearly showing how absurd that was. "Hardly."

"Hmmm. Are you sure? I could never be just your friend," Dave teased.

"Positive. Haven't you seen him around? He knows you."

Dave's eyebrows rose speculatively. "Is he warning you off me, then?"

I nodded, a small smile toying at my mouth. "Something like that."

"I hope you're not listening," he said suggestively. "Aaron was supposed to get me your number months ago."

"To be fair, he did mention you." I didn't want him to haze Aaron because of me, so I made sure Dave knew Aaron had made an effort. "He said you wanted to go out."

"Yes, I would. Are you up for it?"

Here was my opportunity to stop mooning over Ryan. It took some effort, but I pasted a smile across my face. "Yes. I'd like that."

Dave's smile brightened. "Yeah?"

I nodded, mustering as much enthusiasm as I could manage. "Uh huh."

"Good." The hand that was holding my hand moved to my back to rub up and down, his eyes became hooded. I tried to relax, but I stiffened just a touch.

"Ellie looks like she's had too much to drink. I should probably get her home." I pulled the phone out of my back pocket. I wasn't sure if I was checking the time or looking for a message from Ryan. It was after 1:30 AM. The party would be breaking up soon, and Ellie, sitting next to Nate across the table from me, was giggling at something he'd said. They were huddled together and he had his arm around her.

Dave's gaze was intense on my face, and I could sense he was thinking about his options. "She should probably eat something. Why don't we all go to breakfast?"

I nodded. "Okay. Hey, Ellie!" I called to get her attention. "Do you guys want to get something to eat?"

"Sure!" Nate said at the same time Ellie answered.

"Yes!"

"Great. I just have to see if one of the others will make sure the house clears at two. If we get busted, we lose our charter."

He got up but stopped to squeeze my shoulder before he turned to go. "I'll be right back."

"Okay." Maybe Dave had a better head on his shoulders than Ryan gave him credit for.

Ellie was leaning into Nate and he bent to plant a kiss on her mouth. It was clumsy and sloppy, considering they were both somewhat inebriated. My phone finally vibrated in my pocket.

Where are you?

I'm still at the party. Going to breakfast.

Can we join?

My heart sank as I wondered who was with him. Would I be faced with some girl draped all over him if I agreed? My chest constricted as I tried to suck in a breath. Well, maybe that was just what I needed. I needed immunity to Ryan's pull, and small doses of seeing him with women was probably what it would take. Besides, Dave would be with me.

After a second, I typed in my response.

Sure.

Less than fifteen seconds later, Ryan had answered.

Where and when? Stacks isn't open.

Ryan and I liked this place called Stacks for breakfast, but they weren't open at this time of night, and in fact, not beyond the afternoon on any day.

I know. IHOP? We'll be leaving soon.

Redwood City?

It's the closest one.

Okay. See you in thirty minutes.

I shoved my phone back in my pocket. People were still hanging out, but the party was winding down. Dave came back, his keys in his hand.

"Are you ready? I can drive," Dave said.

"I need to get Ellie's keys. She's not in any condition to drive. So we can meet you there?"

"Why don't we all go together?"

If I were any other woman, I'd probably be clamoring to spend as much time with this man as possible, but the truth was I didn't know him that well, and with Ellie this out of it, it would just be better to drive her car to the restaurant and go home from there.

"Why don't you and Nate follow us in your car?" I suggested. "We can go to the IHOP nearest our place." Dave's lips pressed together briefly. It was clear he was annoyed, but Ellie was in no condition to drive. I stood up, walked around the table and took a hold of her arm. "Come on, Ellie. It's time to go."

I helped her up, and Nate caught her when she tripped trying to step over the bench of the picnic table. She started laughing outrageously. I hadn't seen her this intoxicated since freshman year and we'd gone to our very first college party.

"Okay," Dave agreed, finally. "If you promise we'll go out next weekend."

Within minutes, Ellie was piled into the front seat and Dave and Nate were following behind us on the way to breakfast.

"Why didn't you just let me go with Nate?" Ellie's voice was slurred, and her head lolled against the passenger door window.

"You're a little drunk, Ellie."

"Oh, God. I feel sick."

"You need to eat."

"Ugh," she moaned, putting a hand to her head. "I'm gonna throw up."

"Really?"

"No." She moaned. "I don't know."

I was almost to the restaurant and soon I was pulling into the parking lot. Ryan's CRV was already there, and he and a guy I didn't recognize were leaning on it, waiting for us. No women anywhere in sight.

I pulled into a spot three away from Ryan and he started walking toward the car just as Dave parked in a spot behind Ellie's car.

Ellie's door flew open, and she stumbled out before I could get around to help her myself. Ryan was there instantly, and his arm went around her shoulders.

"Hey, El. Are you okay?" he asked.

"No. I need the bathroom."

Ryan glanced at me then at Dave and Nate. "Hey," he greeted them. "Come on, Ellie. I'll take you in. Jules, you should come with her."

"Yeah. Dave, can you and Nate grab us a table?" I asked.

"Sure," he said.

Ryan's eyes shot briefly to my face. "This is Shawn," he introduced briefly, as we all started walking into the restaurant. The parking lot was starting to fill up with the bar crowd. We all went inside, and Ryan steadied Ellie. "Can you walk?"

"I think so."

I took her arm and started to pull Ellie in the direction of the bathroom on the other side of the restaurant. "Come on," I told her. "Be right back." I looked apologetically as we began to walk away. I just hoped Ellie didn't lose her cookies before we got there.

*****

Ryan ~

This was damn awkward. At least, it felt awkward, though the other guys seemed oblivious.

My fear that David Kessler would be at the party was confirmed. I pressed my lips together in irritation. He'd sure as hell wasted no time. I made small talk with them and more formally introduced Shawn. Nate knew him from another one of the science courses we shared, but Dave was a business student, so they hadn't met. The hostess showed us to a table and I threw my coat over the chair on my right. Dave took the one on the other side of it. When we sat down, she placed menus in front of all of us and left two in front of the two empty chairs.

"I'll send the waitress over when the ladies get back from the restroom. Enjoy your meals," she said then left.

I could feel Dave's eyes boring into me, so my eyes snapped to his and held. He was throwing down a challenge, and I met it, unflinchingly. He was obviously threatened and I inwardly rejoiced. He huffed, which told me he knew exactly what I was thinking.

"How long have you known Julia, Ryan?" It was a barely veiled throw-down that I was more than willing to pick up.

"Long enough." I knew it was a pissy response, but I didn't give a damn. It wasn't any of his business that I'd met her the beginning of second semester last year, and really, why did it matter? My eyes were still trained on his face and my expression was stoic.

"Funny, I was thinking the same thing. She's great."

"I agree," I said steadily.

"Ellie's awesome, too," Nate interjected, sensing the tension between Dave and me. I opened the menu and tried to concentrate on the images and words.

"She looked a little green around the gills tonight," I answered.

"I guess I gave her too much beer, but we were having a good time," Nate answered.

My eyes flashed up to David's again. "Julia seems fine."

"Where did you guys go tonight?"

"We went to the Brewery and played pool," Shawn interjected.

"Yes since we couldn't come to your party. That's quite a racket you've got going there." The corner of my mouth twitched.

"What do you mean?" Dave wanted to know. By now we were all looking over the menus and the waitress came back to get our drink order. I ordered coffee for Ellie, Julia and myself and she left us, saying she'd return with the beverages and take our food order.

I leaned back in my chair, still intent on answering his questions. "Don't patronize me. You know." I was stoic in my response. "Not letting other dudes attend your party gives you a captive audience with the girls."

Dave smirked and shrugged. He was a slick bastard. Where Nate was all loose and sloppy, David Kessler was put together and edgy, despite his casual state of dress. "It works. I've been trying to talk to Julia for two semesters."

Shawn was a quiet and introspective type and pretty oblivious to what was going on. He was dealing with a bad break-up and kept pretty much to himself. On the other hand, Nate could see all my muscles were coiled, and it made him uncomfortable. He was bristling in his seat.

"I'm aware," I answered flatly. I had no right to tell him to keep away from Julia, but I wanted him to know I'd be watching what went down. "She's a class act."

"Yes." His eyes narrowed.

"Look, I've heard about you and I've seen you in action. Treat her right and we've got no problems."

"What's between you two? Crash and burn, huh?"

"No. I've got no beef with you, Kessler, but Julia is a good person. She's not just a piece of ass. Got it?"

"Ryan, lighten up. Women are pieces of ass. I can't believe you haven't tried to hit it."

I saw Julia and Ellie emerge from the bathroom so I had to say what I had to say, then shut the hell up. "I'll only say this once; treat her with respect or you'll have me to deal with."

"Oooh," he mocked, putting both hands in front of him and wiggling his fingers, in a big "fuck off."

My blood began to boil, but a sly smile slid across my mouth. *The little prick!* Part of me wished he'd push me just a little bit further, though my logical mind told me to back off. Not that I gave a fuck what he thought, but this was a public place and worse, Julia was here. I didn't need to make an ass of myself in front of her.

"I'm not fucking around." My voice was low, so the girls wouldn't hear, but laced with a growl. I felt claustrophobic and wanted to reach across the empty chair between us and slug him across the mouth.

Ellie pulled out the chair between Nate and Shawn and plopped into it, at the same time I nodded to the chair next to me, silently indicating that Julia should sit next to me. Dave Kessler on the opposite side couldn't be helped at this point.

"I ordered you both some coffee," I said to the girls.

"Sorry," Ellie muttered. She leaned on her folded arm and looked like she was about to pass out.

"Thanks, Ryan," Julia said.

The waitress returned, we all ordered breakfast, and the conversation was full of generalities. It was normal to talk about nothing but bullshit when you didn't know the people you were with very well; that was the way you got to know them, but I leaned back in my chair and zoned out.

To David's chagrin, I pushed my open menu in front of Julia. I didn't intend to piss him off, but he visibly stiffened. Julia didn't notice either my action or his demeanor because sharing a menu was just something we did and wasn't out of the ordinary. If I put myself in the other guy's shoes, I'd have been pissed, too. I knew I needed to stop over-stepping my place, but habits were hard to break. If the guy hitting on Julia was a good guy and I knew it, maybe I wouldn't feel so territorial, but this asshole wasn't going to get what he was after from her as long as I was around.

When the meal came, most of us started to eat, and I shut my mouth and tried to stay out of Julia and Dave's interaction. It wasn't easy, and I was torn. I found myself just wanting to get the hell out of there, but a bigger part couldn't leave her alone with him. Kessler was smooth, I had to give him that. He sidled up close to her side and talked to her in low tones designed to keep me and anyone else from hearing what he had to say. I knew her as well as I knew anyone, and I could tell by her nervous laugh and flushed cheeks he was flirting hard, maybe being too pushy. My fist clenched around the napkin I held in my hand.

Ellie was leaning on the table with her head resting on her folded arm, her eyelids drooping heavily and I used her as an excuse to draw Julia's attention away from the asshole on her other side.

"Ellie, are you okay?" I shot Nathan a disapproving look. "Dude, you shouldn't have let her get so wasted."

He looked incredulous. "We were having fun. You're too uptight."

"I'm okay. I do want to go home."

"Nate, why don't you drive Ellie, and I'll follow you with Julia," Dave suggested before turning toward Julia and taking her hand. His voice lowered a couple of decibels. "I want to be alone with you for a while."

Thankfully, Julia shook her head. "She'll need me to help her into the dorm and into bed."

I wanted to say that I'd help, but I had to take Shawn back to his place, and I'd damn well be checking up on them once that was done. Dave was able to hide his annoyance from Julia only because her focus was on Ellie, but I saw right through him.

I leaned in toward Julia. "I'll take Shawn home then check on you guys."

"You don't need to, Ryan." Julia smiled softly, but there was sadness behind her eyes that nagged at me.

"What if you can't get Ellie inside by yourself?"

"Dave and I can follow them, and we'll make sure they get in all right," Nate said.

"Sounds like a plan," Dave answered with a smug smile and inwardly, I seethed.

We all finished the meal, and while I was drawn into the conversation with the others, my ears were straining to hear the low conversation between Julia and Kessler. He was making plans to take Julia out the following weekend.

I inhaled a breath, hoping it would ease the uncomfortable tightness in my chest and fix the erratic heartbeat that was close to making me sick. I'd have to deal with the insane attraction I felt for Julia, and I'd have to find a way to get over it. I ran a hand through my hair, my cheeks puffing out as I let out the air in my lungs.

I made a silent pact with myself. I'd have to focus on school and concentrate my social energy on dating. Being out with other women would accomplish three things; my social calendar would fill up with activities it would be impossible to include Julia, it would get my head back around our friendship, and it would ease the physical ache that was becoming a problem.

~8~

Hard Facts

Julia ~

Somehow, I was surviving. I was trying hard to balance being Ryan's friend but the signals coming off him were so mixed; I was confused more often than not. He acted jealous, but there was a definite divide between our friendship and his social life. We kept to our Sunday coffee schedule, but soon, we wouldn't have Lit together, and it was getting impossible to plan classes together because our majors were so different.

I was sad and frustrated, torn between screaming at him, crying my eyes out when I was alone and never seeing him again. The latter was impossible, even if being with him was starting to hurt. It ached when I was with him and when I wasn't. After coffee today, I agreed to come back to Aaron and Ryan's apartment to make dinner for everyone. Afterward, I spent two hours quizzing Ryan to help prepare him for his Organic Chemistry final, and now, we were both studying for other finals.

My eyes fell on Ryan. He was sprawled out on his bed, face down, reading a book on his laptop and I was sitting at the desk in his room trying to work on one of my communications papers. The cords from both of our computers were plugged into the wall behind mine in a tangled mess. The light in the room was low and most of it came from our respective computer screens.

I closed my eyes. They were burning from the hours spent staring at the screen and the muscles in my neck and shoulders were screaming as well. The light from Ryan's computer turned his perfect features into a plethora of contrasting light and dark shadows. I rubbed my neck as my mind committed his image to memory because it would become the next portrait in my ever-growing portfolio. I'd be sunk if Ryan ever saw those drawings. I'd be sunk if Ellie, Jenna or anyone else saw them. They were so personal, and other than the fact my feelings would be outed, I just didn't want anyone else to see them. With summer looming in front of me, I'd have three months without Ryan, and no doubt the number of drawings in my portfolio would increase.

I'd been trying to get over it, trying hard not to be in love with him, but I measured every other man against him. I knew it was toxic, but I couldn't help it and I couldn't talk to anyone about it. Ryan was so perfect. My heart seized just looking at him.

I was basically forcing myself to date Dave Kessler on a regular basis, and it had been more than two months since that uncomfortable night when I was sandwiched between him and Ryan at the IHOP. Now, Ryan made himself scarce whenever Dave was going to be around, and it was some unspoken agreement between us.

If only I could really care about Dave. I let him touch me, I made out with him with heavy petting, but when it came down to it, I hadn't been able to go through with full-blown sex. Stupidly, I felt guilty, and so, when Dave pressed me, I said I just wasn't ready. He wasn't Ryan. Even as I thought it, I wanted to punch myself. I could see Dave's irritation written all over his face whenever Ryan would call or text me when Dave and I were together. He was starting to catch on and we'd had three fights over Ryan since we'd been seeing each other. One just earlier today when Dave wanted me to go over to the frat house, but I'd already made plans to study with Ryan. It ended with me ending the call mid-sentence, and I'd kept my phone off most of the day since.

Finals were next week, and I was silently grateful to be going home to Kansas City for summer break. My mom and dad were divorced and I'd grown up there so when I picked a place for college, I wanted to be closer to my dad. Ryan was staying on campus and taking summer classes, but maybe the distance away from him would do me good.

It was late, and when I yawned, Ryan caught it.

"Are you tired?"

I nodded and laid my head down in my folded arms, but turned to look at him. "Yes, aren't you?"

Ryan shut down his laptop and set it on the floor before turning and crawling toward the end of the bed closest to the desk. He flopped back down on his stomach and propped his chin in his hand, his blue eyes darker in the dimness of the room.

"Yeah. You're preoccupied. What's up?"

My heart fell and soared at the same time. Part of me wished Ryan didn't know me so well, but there was nothing I loved more than being with him.

My shoulder lifted in a half-shrug. "Just thinking about summer and stuff."

Ryan rolled onto his back and shifted over on the bed, leaving a pillow free, he patted the bed next to him. He silently invited me to share it. I couldn't help myself. I longed to feel the heat of his body only inches away, to smell the scent of his skin, to be closer. I moved the few feet necessary and lay next to him. He threw the old sleeping bag he used for a comforter over us both. It was unzipped and so covered most of the bed. I turned onto my side toward him, cuddling the bag closer and looking into his face. I could feel the heat radiating between us and filling up the space beneath the blanket, but I was careful not to touch him.

"Stuff?" he asked in a murmur. He reached up and grabbed the small remote he used to turn on the iPod docked on a shelf by the TV across the room. Soft music flooded the room and before I could stop myself, images floated through my mind of Ryan making love to faceless women in this room with music playing, in this bed.

I inhaled a shaky breath and nodded. "Yeah."

"Are you worried what will happen with Dave over the summer?"

I shook my head, my eyes never leaving Ryan's face. "No. I guess I should, huh?" Self-preservation should have taught me to be a better liar.

He shook his head, his hand reaching out to squeeze my upper arm that was beneath the covers. "He's not the guy," he said simply.

He was right. Dave wasn't the guy. I was looking at the guy.

"You may be biased."

He nodded. "I told you in February what I thought."

I frowned at him. "Yes, but do you think you get a say?"

"As your friend, I want what's best for you."

Smack! I was starting to hate the F word. I huffed loudly and flopped onto my back. "So?"

"So, he's a user."

"It hasn't been like that."

"He's a user," he said it again, so matter-of-factly.

"You're a fine one to talk, Ryan. I never see you with anyone. I mean, being friends and all, you'd tell me if you had a girlfriend. You'd bring her around me. Right?"

"You don't bring that asswipe around me." His voice was irritated.

"You're never around. It's not like I tell you to stay away."

"I'm not a fan of animosity. I don't tell you not to be around, either, but it's easier, isn't it?"

I turned toward him again. "I suppose. Do you have a girl-friend I don't know about? Because if you did, wouldn't I at least know about her? Jenna would tell me." He didn't say any-thing and just lay there looking at me. "She's said you've been out on a few doubles with her and Aaron, but it's always a differ-ent girl."

"So?" he asked indifferently.

"So, you're no different than Dave. He's been seeing me for two months. Your record is what? 6 hours?" I knew my voice was filled with sarcasm, but I couldn't hide it.

He didn't look mad at me, but he studied my face. "The truth is, it's weird to talk to you about it."

The breath left my chest. Did he think I'd fall into a sobbing heap around him and his bimbos? If so, could I be more humiliated?

"Why? I know you're with a different girl every weekend, so why don't you want to introduce me? You think if I don't meet them, I'm somehow oblivious?" I forced out a harsh laugh. "*Please*, Ryan."

"Julia, that's not it. And, yeah, I take girls out, but I'm not preying on women."

"Yeah, so you've said. And, I know they practically beg. Forgive me. That's so much better." My chin jutted out of its own volition. I was pissed, and I started to get up, but Ryan's hand shot out to stop me. His fingers wrapped around my arm.

"I wasn't trying to hurt your feelings. I just think you and I are close, and it's weird for them. It's easier to keep you and me separate from that stuff."

It was weird and painful for me, too, even if he wasn't aware of it. Honestly, I didn't need or want to be around it, but part of me hurt when I thought he was hiding things from me. I was sitting there, still as stone, and his hand remained around my arm. I finally pulled it free. "That has its drawbacks, too. Dave and I had a huge fight today. He's pissed that I don't want him to join us when I make plans with you." If it was all copasetic, we should all be able to hang out together. The women would have to deal, and Dave would have to deal. The issue was that Ryan and I were close, and it was hard to dial it back. "He doesn't want me spending time at your house alone with you. Like this."

"Fuck him."

"That's what he says about you."

"I'm sorry."

"Really?"

"No. I don't give a fuck if that pissant is uncomfortable."

"That is exactly why I can't bring him around you!"

"Are you guys serious or what?" His words were more measured.

"I don't know." I sighed. "Didn't you just tell me he wasn't the guy?"

"See? You were listening."

"But, it still doesn't solve our problem. You and I should be able to be friends and still have relationships at the same time."

"If you really like the guy, I'd deal with the prick."

"Ryan." I was exasperated. I felt like a lab rat running on one of those wheels inside a cage.

"If he treats you right, then I'm fine with him."

"You won't be a jerk? If we do start hanging out?"

Ryan sighed, and even in the darkness, I could feel his internal struggle as if it permeated the air around us. I wanted to reach out and touch him; my palm burned with it.

"Then you do like him." It was a statement, not a question.

"I'm not sure. He's nice."

"As long as he's genuine, and he hasn't—uh..." He paused and grabbed my hand. "Julia, I don't know how to say this without it coming out wrong."

"Just say it, Ryan." As well as we knew each other, it was almost ridiculous that he didn't just say what was on his mind, though this subject hadn't been a big topic of discussion for us before now.

"If he's only trying to get you in bed, and then he treats you like hell afterward, I will beat the living shit out of him," he blurted. "Not just him. Anyone who treated you like that."

I couldn't help but let out a small laugh. If Ryan only knew how I felt about that.

"I thought you'd be pissed I said that," he said, surprised.

"I'm not really sure how I feel about it." I lay down again and pulled on the edge of the sleeping bag. Ryan shifted to give some of it up. "I mean, I've thought about it. Sex doesn't mean anything."

"Maybe not to some people, but you're different, Julia."

"You do it, right? So why not me?"

"I don't want you getting hurt. It's not the same for dudes. Women can't separate love and sex like men."

"Really? Then whom are you screwing? You insist you're not hurting anyone. That's a contradiction."

"Well, I mean..."

"Ryan, you can't have a double standard between men and women, then apply one set of rules to me and another to the girls you sleep with. Right?"

I could tell Ryan was smiling because his white teeth flashed. He couldn't weasel out of it. I nailed it. My phone started ringing, and I ignored it. I wasn't in the mood for round two with Dave.

When Ryan didn't answer, I decided to take a risk. I was going to test his feelings and throw it out there. "I kind of wish I could have sex with Dave and still be best friends with you. Because…"

"Yeah, I get it."

"Do you?"

"Yes."

I felt like I was about to tell my deepest secret. "Have you considered that we could be friends with benefits, Ryan?"

His head snapped around, he hesitated for the briefest moment, and his eyes narrowed. "No, it can't happen. You're the best friend I've ever had. Even more than Aaron," he said seriously. He said it couldn't happen, but he didn't say he didn't think about it.

"So?"

"So, that means a lot to me."

"And you hit it and leave. It wouldn't be so easy to leave me and still be my friend. Right?"

"Not exactly. Thanks for your high opinion of me."

"I do have a high opinion of you, but I think you're no different from any other guy who fucks for the sake of fucking. You don't have to deny it."

His eyes sparkled, and I could see the wheels turning around behind them. "In a way, yeah, but do you think I do it on purpose? I mean, it happens, but I don't deliberately target girls to get into their pants. And if something more were to come of it, I wouldn't avoid it necessarily, but it would be a complication. I'm focusing on school, and I only have time for one woman in my life. That's you."

My heart swelled, but what was he really saying? "What does that mean, Ryan?"

"It means I like everything the way it is."

I nodded, resigned to our plight. "Me, too. It would make things easier, though. At least, I wouldn't get yelled at for spending time with you."

"How do you feel about this guy?" His expression was serious and concerned.

"He's okay. He's attractive, and he's been nice, when he's not jealous of you."

"Jealousy means he won't go for sex without a relationship. Maybe he genuinely cares about you Jules. I'm surprised as shit I just said that." Ryan's voice was gentle.

"I guess," I replied. I wished it mattered to me.

"Jules, think about it over summer break, and if, when you come back in the fall, you want to spend less time with me to make it easier with Dave, I'll understand."

"Ryan, we tried that already, didn't we?" My throat tightened painfully and the back of my eyes began to sting. I didn't want to be without Ryan. I knew he was the reason I couldn't be open to a relationship with anyone else, but it didn't matter. It didn't matter that I spent so many nights crying, alone with my broken heart and sketchpad. Ryan was all that mattered. Moments when we were together like this were all that mattered. "It didn't work well for either one of us."

"I know, but I don't want to keep you from being with Dave if that's what you really want."

"I don't know what I want."

"Okay. But I'll stop being such a selfish dick. If you don't want to be with him, that's one thing, but you shouldn't be kissing him off because you and I are friends. That's not fair."

"Okay." My heart clenched. This meant that if he found a girl he really cared about, the friendship would take a backseat to that, too.

"But, I'll still kick the shit out of him if he hurts you."

Ryan ~

Julia was sleeping in my bed and being so close to her was getting to me. I crawled out of bed and went to find some water. She was still fully dressed and I had sweatpants on, but I could feel the heat radiating off her, and my dick reacted as if she reached out and closed her fist around it. I couldn't take it.

I filled a glass with tap water and took a swallow. I loved having Julia here. I loved our talks, even if the subject got a little too close for comfort.

Friends with benefits.

I could hardly believe Julia brought that shit up. I'd thought about it at least a thousand times. I'd beat off to the thought of sex with her a hundred times, probably. Thoughts of Julia naked and writhing beneath me, sighing my name in satisfaction, her hands on my flesh, and her hips rising to meet mine were all delicious torment. My dick swelled and stood at painful attention, even now. *Fuck!*

The problem hadn't gone away despite our concerted effort to reduce our time together. Maybe it made it worse. I thought about her all the fucking time. I groaned and leaned both hands on the counter after I put the glass in the sink, sighing deeply. I didn't know what to do about it, other than keep doing what I was doing. My hand closed around the aching offender, wishing to God I could turn it off like a switch. Maybe these overnights weren't such a good idea, but damn if I didn't like having her here. I liked her company, and I always looked forward to seeing her. It wasn't that I could take it or leave it. It was that I needed to see her, or at least know I would see her; or I wasn't content.

There was a knock on the door, and the sound startled me. I rushed to the door, searching around for something to throw on. Normally, I wouldn't give a shit if I answered the door shirtless, but my raging hard-on posed a problem. There was a dirty button-down I'd discarded two days before laying on the big chair in the living room and I scrambled to grab it and throw it on before whoever was at the door knocked again. Julia, Aaron and Jenna were all sleeping, and it was 3 AM, for Christ's sake.

I buttoned the bottom three buttons in a hurry as I walked to the door. "I'm coming!" I said in a loud whisper. "Who is it?" I asked when I was next to it.

"Dave Kessler."

My eyebrow shot up. Of course it was.

I opened the door but left the chain bolt in place. "Yeah?" I asked through the crack in the door.

"Open up, Matthews."

"No. It's three in the damn morning."

"What are you, a hundred?"

"No, but I have a final in five hours."

"Is Julia in there?"

"Uh…" I hesitated only briefly. *Fuck it*, I thought. "Yep." I was about to do the unthinkable, and only the degree of nastiness was in question. "She's asleep in my room."

I peered at him steadily through the door, my left arm raised above my head as I leaned on the wood. His face turned a mottled red.

"I want to talk to her. Now."

"Not happening. We were up late, and she also has an early test. Talk to her tomorrow."

His fist slammed into the door hard, making a loud crash.

"Don't be an asshole," I said calmly. "You'll wake everyone up. Just go home."

"Come out here. Let's go!"

I huffed and my lips twitched. *Was this dickhead for real?* "Go home, Dave. Talk to Jules tomorrow."

He banged the door again, trying to shove it and break the chain, but I was a counterweight on the other side, and it didn't budge. "Open the door, Matthews! Just what the fuck is going on with you and Julia?"

My eyebrow shot up. "Look, idiot. I can come out there and you can try to fight me. You'll lose. Or, I can call the cops and you can get your ass hauled away. Third option," I lowered my voice and slowed down my words, "—you can talk to Julia tomorrow."

"She didn't answer her phone all day. I was worried about her."

"Yeah, she said you had a fight." He stiffened at my words. "When she's with me, you don't have anything to worry about."

"What the fuck is between you two? Is she fucking you behind my back when she won't let me touch her?"

I guess I could see why he was so livid, but he'd overstepped. I'd be furious if the positions were reversed, and there was part of me that wanted any excuse to kick his ass. I opened the door, pulled back my arm and hit him hard—one blow square in the nose. He stumbled back then landed on his ass with a thud.

I leaned down so I could lower my voice. "Think, asshole." I touched my temple as he glared up at me. "If Julia and I were fucking, do you think for one second she'd be seeing you at all?

If she's not letting you touch her, then you have a major problem that has zero to do with me. She isn't at your beck and call for one day, and you run over here with a chip on your shoulder?" I laughed out loud. "Get over it."

While I was talking, Dave got up from the floor. "You're such a condescending dick, Matthews."

"No, I'm not. I just know Julia. She said you're nice, and she likes you, but she's not into you. I think it's obvious to both of us."

"Fuck you!" Kessler was even angrier now, and with a grunt, he drew back his fist to slug me. I caught his fist in my open hand, and easily used it to push him back and away from me with all the force I had. The muscles in my arm and chest strained, but I was taller and had more leverage. I shoved him further back in the hall, and he stumbled when I released his hand. This time, he didn't fall but landed against the opposite wall.

I went back into my apartment and started to close the door as Aaron walked into the room.

"What's up, Ryan?"

I turned back toward the man outside the door. "You're acting like a bitch. Women like dicks. Grow one." I shut the door in his face and locked it. "Motherfucker," I muttered.

"Who was it?"

"Kessler," I said in disgust. "If he so much as scratches that door, I'm calling the cops. I don't give a shit if he is your frat brother."

Aaron crossed his arms across his bare chest. "Is this about Julia?"

"No. It's about some dickhead having a temper tantrum in the middle of the night." I rubbed the back of my neck.

"Is Jules still here?"

"Yes. She's asleep. We both have exams early, and we were up late studying."

"You'd be pissed if your girl was in some other guy's bed. If you had a girl, that is."

I shrugged. "I guess. But he knows we're friends. We were friends before his ass ever showed up on the scene."

"Things change. People move on."

"Whose side are you on? Does being in that frat mean you're sucking his dick, now?"

Aaron walked past me into the kitchen, and opening the refrigerator, pulled the milk out. He took a long swig from the carton. "I'm just sayin', you'd be pissed if you were him, and if she's dating him, maybe he has a right to be mad she's staying with you overnight."

"Whatever, Aaron."

"Do you ever consider that Julia doesn't date because of you?"

I stopped and shot him a dirty look. "I guess you missed it. She *is* dating that prick on his ass in the hall." I pointed to the door. Aaron's expression turned accusatory. "Julia and I have this handled, so stay out of it, Aaron."

"Sure you do. Just think about it, Ryan. What you have going on with Julia is not friendship. You're acting like a jealous boyfriend."

"You don't know shit about it," I hissed at him. "We're doing what works for us, and it really isn't anyone else's business. I'm going to bed."

"With Julia?" He was goading me, and I was done listening.

"Guess so!" I said with my back to him. I was already at the door to my room. He was right. He wasn't saying anything I hadn't said to myself, but I didn't like hearing it. We were both staying on campus for the summer, and Jenna and Julia were leaving. I needed to use the time to get my head on straight and get control of all the emotion that seemed to boil over whenever Julia was around. I wanted to see her, but I wanted it to be easy and relaxed. Thinking back over the time we'd known each other, I was always attracted to her, but it was getting worse. We were closer, we'd admitted as much as we could comfortably admit.

The door closed behind me and the room was doused in darkness except for the glare of the red digital numbers on the old clock my mom gave me two years ago. I could make out Julia's form curled under the sleeping bag, so I crawled over her, and lay down on the bed near the wall. I pulled part of the covers over me, threw my arm over my eyes then tried to go over the material that I'd stored in my head for my upcoming exam. Maybe isotopes, molecular orbital theory, and reactive intermediates could keep me from fantasizing about the woman lying a foot away from me.

~9~

Perspective

Julia ~

It was a new school year. Ellie and I were getting an apartment off campus, and we'd come back a month early to find one. I was excited to get back to Stanford, to Ellie and the gang... to Ryan. Dave and I had gradually stopped talking, and I almost felt guilty because I had a huge sense of relief. As much as I'd tried, I couldn't distance myself emotionally, even if the physical distance was fifteen hundred miles. I couldn't convince my heart to forget about Ryan, so I finally gave up trying.

Two months of being apart with only Skype to connect us once a week hadn't changed anything. Sunday Skype like Sunday coffee; we never missed it. We still texted a couple times a day but not as often as when we were both at school. The nights on Skype felt no different from when we were together. We laughed, watched movies together, and talked about everything. He'd emailed me copies of his class notes and I even helped him study over the computer screen. The time and distance made it easier to move past the embarrassment I felt over the sex discussion we'd had before I left, and we were back to being us. We were Ryan and Julia... Julia and Ryan. Nothing was going to change it, so I accepted my fate. I would enjoy the time with him, suck it up when my heart broke, and be thankful for every second we had together.

When I'd flown into San Francisco, my dad was working and I expected Ellie to pick me up at the airport, but Ryan was there instead. It was a happy surprise; I couldn't help melting into him when he hugged me hello, and when he lifted me off the ground my arms tightened and I'd closed my eyes in silent bliss. He smelled incredible and felt amazing. I never wanted to let go of him. It was heaven, though I was flushed, and it was a little weird when we'd separated. I wondered if Ellie told him Dave and I were done because I hadn't, and Ryan hadn't asked about him on our drive back from the airport or in the week since I'd been back. Not even once.

It was Saturday and the whole gang was going to a local flea market and a few thrift stores because Ellie and I needed to furnish our apartment, cheap. Ellie had her bedroom set that her parents hauled up from Los Angeles, we had a couple of mismatched chairs for the living room, and a small television. Other than that, we had nothing. My dad had given me a thousand dollars to buy furniture, but that wouldn't go very far. I'd been sort of pissed at the amount until he told me he'd come to Palo Alto the week before classes began to, in his words, "fill in the blanks."

Ellie, Jenna, and I were sitting in the back seat of Ryan's CRV and Aaron was with him in the front seat. I liked my position in the rear passenger seat. It gave me a good view of Ryan, and I could observe him freely. Ellie caught me looking at him once, and I felt the heat rush into my cheeks. I looked down, then out the window, but she reached over and squeezed my hand. I could only hope I was better at hiding my feelings around the others. It was inevitable that Ellie might be suspicious. I'd seen her watching me when Ryan was around, and it was harder and harder to keep my feelings from showing like a beacon on my face. She knew me better than anyone—save Ryan. My lungs expanded as I took a quick, deep breath. I hoped to God he couldn't tell. I looked back at Ellie and offered a weak smile.

There were several trucks lined up, tailgates down as their wares were being displayed. It was a seasonal thing held on a farm southwest of Palo Alto off Interstate 280, and a big chunk of the property was reserved for parking. Navigating through the throng of people walking toward the entrance was slow, and Ryan chose a parking place toward the back of the lot.

"If we find anything big, it will be hell loading it, Ryan," Jenna complained.

"We'll deal with that if it happens, honey," Aaron responded.

"It's only a couple hundred yards, Jen," Ryan added.

"Okay, I'm not carrying anything heavy, just saying."

"Wouldn't want you to break a nail," Ryan scoffed as he turned off the engine. "God forbid." His blue eyes met mine in the rearview mirror and he smiled. "Jules will do all the heavy lifting."

"Then what the hell do we need you for?"

"Decoration," Ryan answered, amused.

Jenna snorted, and I huffed out a small laugh as I watched his face. He was strong and we all knew it would be Aaron and Ryan doing most of the work if we found anything worth buying.

"Yeah, right," Jenna said dryly.

Ryan came up next to me and threw his arm over the top of my shoulders and around my neck, pulling me close to his side. "Aww! Jules always needs me, Jen." His dancing blue eyes darted to mine and he smiled, his white teeth flashing brilliantly. "Right, Jules?"

"Unfortunately," I tried to sound annoyed, but a smile pulled at my lips, and my heart hammered hard inside my chest. If he only knew. I tried to distract him by pushing away from his embrace and poking him in the ribs. "You're making me all sweaty."

He didn't try to reach for me again, but a secret smile played on his mouth as he walked next to me. "There's a thought," he muttered under his breath.

My mind flashed to our "friends with benefits" discussion, and his teasing sort of pissed me off. He was the one who dashed that idea, so he could just keep his flirty mixed messages to himself.

"What exactly are we looking for?" Jen wanted to know as we came to the entrance gates. There was a small fee to get in, but I didn't have my purse. The last thing I needed was to carry that thing around, and I dug my hand into the front pocket of my denim shorts.

"Furniture, pots and pans, and dishes. Basic stuff."

"You can just cook all the meals at our place, Julia. We have pans," Aaron teased.

"You didn't put that entire wad of money in your pocket, did you?" Ellie asked.

Aaron huffed. "Why don't you say it a little louder, Ellie? Jesus."

Ellie glared at him. "Well?"

She was right. I shouldn't have the entire thousand in my pocket, but I didn't want to be bogged down with a purse. Ryan's hand closed around my wrist before I could pull the money out. He shook his head and instead paid for Ellie and me, along with himself, to get into the flea market.

"Good thing some guys have manners," Ellie spouted at Aaron who looped his arm around Jenna's shoulders, and pulled her toward him so he could kiss her as they walked. It was awkward but it didn't stop Aaron. Ryan and I walked behind them. "Ugh, get a room already. Do we have to watch that all day?"

"Yes," Aaron replied wryly, still trying to kiss Jenna, who started to giggle happily.

We made our way through a few aisles without finding anything. There was a lot of hodgepodge junk that I had no clue why anyone would want, and a few booths had interesting lamps, dishes, picture frames, and other miscellaneous stuff.

I found an old table and chair set that was only a hundred dollars. It wasn't anything to look at but it was functional, and it was really all we needed.

"It's so ugly, Julia," Ellie whined.

I looked at her pointedly. "It's cheap. I have to save some of the money for an art table. That's even more important to me than a bed."

"That's how I feel about my keyboard," Ryan murmured. He was close but his back was to me as he looked through some stuff on one side of the booth.

I wanted the art table, but more than that, I wanted to get Ryan the MCAT study course for Christmas and it was expensive—as in a few thousand dollars. I'd already applied to work at the campus newspaper for this school year, and it would help with day-to-day expenses so I could tap into my savings to enroll him in the class. It was a big gift, but one I really wanted to give him. I'd considered that it could tip him off to my feelings, but he was the best friend I had. Nothing would make me happier than doing that for him.

"I'm surprised you don't want to be a musician, Ryan," Jenna said.

"He *is* a musician, Jen." I couldn't help but say it. He was a musician and a good one.

Ryan turned to look at me. His expression was serious and contemplative.

I wanted to say something to dig myself out of the hole I'd just landed in, but I couldn't find the words.

Jenna rolled her eyes. "I know, Julia. I meant he could have a band."

"He could." I agreed. "So, Ellie, are we getting this table or what?" I tried to change the subject. "We can get a tablecloth to put on the table." I looked more closely at the chairs. The seats were covered in ugly brown fabric, but it looked like I'd be able to pry them lose and recover them. "And we can paint the chairs and recover the seats."

"That's a lot of work."

"Probably right, princess, but you won't be doing it," Ryan interjected wryly, shooting me a look. "I think that's a good plan, Julia. I'll help you paint it. We'll do the table, too."

A happy smile settled on my face, and I nodded. "Good."

I peeled a one hundred dollar bill off the roll of money from inside my pocket, then shoved what was left back into it.

"Okay, as long as you think so," Ellie agreed.

The old woman hosting the stall agreed to hold it for us while we looked through the rest of the flea market, and plastered a "sold" sign she made out of a paper plate on top of it.

When we left the booth, Ellie and Jenna were walking in front of us and Aaron was looking at a booth full of sport's paraphernalia. I gently nudged Ryan's arm with my shoulder. "Thanks."

"Ellie's a little big for her britches. I don't see her forking over the cash."

"Her parents aren't very well off. It's all they can do to pay her tuition."

"Come on, Jules. Stop doing that." Ryan leaned his hip up against the side of a beat up old pick-up truck filled with fresh produce that another vendor was selling. "If she's got it so rough, why isn't she a little more humble?"

"Not everyone is perfect, Ryan."

"No, but she could be more help."

"She's not as creative as me. She takes things at face value."

He nodded and ran a hand through his hair. It was getting hotter as the afternoon wore on. "Right. Ellie sees what *is*. You see what could be."

My heart stopped inside my chest. I wondered why Ryan could always read me like a book, how he always got me when others didn't. Sometimes, the way Ryan talked made him seem so much older, as if he had an old soul that had learned many lessons through many lives. It was just one more layer that set him even further apart from everyone else I'd ever known. He and I were both introspective and maybe that was part of our connection.

"Um… yeah. With a little TLC, anything can be more than it is. Does that make me weird?"

His teeth raked his lower lip, and he shook his head. "No. It makes you, you."

A nervous laugh escaped, and I walked around him to lean on the truck bed at his side. "Yeah. Weird."

"Not weird. Just you, and that's a good thing. Trust me."

Aaron picked up a football and turned toward us. "This thing is signed by the 49ers! The whole team!"

"Dude, how do you know it's the whole team or if it's legit? Seriously," Ryan admonished.

Aaron paused, holding the ball and considered his brother's words.

"It is," the man sitting behind Aaron said. "You can go on-line and verify it against copies of the signatures."

"See?" Aaron said.

"Uh huh, sure." Ryan wasn't convinced and his face filled with mocking disbelief. "Let's get out of here. It's getting hot, and I'm hungry."

We all decided we would take two of the chairs in the back of Ryan's CRV, and Ryan and Aaron would make another trip to get the other two chairs and the table without the rest of us so the back seat could be folded down.

We didn't have dishes yet, so the boys dropped us off at their place. I gave Ryan my keys so they could take the first two chairs, and then the others with table, to our empty apartment. Jenna went inside to start doing Aaron's laundry, and Ellie and I ran out to the grocery store to buy the makings for lunch.

We were in the produce aisle, and I was picking out stuff for a salad and toppings for the grilled chicken sandwiches I planned to make.

"Julia, why don't we buy some of that deli turkey? This seems like a lot of work."

"What? You live on birdseed and raisins. You'd settle for nitrates and saw dust?"

"Gross." Her face screwed up in horror. "When you put it that way, no."

"Thought so. I just wish I had time to marinate the chicken."

I picked out an organic tomato, some lettuce, a cucumber and a red onion. I planned to make a Dijon vinaigrette for the salad, and a lemon and pepper rub for the chicken. If I had more time, I'd use white wine with the rub and let it set in the refrigerator overnight. I sighed regretfully, knowing how much better it could be. Maybe next time.

I didn't have time to make it from scratch, so we picked up some deli potato salad, and in the time I'd spent with Aaron, I knew he'd want something sweet. Ryan liked sweets, too, but they were Aaron's favorite part of the meal. I racked my brain for a quick and easy dessert.

"You go to so much trouble. I don't get it. Or do I?" Ellie asked knowingly.

My back was to her so she couldn't see my eyes widen. "It makes me happy to do things for my friends. Especially when you've all been so helpful."

"I didn't do anything, and it's for our apartment."

"It is, so you should be more gracious and help me. What should we make for dessert?"

"Cookies?" She picked up a package of chocolate chips and turned it over to read the recipe printed on the back.

"Mmmm... It's too hot to start the oven. That's why we're grilling outside."

We made our way down the aisle lined with flour, cake mixes, spices and other baking needs.

"Forgive me, Julia, but why the hell are we in this row then?"

I came across the instant pudding and picked up a box. "Maybe we can get creative with instant stuff."

"Oh, my God! You're not making something from scratch? I die!" She was being dramatic and an older woman, pushing her cart past us laughed.

"I don't have time today." I put the box of vanilla pudding I was holding in the cart then gathered the rest of the things I needed. Finally, we were heading back to our new apartment. It wasn't far from campus, and only a mile or so from Ryan and Aaron's place.

I was busy crushing Oreos inside a plastic bag with a rolling
pin when Ryan and Aaron came in.

Ryan went to the kitchen sink to wash his hands. "What are
you making?"

I looked up at him as he peered curiously at the bag of black
crumbs. I pushed on the rolling pin again and the sound of the
crushing made his eyebrow shoot up quizzically. "Just sandwiches and salad."

He looked at the bowl full of crumbs next to me, and the
empty Oreo package lying beside it. "Mushed Oreos on toast?
Yum."

I huffed and rolled my eyes. "Yes. Can you start the grill?"
Ryan and Aaron roughed it in many ways, but they did have a
grill. Grilling seemed to be a "he-man" requirement. Most guys I
knew could grill if they had no other cooking skills.

I pulled the square pan filled with the vanilla pudding I'd
made from the refrigerator then lifted the bowl of crumbs and
dumped them on top. While I was spreading them to cover all of
the pudding, Ryan smiled. "What is it? It looks good."

"Dirt pudding."

"Pudding?" Aaron interjected from the living room. The
apartment was small so our voices carried easily. "Pudding is for
pussies!"

I laughed softly as I pressed the cookie crumbs into the pudding with the flat of my hand. There was another thick layer of
cookie crumbs in the center, so maybe it would satisfy Aaron.
"Okay, I officially rename this dirt *cake*. Happy?"

"Depends on how it tastes."

"Aaron! Give it a rest. You've got Jenna washing your
shorts and Julia feeding your ass. What do you have to complain
about?" Ryan leaned on the counter near enough that I could

smell his cologne. I was finished, I went to the sink to wash my hands, then returned the dessert to the refrigerator.

"This was just something I came up with in a hurry." I felt almost apologetic.

"Julia, we could have gotten burgers and brought them back."

"I know, but I wanted to do this for you guys. It's no big deal. Are you going to light the grill?" I reminded.

Ryan's eyes were intense as they studied me. It always unnerved me when he looked at me like that, and he seemed to be doing it more and more. I felt naked, as if he could read my mind or steal my soul.

"Aaron!" Ryan called to his brother. "Light the grill for Julia, will you?" His attention returned to me. "Do you want to go to the hardware store for paint and sandpaper after we eat? Might as well get started on fixing it up."

"That sounds good."

It wasn't long before Ryan was grilling the chicken breasts, and Ellie and I were pulling out plates, silverware, and condiments. The guys didn't have much in the refrigerator, but I had purchased everything we needed for the sandwiches.

Ellie opened the plastic container of potato salad and shoved a tablespoon into it.

I sliced a tomato with one of the knives. It was old and dull, so the result was less than stellar. Juice and tomato seeds squashed out onto the plate resulting in a puddle of juice. "Maybe we can go to some thrift shops tomorrow."

"I thought we were doing that after lunch?"

I lifted a shoulder in a half-shrug. "We can, but Ryan offered to help me start working on the table and chairs. You, Aaron, and Jenna could go without us, if you want."

She looked at me steadily as she pulled open the plastic wrapping on the napkins we'd purchased. "You and Ryan, huh?"

I met her eyes briefly then looked away, deciding I should get the lettuce out, and pull some leaves free. I put them next to the tomato slices on the plate.

"Not really."

"Yes, it is."

I shook my head and wiped my hands on one of the napkins. "No, it isn't, Ellie."

"Then why did he insist on picking you up at the airport?"

"I don't know. We're friends. If it was a big deal, I'm sure he would have let you do it." I tried to keep my voice even and not give any of my inner turmoil away.

Jenna had been outside with the boys and came into the kitchen. "I'm starving!" she said then stopped, looking between Ellie and me. "What's up?"

I gave a quick shake of my head. "Nothing."

"I guess you, Aaron and I are going thrifting this afternoon and R and J are working on the table."

"Hmmm. I see." Her blue eyes narrowed.

"Ugh!" I was exasperated. "What's with everyone? Nothing is different between Ryan and me."

Ellie nodded. "Exactly, Julia."

"Yeah," Jenna added.

"What? Ryan suggested we get to work on it. He might not be able to help me as much after classes start. So what?"

"So, it's you and Ryan alone," Jenna said.

"Yeah. *Working.*"

"Did you know Ryan called and asked me if he could pick her up at the airport, Jenna?" Ellie directed the question at Jenna.

"Doesn't surprise me. Why don't you guys just hook up already?" Jenna smirked. "You're done with that Dave guy, right?"

"Yes. So what? Ryan and I are friends and we have this whole dynamic with all of you guys that I don't want to mess up. Also, he doesn't want to." I resisted the urge to shrug. "We talked about it last semester, so can we drop it, please?"

Both of the girls looked surprised. Jenna's eyes got wide, and Ellie's mouth made a silent "oh."

"He doesn't want to." Jenna's tone was skeptical. "Um, not buying it."

"You asked him, Julia?" Ellie was incredulous.

"It was a joke, but it's clear he doesn't want to go there."

"Did he laugh at you?" Ellie was more naïve than Jenna, who continued to study me. I could almost feel her eyes boring a hole into me.

"Guys don't turn down sex. Like, *ever*," Jenna said dryly.

They do when they're your best friend, my mind screamed. "Like I said, it was a joke. Can we stop talking about this before the guys come in? I'm sure the chicken is almost done." I couldn't see Ryan or Aaron given that their apartment was in the basement and the grill was in the backyard, and the last thing I needed was Ryan walking in on this conversation. "Can we drop it?" I asked again.

Ellie refused to let it go. "Ryan isn't indifferent to you, Julia. It's written all over him."

I sucked in my breath. *If only that were true.* I knew he cared about me, but sexually, I felt as appealing to him as a cardboard box. "Nah. Ryan's a magnet for women. He doesn't even realize it."

"Bullshit. He knows, all right," Jenna replied. "I've seen him in action when Aaron and I go out on doubles with him. Those poor girls don't stand a chance when he turns it on."

"Even when he doesn't. The day Julia and I met him, a girl in our class was practically falling over herself to get him to notice her." The conversation had become between Jenna and Ellie, and I was more and more uncomfortable. "It was sort of embarrassing to watch."

My face began to burn, and I knew it would soon be turning red. "Okay, enough. Ryan is really good looking. Women want him. He and I are good friends. The end. I have to go to the bathroom. I'll be out in a couple minutes."

"Julia," Jenna called after me as I hurried down the hall. "We didn't mean to upset you."

I ignored her and kept going, their voices becoming muffled when I shut the door behind me. My chest hurt as I glanced in the mirror. My face was flushed, and my heart pounded so hard it felt like it might fly from my body. The situation was excruciating enough without my best friends hammering me with it. I didn't want to talk about it. Nothing was going to change, and I'd made peace with accepting it, but that didn't mean it didn't hurt.

I turned on the water and put my hand under the running stream. I pressed a cold, wet hand to my forehead then to each of my hot cheeks. I had to get this under control and fast.

*****

Ryan ~

Julia was quiet through lunch. Everything was delicious. The dirt cake thing she made was amazing. We sat in a circle, each of us scooping up mouthfuls of Julia's concoction from the community pan. Everyone showered Julia with accolades, especially Aaron.

"Holy shit, Jules!" he said between mouthfuls. "Oh my God."

"Are you coming in your pants, or eating?" I admonished sardonically. "Jesus, Aaron."

Jenna and Ellie laughed out loud, and Julia's lips curled up in a coy smile. She didn't say much as we cleaned up the mess, throwing the paper plates in the trashcan Aaron and I had stashed in one of the lower cupboards. Ellie gathered the utensils and put them all in the sink. Even though they were plastic, they planned on washing them for re-use.

I wondered what happened to change Julia's mood. We all left at the same time, Aaron, Jenna, and Ellie left in Ellie's car, and Julia was with me in my CRV. The air conditioning was on and the windows closed, but she was looking out of the one on the passenger side.

"Do you feel okay, Julia?"

"Hmm?" She turned her head toward me. "What? I'm fine."

"You look so deep in thought. We can do this another time if you want."

She shook her head. "No, it's okay. I was just thinking. I've been going over the class schedule and I want to take some more art classes, but I only have four hours of electives left. I'm just figuring out if I should even bother."

I was skeptical. Julia never let class stuff preoccupy her as she apparently was now. She was always so decisive. I knew she'd been disappointed when she couldn't double major in art and business because of the way the two colleges were structured within the university, and they didn't allow crossovers, but she hadn't mentioned it in months. When she said she wanted an art table earlier that day, I decided then and there I'd buy one for her birthday the coming month or for Christmas. It made me feel a little giddy knowing I'd be able to give her something that would make her so happy.

"I know how much you love art." I'd seen a few things she'd drawn. One day last spring, we'd had a picnic at one of the local parks, and she'd drawn some sketches of two children playing near us. I'd been shocked at how truly good she was. The drawings were fast, but with a little more work, they'd look like photographs. She was very talented, and it just made me want to be closer to her still. We had so many things in common. We loved the same music, were close to our parents, and we both had big dreams for the future.

"I do, but it's hard. None of it will count toward graduation beyond the four unrestricted elective credits, and I already have that from my freshman year. That, and that one Human Anatomy class."

"I saw a bit of your drawings. You're very good."

She smiled softly. "Thank you, Ryan."

"I mean it. It's my responsibility as your best friend to tell you if you suck at something." I tried to tease her because her introspection was killing me.

"Does that work both ways?"

I shot her a quick glance, a grin splitting my face. "What do you think?" She had her hair all pulled up in a bun on top of her head, tendrils escaping in all directions. I wondered if women made their hair all messy to be provocative, because it worked. The curve of her neck and her bare arms in the shirt she was wearing—the tight material clung to the curves of her breasts and left a hint of cleavage in view, all made me ultra-aware of my attraction to her. My hands gripped the steering wheel harder, and my cock jumped against my will. Fuck, I needed to quit it.

"Yeah." I tried to distract her from noticing my discomfort by redirecting the conversation. "What color should we get for the table and chairs?"

We decided to go to a fabric store first and see what type of material she could find to reupholster the seats before Julia would decide what color paint to buy for the wood. After we found some patterned fabric with teal and cream circles on a brown background, we decided on dark brown.

I had to remind myself five times during our hour and a half shopping trip to stop looking at all of the bare skin she had going on. It was hot, and besides the skimpy burgundy top, she had on jean shorts and flip-flops. I caught myself staring twice.

My determination to be her friend was still firmly in place, but over the summer I'd missed her more than I wanted to admit. The time apart might have made my dilemma worse. Yeah, it was definitely worse. I realized how much I missed her face and even her scent. I kept myself busy with school and dating, but I always looked forward to our Skype sessions and I stopped whatever I was doing when one of her texts came in.

On the way back to the apartment, we stopped to get a newspaper to lay out on the living room floor to protect it while we painted. It was the biggest area in her apartment and would be the easiest way to spread out. We'd gotten some sandpaper in a couple varying degrees of roughness, a putty knife, brushes and a quart of brown enamel paint. I got to work using the putty knife to scrape off as much of the old paint as I could while Julia worked on reupholstering the seats.

I started to sweat and some of the sharp paint shards poked and sliced at my fingers. I stopped and peeled off my shirt, cranking up the rock-n-roll on her iPod; I used it to wipe sweat off my face and chest. She was singing along to the songs, and I tried to ignore the way her ass was in the air as she laid the fabric out and measured it so she could cut it to the appropriate size. I turned my back and kept pushing the sandpaper forcefully over the hard surface of the wood.

"I'm going to need one of those big staple guns, Ryan. Shit! We should have thought of it before."

My phone was on the counter in the kitchen and I could hear it vibrating from an incoming call. "There is no way we'll get finished with this tonight anyway Jules." I got up and walked to my phone.

I sighed when I saw it was from Darcie, a girl I'd been casually dating during the summer. Okay, if I were being honest with myself, I was casually having sex with her, and I hadn't mentioned her to Julia at all. I hadn't tried to see her in the entire week Julia had been back. In fact, I'd barely given her a thought because I was spending so much time with Julia. It was a miracle she hadn't called before this. I hesitated as it rang in my hand, wondering what I should do. I looked at Julia who was using one of the pieces of fabric she'd already cut as a pattern to cut out another seat cover.

I turned my back to Julia and flipped on my phone.

"Yeah?" The music was loud, but I didn't want to raise my voice.

"Hey, lover. Did you forget about me?" Darcie's voice purred on the phone. She was pretty and smart, but for some reason, I couldn't see her as more than a sex partner. I'd wanted to. I'd tried for two months to turn it into more than sex, but it didn't happen.

"I've been busy. Sorry," I said, glancing over my shoulder. Julia was sitting on the floor working on the cushion of a chair, unrolling a big bolt of the white batting she purchased at the fabric store. A rush of guilt washed over me, but I wasn't sure if it was for Darcie or Julia. It was ridiculous either way because

Julia was my friend and I hadn't known Darcie that long. We'd dated quite a few times, but she wasn't my girlfriend.

"Too busy for me?"

"I've been helping some friends move."

"Is it anyone I know? I can come help."

"Uh, that's okay," I said shortly. "And no, you don't know them, and we've got it handled. Aaron and Jenna are helping too."

"Well, come over when you're done. My roommate is gone." Her voice was honeyed and suggestive. Two weeks ago, her cloying tone might have gotten my dick hard, but right now, in this second, with Julia twenty feet from me, it just felt wrong. I shook my head and sighed. This was part of the problem. I had to get over feeling like this if I wasn't going to go crazy. Julia and I had agreed we weren't crossing the line beyond friends, so I needed to shake this off.

"Yeah, okay."

"Yay!" Darcie said, happily. "What time? I'll make sure I'm ready."

What she meant was she'd be ready to have sex. She was all about sex. I wasn't sure if she really liked it or if it was just what she thought she needed to do to keep a guy interested.

"Ten?"

"Okay."

"Listen, I gotta go. I'm in the middle of something."

"What?"

"I'll tell you about it when I see you."

"'Kay. See you later, Ryan. I'm excited to see you."

"Yeah. Bye." I hung up the phone and walked back into the living room. My apprehension must have shown on my face because Julia looked concerned.

"Is everything okay?"

"Yes. It was just a girl I've kind of been seeing this summer."

"Oh," Julia said. Her hands paused in her work for a beat but then she continued with earnest. Her head was bent, and I couldn't see her face.

Heat infused under the skin of my face. I felt ashamed, as if I'd done something wrong. I started sanding the table again, but I felt like shit. I wasn't sure what the fuck was going on or why I was so hesitant to tell Julia about Darcie. Darcie and I were casual, and I didn't really see it going anywhere.

I moved around the table to work on the other side, and Julia was now in my direct line of sight. She kept working without talking or looking up at all. Deep down in my gut, I wanted to talk to her about Darcie—to tell her it wasn't a relationship, but it went against my earlier vow to shake it off. I needed to just blow this off, and go about life as usual.

We kept working without talking, letting the music behind us be the focus. When Julia started singing again, I felt easier, and the tension inside my stomach started to ease. I wasn't sure if she was hurt or just uncomfortable, but I'd figured out a long time ago that keeping my dating activities and my best friend separate was the easiest thing for both of us. Thirty minutes later, Aaron, Jenna, and Ellie burst through the door.

"Hey! Julia, we found a sofa for only seventy-five dollars! I have a lamp and a coffee table, too!" Ellie's excitement was evident on her face.

Jenna came in with a couple bags of stuff and dropped them on the floor. "I found some old shirts we can use for rags to clean and for painting."

Julia looked up, directing a smile at the girls, but didn't look at me at all. "That's great! I'm almost done cutting the fabric and batting for the chairs, but I need one of those big staple guns to finish attaching it all to the wooden base. Do you like the fabric? I tried to stay fairly neutral with just a pop of color. I figured we could add more with the accessories as we add on to everything."

"That's a great idea. I really like it. Ryan, looks like you've been busy, too!" Ellie came to inspect my work. I had most of the old paint scraped off and the tabletop sanded down, but the table legs and the chairs still needed sanding before we could start painting.

"Still a lot to get done." I was shirtless and sweating, my throat parched. "Did you guys bring anything to drink?"

"Aaron has a twelve pack of beer and some soda," Jenna said.

Just as she spoke, my brother appeared in the doorway carrying the two boxes of cans, topped off with three bags from McDonalds.

"We have to go back and get the sofa, Ryan. It will still hang out of the back of the CRV, but we can tie down the hatch-back," Aaron said, walking to me, and looking around the room.

"Okay. No problem." I threw the sandpaper I was holding in the trashcan that was sitting near me, but between the table and where Julia was working on the floor. She had been using it to put the fabric and batting scraps in as she cut out the seat cushions.

It was almost dinnertime, and my stomach was grumbling. I left the girls in the living room and went to help Aaron. There was nothing to set anything on save the countertop, so I took the burger bags off the pile in his arms and set them down. Together we unloaded the soda and beer into the refrigerator.

"Did you get a lot done?" Aaron wanted to know.

"Yeah. But the sanding and painting won't be finished to-night. Maybe tomorrow if we all work on it."

"We could work on it late tonight."

"I can't."

"Why?"

"Let's eat, and I'll talk to you about it on the way to get the couch." I was already popping the can of a beer and unwrapping a burger. I took a big bite.

"Hey, girls! I have food."

The girls were talking among themselves when they walked into the room. Julia went to the refrigerator and took out a Diet Coke. "Thanks for getting the burgers and drinks, Aaron."

He smiled wide. "No problem! As much as you feed me, I owe you more than a burger, Julia."

"I like doing it," she said.

"Because you're awesome! Give Jen some lessons."

"I'll give *you* some lessons," Jenna retorted dryly.

We all laughed then sat down on the floor, crossed-legged and leaned up against the cupboards for a backrest, as we ate our burgers and fries.

"We have to pick the sofa up tonight. Can you guys do that?"

"Sure. We can go when we're done eating. When we get back, Julia can finish the seats, and if all of us work on it, we should be able to get the sanding finished tonight, and then we can paint tomorrow." I took the last bite of my burger after I'd finished speaking.

"I wanted to go out tonight," Jenna said, her words directed at Aaron. "It's Saturday night."

"I sort of promised Jen we'd go to a club tonight, Ryan," Aaron agreed.

"Yeah, it's okay, Ryan," Julia said.

"I'd like to go out, too!" Ellie added. "We can all go."

"Um, I was going to work on this until I get the table done, but the rest of you go." I looked right at Julia. Her big green eyes met mine. "You, too, Jules."

She shook her head. "No way. I'm not letting you work while I go out. I'll work, with you."

"Okay, but just a few more hours, and then we call it a night."

"Sure," she said.

I got up and walked into the other room to throw the wrappers and empty box from my fries in the trash. "Aaron, are you ready? Let's get the couch. We'll push it up against the wall in here until we're done working on the table and chairs."

"Just a couple more bites, Ryan." He was almost finished with his second burger.

"Ryan, will you stop and get me one of those staplers if I give you cash?"

I was ready to tell her she didn't need to give me money for it but stopped myself. At least in front of everyone else, I wouldn't say I'd buy it. I'd just return her money to her later.

"I don't know how much it will be, but here is thirty dollars." She handed me the cash and I shoved it in my pocket.

"Is the thrift shop anywhere near a home improvement or hardware store Aaron? Which one did you go to?" I asked.

"Thrift World. The one on Baker Street. I think there's an Ace about a mile from there," Aaron answered.

I nodded and pulled my shirt back on. I hoped it didn't smell too bad, and I lifted my arm to sniff it.

Jenna let out a hearty laugh. "Are you stinky, Ryan?"

"I can't tell," I said honestly. My face twisted wryly, and I walked up to Julia. There was no one else in the room I would ask if I stunk. No way. "Well?"

"Oh, I get the honors? Thanks *so* much." She smiled and leaned in, sniffing twice. "Nope, you're okay. No more stinky than usual." She shoved me in the shoulder, letting out a small laugh.

I noticed Ellie studying the interaction between Julia and me and I met her eyes steadily. "What? Do you want a sniff, too?"

She huffed. "As if, Ryan!"

"Okay, then stop with the looks."

Julia had resumed her work on the floor, and her head popped up to look from Ellie to me and back again.

"I just think it's funny. You and Julia. It's like you're—"

"If you say brother and sister, I might have to hurt you," I retorted before I could stop myself, but my tone was teasing. I dug my keys out of the front pocket of my khaki shorts.

"I was going to say an old married couple."

"Hardly, Ellie," Julia said. I couldn't tell if her laugh was nervous embarrassment or mocking.

I ignored her comment.

"I agree with Ellie!" Jenna said with a grin. "I don't understand you guys at all. You should just date."

It wasn't her place to understand anything, and I didn't care what any of them thought about our relationship. Again, I got that weird feeling in my gut that I hated. Julia's head was down again and I couldn't tell what she was thinking. "Aaron, you ready?"

"Yep." He threw the papers from his burgers on the counter and followed me out the door.

When we got in my CRV, I looked at Aaron right after I shoved the key in the ignition. "Aaron, can you ask your girlfriend to stop saying shit like that?" I was irritated and it showed.

I pulled out of the parking lot of their building and made a left turn.

"I'm sure she meant nothing by it, bro. She sees how you and Julia are together, that's all. We all do."

"You don't know shit. My relationship with Julia is nobody's business."

"Why are you getting so pissed, Ryan?"

I took a deep breath. "I'm not. It's just that it's hard enough without the rest of you interjecting crap we need to address. Just leave us alone."

"I've been thinking it for more than two years. Why the fuck aren't you with her, again?" I shot him a dirty look that told him to shut the fuck up, but he didn't. "I mean, you're *with* her."

"No I'm not. The reason I can't go out tonight is because I'm seeing Darcie."

He was quiet for a moment, and I concentrated on the road.

"How do you feel about Darcie?"

If I told the truth, I'd sound like a dick. "I like her. She's sexy, and we have fun together."

"And how do you feel about Julia?"

My jaw shot out. Leave it to Aaron to make me think about it. I shook my head without answering.

"Well?"

"Well, what? What do you want me to say?"

"I want you to answer the question."

I swallowed and pulled into the parking lot of the thrift store.

"I care about Julia. She's my best friend."

"You don't think she's hot?"

I parked then turned toward Aaron angrily. "Yeah! I think she's hot, but that just complicates everything!"

"When you're fucking other women, are you thinking about Julia? When you beat off, are you thinking about her?"

I glared at him. I'd never wanted to punch my brother before, but I was inches from it. This wasn't anything I hadn't already thought about.

"That doesn't matter, Aaron. My romantic relationships don't last long and Julia is someone I want around for good."

"Listen to yourself, Ryan. Jesus, I feel like Dr. Phil. Your relationships tank because you're not *in them*. Julia is the reason you don't care about anyone else. Don't you get that?"

My skin felt on fire, heat rushing up from my chest and over my neck to finally burn my face. It physically burned. I sighed and looked out through the windshield, the muscle in my jaw working overtime.

"You're in denial. We all see it."

"I'm not going to fuck up my friendship with Julia and I'm not going to tell you that again! Just drop it. Don't bring it up, and tell Jenna to keep her mouth shut!"

He shook his head in disgust. "When you're fucking Darcie tonight, you remember what I said. See who you're thinking about."

"I said, shut the fuck up, Aaron!" I was pissed, but was I angry at Aaron or myself? I didn't know. "I know what I'm doing." My tone was fierce, and I was furious he was making me face something I'd been trying to tamp down for-fucking ever.

He looked at me in disbelief. "Okay, whatever Ryan." He pulled on the door handle and started to get out of the car. "You're hurting Julia, in case you didn't notice," he shot at me, frowning.

I shut off the engine and got out. I was still fuming, but felt sick inside as we started to walk into the store. Hurting Julia was the last thing I wanted to do.

"But, what-the-fuck-ever," Aaron muttered under his breath.

Inside, I wanted to look around and found an old pair of jeans I could wear the next day to paint in and threw them over my shoulder. I still hadn't spoken to him, but when Aaron saw what I was doing, he followed suit. I went to the men's shirt section and found a button-down with short sleeves. It was an ugly plaid and in a small size.

"That won't fit you, Ryan," he muttered.

"Thanks, Mr. Obvious. It's not for me." I flushed at the implications of the impending purchase.

He nodded knowingly, his brows rising and his mouth pressing into a thin line. "I bet you a hundred bucks it isn't for Darcie."

I walked around him without a word and went to the register to pay for the pants and shirt.

Aaron handed over the paid-in-full receipt for the couch. "We're here to get this. I was here earlier."

"Sure. We have a loading dock of sorts at the back of the building." She pointed to the rear of the building. "Drive around. I'll open the door and meet you there."

Aaron went with the girl, and I went to my car. The heat that accumulated inside from the beating down sunshine made the inside suffocating. It didn't help that I felt like a thousand pound weight was on my chest. I turned on the engine and cranked the A/C. "Fuuuuuuck!" I yelled. I threw myself back in my seat and rubbed a hand over my face. "God damn you, Aaron!"

I sat there for a good five minutes before I felt in control enough to drive around the back of the store to pick up my brother and the couch.

*****

Julia ~

It was dark, but I had three candles burning that flickered on the walls and ceiling. I was lying on the new, old couch, alone in my new apartment. Aaron, Ellie, and Jenna had left to go to one of the dance clubs about three hours earlier. Ryan left an hour ago after his phone wouldn't stop ringing.

It was awkward, but I'd finally gotten it out of him that the person calling was a girl he'd been dating all summer. While it hurt, I wasn't shocked. I wasn't surprised he didn't tell me about her any more than I wasn't surprised I didn't tell him I broke up with Dave.

My chest felt hollow, and my throat ached. My eyes burned with unshed tears. I was trying so hard not to cry. Fuck crying. Fuck feeling like hell. I was staring at the flickering shadows the candles cast off of things around the room, but it all blurred in front of my eyes as they filled with tears.

It ripped my heart out to think of him with someone else. I felt like I was dying. I couldn't breathe as I rolled onto my side and pulled my knees up. I wrapped my arms around them, closed my eyes, and the tears were forced out, rolling down my face. One dripped from the bridge of my nose and onto the arm of the couch, which my head was resting on. It was uncomfortable without a pillow, but I barely noticed. I drew in a shaky breath, that felt like a knife shredding my lungs as they resisted expanding.

It didn't matter that I'd told myself I was going to deal. It still hurt like hell. I loved him more than was healthy, and I bottled it all up inside. I sniffed as the tears dripped silently from my eyes until finally, the sobs started to shake my shoulders, and the sound of it filled the room. I couldn't help it, and maybe letting it out was the release I needed. All of this pent-up misery had to go somewhere. Ryan caused so many emotions, and I was addicted. Addicted to the rush of seeing him, addicted to the love I felt, addicted to his face, and addicted to the way only he could make me feel... and even to this awful, debilitating pain. I even needed it in some sick way.

It meant I loved him, and to nullify the pain would mean losing the love. Maybe losing Ryan. It would mean being away from him, of ending our friendship, and even then, I'd hurt. I wasn't sure quitting him cold turkey would be any better than this. I'd be miserable every minute and not just the evenings like this. Until graduation, knowing he was close by, it would be worse trying to stay away from him than dealing with this shit whenever he went out. I gasped for breath and sat up, wiping at the tears on my cheeks with both of my hands.

I went to the kitchen to get a glass of water, but seeing the few beers still left in the fridge, I took one of those instead. I hated beer, but maybe it would help me sleep. I wanted sleep— deep enough not to dream. I popped it open and took a long chug. It tasted bitter, and I grimaced. Still, I chugged down half of the can. I needed something to occupy my mind. There was only one thing that worked on nights like this. I set my beer on the floor under one of the windows next to where the candles were and picked one of them up. My bare feet padded into my bedroom to find my sketchpad and charcoal pencils before retracing my steps.

I set the candle down then settled next to it, on the floor and leaning against the wall under the window. I opened the pad and picked up a pencil. I'd decided on a soft rock playlist on my iPod, and the soft strains of *Mirrors* came on. It was a cover version of the Justin Timberlake song that Ryan had found by accident, and we both liked it better than the original. It was acoustic and Ryan had even played along with it once. Without sheet music, he'd been able to follow it perfectly.

The harmonies were calming. I sucked in my breath and threw my head back trying to form in my head, the image of what I wanted to draw. The song filled the room and reminded me of Ryan. Of us. There was no way I could not see him. Regardless of this fucking struggle, I had to come to terms with it. I knew I could count on Ryan, and we'd always be there for each other, no matter what. That fact would have to get me through nights like this.

I started to sing with the song as I put his image on the page. I felt calmer, my heart settled and the ache began to ease.

It was midnight when I finished and put the new portrait of Ryan into my portfolio. I leaned it up against the wall, wishing I had an art table to stash the sketchpad and pencils in. Instead, I took them with me to the bedroom to put them away in the lower drawer of the dresser. A hot shower and bed, then the sun would rise on another Sunday. Ryan would come over, and we'd finish the work on the table set... Maybe I'd make breakfast if he came early enough.

*****

Ryan ~

I did it. But once it was done, I had to get the fuck out of there. *Goddamn Aaron.* He was right. I felt intensely claustrophobic with Darcie's fingers grasping and pulling at my back and arms. I'd had to turn her over and take her from behind just to get through it. It was ridiculous. I'd been with several women in the past two years, and yes, maybe I did think about Julia from time to time. I couldn't lie to myself about it. But tonight, she was everywhere, in everything.

Maybe there were times I deliberately had sex with someone because the feelings I had for Julia were becoming too much
for me, but besides that, Aaron's words were still raw and
screaming at me. The minute Darcie and I were done, I wanted
to leave. I felt like a dick on multiple levels, but it didn't matter.
I'd rarely stayed all night during the summer either, but now,
tonight, there was no way in hell it could happen.

It was barely midnight. I'd arrived later than I planned and
was with her less than an hour. Still, I had to leave. I got up,
peeled the condom off, and threw it in the trash. Darcie's apartment was on the opposite side of campus from mine and Aaron's
and now, Ellie and Julia's.

"Ryan?" Darcie called softly from the bedroom. The bathroom wasn't connected, and thank goodness, her roommate was
out because I was naked.

"Yeah?" I called back, turning on the water. I splashed
some on my face then used toilet paper to clean off my cock as
best I could before throwing it in the toilet and flushing it.

"Come back to bed."

I walked back into the dark bedroom and fumbled around to
find my clothes. "I gotta go," I said, sitting down on the edge of
the bed to put on my boxer briefs then quickly stood to pull them
up. I bent to retrieve my jeans.

She propped up onto her elbow, the white sheet outlined her
body but I couldn't see her expression without a light on. I
couldn't see her red hair or her eyes. I didn't want to. "You were
late getting here, now you're leaving already?"

"Yeah. I have work to do early tomorrow. *Today*," I added.

"So, what? I'm just a quick fuck tonight?"

"Darcie, you asked me to come over. I told you I was working." I was impatient, threw my T-shirt over my head, and
shoved my arms in the sleeves.

"I know. Cuz I wanted to see you. I haven't seen you at all this week. What's different?" I could hear the disappointment in her voice.

"I'm sorry. I'm busy this week. I'm helping some friends set up their apartment before classes start."

"Who are the friends?"

"Mainly, it's my best friend, Julia Abbott."

"A woman?"

"Yes." I ran my hand through my hair. "We found some old furniture and we're trying to restore it. It's a lot of work, and I promised I'd be there early."

"Why haven't you mentioned her before?"

Fuck, did I want to tell her the truth? What the hell, my mind couldn't come up with a lie. "Because I keep Julia separate from the women I date."

Darcie sat up further, gathering the sheet to cover her chest. "Why? Is she jealous?"

More word vomit truth was coming and I couldn't stop it. "Not necessarily. You might be, though."

"Is she some sort of beauty queen or something?"

"Or something," I agreed. "Look Darcie, I really don't want to get into it."

"Maybe I do." She reached over and turned on the lamp on the nightstand.

I sighed and put my hands on my hips, exasperated. "Okay, fine. What'd ya want to know?"

"So she is pretty?"

"Yeah, and smart and cool. I can tell her anything."

"Not everything, if you didn't tell her about me."

I met her eyes steadily but shook my head. "No."

She looked hurt and angry, a frown on her face. "Why isn't she your girlfriend if she's so great?"

"*Because* she's so great is the reason." Shit! I knew that was the wrong thing to say as soon as the words were out. I didn't need a light on to sense Darcie's anger. "Just... I gotta go."

"You've got problems, Ryan!" Darcie spat. "You're a dick for treating me this way!"

I turned back around on my way out the door, getting pissed myself. "How did I treat you? Other than I didn't tell you about Julia? We've only been out a few times, and you wanted to have sex as much as I did. We both know it. I'm sorry you're upset, but I didn't do anything to you."

I walked out of her room and to the door of her apartment without a backward glance, hoping she'd never call me again.

When I got home, I went into the shower and let the hot water rush over me, soaking my hair. I wanted to get any remnants of sex with Darcie off my body. I soaped down then leaned against the side of the shower stall, my hand falling onto my heart.

Ugh! I thought. I had to get a grip. It was true I had to help Julia finish painting the table the following day, and despite the orgasm I'd had, I wasn't ready to sleep. Aaron wasn't back yet, and I wondered if he would be. Maybe he'd be staying at Jenna's place.

I rubbed my hair dry and pulled on some old sweats but no shirt. I didn't bother combing my hair, but I did brush my teeth before going into the living room and grabbing the remote. I threw myself down on the couch at an angle. I began flipping through the channels. I felt off balance, and it fucking sucked.

It was worse since Julia and I had the "friends with bennies" talk last semester. It was as if now it was a real possibility I'd be able to be with her like that. *It could happen.* She wouldn't have brought it up if she hadn't thought about it. She must want it to happen, and I wanted it too. Badly. But I wanted her in my life more than I wanted to fuck her. I might even need her in my life. She was the balance and that was why I was feeling so fucked up right now.

"Shake it off," I said to myself. "Shake it off."

"Shake what off?" Aaron asked. He'd come in quietly for him and I barely heard the door open.

"I'm not talking to you."

"Real mature, Ryan."

"What do you want from me, Aaron? What's your purpose in this?"

"Nothing. Just trying to keep you from doing something you'll regret."

"Too late. You said enough earlier."

"Ah," he said knowingly. "Did you see Darcie?"

"Yep," I answered shortly, not elaborating as I flipped through more of the cable channels.

"Did you screw her?"

"No comment."

Aaron went to the kitchen and came back with a glass of water. "How'd that make you feel?"

"Fuck off, Aaron. I don't want to talk about it."

"Well, you aren't going to talk to Julia about this, and you need to talk. You're wound up."

I sat up and threw the remote on the coffee table. "Okay. Yes, I was with Darcie. And thanks to you, I couldn't get Julia out of my head!" I threw my hands up as I scowled at my brother.

He laughed and sat down on the chair closer to the TV. I wanted to punch him in his smug face. "Oh, it's not because of me... it's because of her, shithead."

"Look, Aaron, I don't want to talk about it anymore. It's be-tween Julia and me. Just stay out of it, got it? It's none of your business." I hoped my voice relayed some of my frustration and my need for him just to respect my wishes. "It's hard enough as it is."

"Yes, I can see that."

"But nothing is going to change, and you just make it worse. Let us handle it."

"Ryan, you and Julia are inevitable. When are you gonna accept it?"

"I have. I know we're going to be in each other's lives forever. No matter what I have to do or not do," I said earnestly. "She might get hurt if we move this beyond friendship and it doesn't work out. I couldn't live with myself."

"You might get hurt, too. Isn't that what you mean?"

"Maybe, but I don't matter. Julia does."

"You're both hurting already."

We were. I knew it, but it was a different kind of pain than not having each other. "What? Are you a girl, now? We're fine. We've discussed it. Just stay the fuck out of it. Please." My throat got tight. This was, maybe, the most honest I'd been about my feelings about Julia. To myself or anyone else, and it hurt. I was sick of repeating myself to my brother and hoped he'd let this be the end of it. "Just let it go."

Aaron stood up and walked behind the couch. He put a hand on my bare shoulder and squeezed. "Okay. I'm going to bed."

"Night."

"Are we working at Julia and Ellie's tomorrow?"

"I don't make plans for you, but I am. Before I left, she said she'd make breakfast."

Aaron stopped halfway down the hall. "What's she making?"

"Muffins, eggs, and bacon, I think."

"I'm there, then. Did she like the shirt you bought her at the thrift store?"

"I bought it for painting, Aaron. Obviously, it was a dude's shirt."

"I know why you bought it. Did she like it?"

I remembered the way her face lit up when I gave it to her. "Yeah. Yeah, she liked it."

~10~

A Night out at Stanford

Ryan ~

I hated this fucking place! The music pounded in my ears and it was almost packed body-to-body. The sort of uncomfortably packed that was only okay if you were drunk off your ass and you didn't care if some other dude rubbed up on your date. The club was swanky, bordering on cheesy, but to me, it felt like a throwback to a 1970s disco, circa Saturday Night Fever. Except not as cool, and the sort of mind-numbing rhythm that was just a beat littered with a series of grunts, held little resemblance to actual music.

Normally, I wouldn't be caught dead here but my date Leah, picked the joint, not me. It was dark, the walls deep burgundy with a dance floor in the back of the large room that was just a continuation of the wood floor. The DJ and twenty or so couples bouncing up and down were the only things that set it apart from the rest of the room. Low couches were lined up around square tables, and they were littered with women and men who were drinking too much and carrying on together. I almost visibly cringed.

Fingers tightened possessively around mine as I led my date through the throng, shouldering my way in between the crowd toward a vacancy on one of the couches near the dance floor. I would have preferred a greater distance from the speakers, but as my eyes adjusted to the dim light, I realized actual seats were hard to come by, and it was so busy, people were lined up against walls and stacked up two and three deep at the bar. The darkness was broken by only a few flashing lights that reflected off the mirrored ball above the dance floor. My brain fought back the urge to turn around and leave, but instead, I motioned for Leah to take a seat.

"I'll go get drinks. Do you want one?"

She lifted her eyes to mine. She was pretty with delicate bone structure and bouncy blonde curls that barely reached her shoulders. She was also model-thin, and besides wasting twenty bucks on a meal she hadn't touched, it just wasn't that attractive.

Her father was a bigwig in the California legislature but, from what I gathered from her dinner conversation, her mother spent all day in the spa and did little else. My father might approve on the surface, but my mother would raise a cynical eyebrow, especially after meeting my best friend. Substance—Julia had loads of it, and most of the women I dated weren't worthy to stand in her shadow. I'd fucked my chances at ever getting my mother's approval on anyone else after taking Julia home for Christmas last year. Maybe that was why I didn't bother.

The woman in front of me looked properly primped and groomed, completely coiffed, even if her bones did poke out more than I preferred. I knew, all too well, that appearances could be deceiving, and while I'd hoped for depth, her personality was a little too narcissistic for my taste. Sure, my friends gave me shit about my looks all the time, and I played into it for fun. Mostly because it made Julia blush and I loved to tease her. I had a hard time admitting it, even to myself, but a part of me puffed up that she found me attractive. It was mutual, and we both knew it, but somehow we managed to push it aside when we were together. As much as I'd tried to deny it and overcome it, I was still suffering a serious pull to her. It was a much-needed balm to let myself believe Julia had to deal with the same bullshit I did.

I'd only known Leah since the semester began a couple weeks earlier, but I'd already gathered she detested being Mommy and Daddy's perfect little princess and was looking to rebel in a big way. She might look fragile, but the beginning of the evening had shocked the shit out of my expectations. The suggestive expression in her eyes and the way she continually found excuses to touch me left me with little doubt the evening could end up between the sheets if that's what I wanted. Intuition was telling me to keep my dick in my pants or I'd be sorry. My father had schooled both Aaron and I to be wary of women with little or no ambition.

Her red-tipped fingers wound around my bare forearm, below the rolled up sleeves of my midnight blue button-down—a shirt Julia had given me this past Christmas. Already, it was one of my favorites. She had a blouse in the same shade, and I'd mentioned that I loved the color, but I meant I loved it on *her*. She said it matched my eyes, and my heart hammered a little at the admission. She was amazing. She'd given me the shirt and paid for an online study course for the MCATs. I'd looked into it myself and knew it was more than a couple thousand dollars. I'd been shocked at her generosity, though later I realized she was just being Julia. My parents would have paid for tutors or anything else I needed to prepare, but my original plan was to pay for it myself. I was so moved that Julia had done it. She'd loved the art table I got her, too, but it couldn't compare with the MCAT course. It was funny. She didn't buy herself an art table because she'd used all her money to pay for the course and I bought her the art table in lieu of the course, knowing my parents would buy it for me. It still made me smile thinking about it. It was like a modern day Gift of the Magi, and Aaron rubbed my nose in it every chance he got.

Julia and I were still managing to keep our dating lives and our friendship separate. It was tough because I wanted to know everything about her, but the truth was, ignorance was probably bliss and I'd be a stupid ass if I pushed to know more. She was incredible and other guys flocked to her like crazy. I saw it everywhere we went.

Leah's mouth moved, but I couldn't hear her over the din or my wandering thoughts.

I leaned down, and her thick perfume wafted around me. It was strong and just like Leah; subtle when you observed it from a distance, but a little too overdone up close.

"What?" My words were just shy of a shout.

"Whatever you're having is fine." She echoed the volume of my voice.

I huffed silently and nodded with a fake smile as I turned toward the bar. She couldn't even decide what she wanted to drink? I was bored, if I was honest, and now I was pretty much guaranteed to end up with a pounding headache before the evening was over. I found myself wishing I'd stayed in and just invited Julia over for pizza and a movie instead.

This past semester we'd perfected our silence pact and now it was an unspoken rule there were some things we just didn't talk about. While at times it killed me, it meant we could spend more time together. Lately, it had occurred to me we were getting way too close, and our comfortable friendship was beginning to become more. I wanted to hang out with Julia. She was fun, funny, gorgeous, and smart. The harder I tried to keep things on an even keel, the more I noticed her tight little ass or the way she used the tip of her tongue to lick hot chocolate off her full lower lip. It was getting more difficult to be around her and not touch her. The yearning was becoming unbearable. It felt like the natural progression of us, and she excited me more than any plastic Barbie doll-wannabe ever could. But that was just the problem. If it was bad last year, now it was excruciating. It was sort of a blissful torture that I needed like some sort of intoxicating addiction. If I weren't careful, it would only be a matter of time before I did something stupid.

I inhaled deeply and ran a hand through my hair on my way to the bar. It was in the back, opposite the door. I leaned in to get the bartender's attention and ordered two bottles of Budweiser.

"Can I get a glass with one of those, please?" I asked loudly.

"Sure."

As I waited for him to bring the beer, I pulled out my money and unfurled a ten-dollar bill. A cocktail waitress standing next to me was loading up a bunch of lemon drop shots on her tray before she returned to the floor. My mouth quirked as I handed over the money and prepared to take the beers, one of them with a glass resting upside down over the neck.

Of course, I berated myself silently. The corner of my mouth curled in a sarcastic grin. Another reminder. Lemon drops were Julia's favorite shot. *Could I not get a fucking break?*

I turned around, lifting my beer to my lips at the same time, ready to take a long pull on my way back to the table, when a hard hand on my chest stopped me dead in my tracks, and almost spilling beer down the front of my shirt.

"What are you doing here?"

I looked down into Ellie's accusing gray eyes, her left eyebrow was cocked sharply.

"Uh…" I began, bemused, but automatically my eyes began scanning for Julia. "Having a beer? Didn't know you owned this shithole."

Ellie's hands rested on her hips and her jaw set. "You never come here. That's why... Oh, hell!"

"Yeah, I hate this damn place. I'd never pick it, but my date wanted to come. Is Jules with you?"

"She's having a good time, and she doesn't need you hovering."

My brows knitted together in a frown as I looked down on the much shorter woman. "I'm not! I don't." I finally took a swig from the bottle, only to gaze around the bar.

"Yeah, sure you don't."

"What's your problem?" I asked, irritated.

"Just let her be, Ryan. It would be better if she didn't even know you were here. She'll be too busy worrying about you to have a good time."

"Whatever. Since when is hanging out with you guys off limits?"

"Since you started going all Neanderthal ape-shit when any-one male even glances in Julia's direction."

I ignored the implications and flushed, uncomfortable from her shrewd observation and now worried that she'd said some-thing similar to Julia. Or worse, that my feelings were obvious to everyone. Ever since the "Dave" situation, I'd tried hard to lighten up. That was nearly a year ago now, and though I was uncomfortable then, the closeness I shared with her now was compounded.

I rewarded Ellie with a wry look. "Is there something that will freak me out?" The hair on the back of my neck was begin-ning to prickle.

"See, that's just it. *Nothing!* She's an adult. Nothing should freak you out, Ryan. She gets to do what she wants, and as her friend, you should support her."

"As long as she isn't getting hurt, it's cool." I dismissed her with a roll of my eyes, but the very direction of this conversation had me feeling uneasy.

"It's cool." Ellie mocked dryly, staring up into my eyes with a shake of her head, and apparently waiting for me to slap a condition on what I'd just said. I was getting tired of the inquisition.

"Yesssss," I hissed. "Can I go back to my date now, Ellie? Christ!" I began to move around her as she still stood in my path, but she grabbed my arm. "What?" I was starting to get pissed and wondered what the fuck she was trying to keep from me.

"Where are you sitting?"

I used my beer as a pointer. "Over there, on that couch near the dance floor."

"Shit."

"Why? What is it I'm not supposed to see? Is some asshole trying to get her drunk? I saw that tray of lemon drops head out from the bar a minute ago."

"She's having fun and dancing. Letting loose a little. If she sees you, just chill and let her be."

My mouth settled into a firm line as I noted the direction of Ellie's glance. If she was worried about my reaction, then something was worth worrying about. I did a half-turn, and my eyes narrowed as I searched the crowd and finally landed on Julia.

She was standing near a table on the opposite side of the dance floor from where I'd left Leah lounging on one of the couches. My breath hitched as I looked her over. She looked stunning wearing a short, black sequined dress with miles of bare leg showing. I couldn't see her feet from where I was standing, but I knew she'd have on some sort of amazing high heels. Her hair looked wild, as if she'd just been freshly fucked, and I nearly dropped my beer, realizing just how often I'd fantasized over that very image. I lifted the hand still holding my beer and wiped at my mouth with the back of my wrist.

"Holy fuck," I said under my breath.

"Yeah," Ellie muttered and shook her head again. "This is not good."

I watched Julia's head fall back as she laughed at something the man next to her said, her hair tumbling down almost to her waist. Then he handed her a shot. Julia took it, clinked her glass with his, and threw it back before setting the glass back down on the tray.

"Ryan!" Ellie waved her hand in front of my face until I looked at her again. She pointed toward my date. "Go on! You're being rude to that girl."

My chest felt weird; curiously tight, and my heart was thudding sickeningly in my chest, like a tennis ball that'd been caged inside a tin can and kicked down a steep hill. It was strangely painful and completely foreign. I was used to feeling protective, and I didn't usually like the guys who were with her, but this was starting to hurt. Physically hurt.

I'd known Julia over two years, and this wasn't the first time I'd seen her dressed up. I knew she was hot. I had eyes, and my dick had a mind of its own, despite my attempts to quell it since the second we met. But what was fucking me up was that she was here without me, and she was having a great time. In this steaming den of hormonal college guys just looking for their next conquest, all of them leering at her legs and the soft curves swelling under the clingy fabric that sparkled softly in all the right places. She was a prime target. It didn't hurt that her face was so beautiful, and her hair was long and screaming to be touched. I glanced at the men near her and the ones lounging on the couches openly ogling her legs, and my chest was ready to explode and my face felt hot. I felt like every male eye in the place was trained on her. It would only be a matter of time before one of those jackasses tried to touch her in a way I wouldn't like.

Ellie shoved me gently in the chest with both hands, and I dragged my eyes away from Julia back down to her face. "Can you just be cool? Ryan?"

"What? Who are those guys?" I didn't recognize them, but the taller of the two, the dark-haired one who'd bought the tray of shots, was leaning in to speak to her, and his hand settled lightly on her hip.

"They're just guys to dance with. They're students at Stanford, too."

My eyes honed in on the one touching Julia. "I've never seen them before."

"Yeah, well it's a big campus. So, we good?"

I cleared my throat. "Yeah. But if something happens... come and get me."

"Ryan." Ellie rolled her eyes in reproach.

"It's either that or Leah and I can just join the party right now." She looked pissed, and I didn't give a fuck. "That's the best I got. Take it or leave it."

"I'm sure your date would appreciate that, Ryan. God!"

"I barely know her, Ellie. Julia comes first."

She looked me square in the eye. "Would it matter if you'd known her for ten years?"

"Probably not," I said without thinking, still watching what was going on at the table across the club.

Ellie sighed, her chest visibly heaving. "Well, at least that's honest."

I ignored her and turned away toward my date; who was bouncing around as she did some ridiculous chair dance. *Fucking embarrassing*, I thought. She looked ridiculous. No doubt, she'd probably drag me to dance, which would shoot Ellie's request I keep a low profile, all to hell. I did a mental shrug as I handed Leah her beer. This place was small, so it was likely Julia would see me anyway. I wasn't exactly sure I didn't want her to. I wanted her to know I was here if she needed me, but it felt strange to be around her when we were each with other people. It was uncomfortable, and I continually found myself wishing it were just the two of us. I had an overwhelming urge to storm across the bar and make sure that dude knew he'd better keep it on the up and up with Julia, but that would only be awkward and embarrassing. I couldn't do that to my date, or my best friend. Instead, I settled down and bored holes in his back with my eyes.

The couch was too low for me. The thing was maybe 18 inches off the floor, and my legs felt cramped between the edge of the seat and the table. Leah smiled and rested her hand on my chest in an awkward attempt to re-establish my attention on her. I smiled weakly, pulled out my cell phone, and fiddled with it, fighting the desire to send Julia a text. It wouldn't be the first time I'd been out with a woman and sought out opportunities to check up on her. Right now, I didn't stand on pretense or formality. My fingers itched to type out a text.

"Ryan, do you want to dance?"

My brows furrowed at Leah's words while my thumbs hammered the keys of my phone. "Maybe in a while," I threw out offhandedly; distracted between my phone and watching what Julia was doing. Ellie was seated at the table, and Julia was still standing next to it. Her companion leaned in and whispered something into her ear. It was way more intimate than I wanted to witness, his hand skirting up her bare thigh toward the hem of her dress. I hesitated half a second before I pushed send. I pulled at the front of my shirt as my chest tightened painfully.

What are you doing?

When she found out I was here and already knew exactly what she was doing, she'd be pissed that I'd ask, but I wasn't thinking much beyond needing to see if she'd tell me the truth.

The music changed to a slow pulse with more of a melody. I watched the guy take Julia's slender hand in his and tug her slowly toward the middle of the dance floor, closer to me. My eyes roamed over them both; jealousy took a tighter grip deep down in my gut and my muscles coiled. At the bar, I'd barely glanced in his direction, but now with Julia, he had my undivided attention.

"I really like this song," Leah murmured, her fingers now worming their way in between two of the buttons on my shirt to scratch lightly on my bare chest. "Mmmm... you feel nice." Her voice was beguiling, and I realized she was trying desperately to get me to pay attention to her. I chugged the last couple ounces of the beer from my bottle and waved the empty bottle at the waitress. I held up two fingers, and she nodded in understanding.

It took every ounce of strength I had to pull my eyes away from Julia, but if I didn't, I wouldn't be able to stop myself from doing something I had no right to do. I turned to Leah, pulling her fingers from my shirt to enfold them with my own. I smiled at her, trying to concentrate on her dark brown eyes and not the asshole wrapped around Julia less than twenty feet in front of me. Leah was babbling on endlessly about a trip to Europe she took with a group of friends over Christmas break, when the waitress brought us our beers. She set them both in front of me and I grabbed the closest one, wanting to get hammered but knowing I wouldn't. How could I take care of Julia if I was wasted?

The music changed again, and I raised my head away from Leah, letting myself glance toward the dance floor and the table where Julia had been. She wasn't there. The guy wasn't either. My breath left in a rush as panic washed over me and I sat up straighter, trying to untangle Leah, who was halfway draped across my chest by now, with one of her legs hitched over my knee.

"Ryan, let's go back to my place," she said, her voice low and dripping with sex. Too bad it didn't do a goddamned thing to distract me. Her hand roaming high on my thigh was only pissing me off when I wanted to be free of her. Her fingers squeezed suggestively as her hand inched closer to my crotch, and her lips nudged my jaw. "If you don't want to dance, maybe we can find something else to do."

My beer slipped from my fingers, and I scrambled to catch it but it was being lifted by another set of slender fingers without the blazing red nails. By the time my eyes shifted up and focused, Julia was leisurely taking a drink from my bottle. Her hooded green eyes appraised me, with my date almost on my lap. I barely noticed Leah because my attention was on Julia, and then her eyes shifted twelve inches right, landing on Leah. Julia hated beer, but still here she was, stamping her ownership with something as simple as a pull on my beer bottle. She probably didn't even know the effect it had on me at such a base level, but I fucking loved it. Something tightened deep inside my chest, and my dick twitched inside my jeans.

"Ryan! Are you gonna let her do that?" Leah demanded indignantly, her eyes flashing haughtily up at Julia.

My lips raised in the slightest smirk. Julia echoed it when her eyes locked with mine.

"Yeah, she... uh, she can do that," I confirmed without emphasis. Amusement at Julia's confidence made me want to laugh out loud. I felt fucking elated.

Leah huffed beside me and angrily flung herself back against the cushions of the couch, removing her leg from mine. "Well, do you know her?"

"Yeah. Yeah, I know her." *Boy, do I know her.*

Julia wobbled a little, and I could see she'd had more to drink than she needed. Still, she grinned at me, her arm bent at the elbow as she curled my beer close to her chest, not drinking, just holding it in place. My instinct was to reach out or stand up to steady her.

Angrily, Leah pushed on my shoulder and spewed venom in Julia's direction. "Are you going to introduce us? Is she your sister?"

Julia started to giggle. "Pffft! Do I look like his sister?"

"Then who are you?" my date demanded, her expression hard. I watched the exchange, anxious to see what Julia would say.

"Oh, we're...." She handed back my beer and walked behind me to sit on the top edge of the back of the couch and slid her hand over the shoulder Leah had shoved. "Well, let's see... we're... mmmm..." Her words were nonchalant but her eyes widened, waiting for me to finish the sentence. "What exactly are we, Ryan?"

"This is my best friend Julia. Jules, this is Leah." I said the words carefully, but couldn't tear my eyes from Julia's face. Her features were filled with laughter and devilry.

"His date," Leah spat.

"Congratulations." Julia focused on Leah and wagged a finger in her direction. She was clearly tipsy. "You need a donut."

A laugh burst from my chest because I couldn't help myself. *You need a donut.* I thought it was fucking hilarious, but Leah was clearly pissed.

"What did you say?"

"You seriously need a donut."

Leah looked indignant and furious, but my shoulders were visibly shaking with laughter when Julia turned her attention to me. "Can I talk to you for a sec?"

"Excuse me," I murmured to Leah then immediately rose to follow Julia a few feet away. "Are you being careful?"

"Is it just a coincidence that you and Twiggy are here tonight?"

I swallowed at the accusation in her tone. She was tipsy, but her eyes still burned into mine. "Yeah. I had no idea you were even going out, but I'm glad I'm here. Who is that guy?" I wanted to ask why she let him touch her in such a familiar way but clamped my jaw shut.

"He's a guy. Collin, I think? No big deal." She shrugged nonchalantly, and her hand came to rest on the front of my shirt. I should have been reassured as her deep green eyes looked up imploringly. "Don't worry, Ryan."

It was all I could do not to cover her fingers with my own. "I worry."

"I know." She leaned in and wrapped her arms around my waist in a brief hug and the scent of her perfume engulfed me. "I'm glad to see you. I'll call you tomorrow."

I wanted to wrap my arms around her and hold her close. I wanted to tell her to be careful, to stop drinking so much, especially around people she didn't know, but my hands fell away, and I shut my mouth as she left me and walked back to Ellie and the two guys sitting at her table.

Over the course of the next two hours, I tried to soothe Leah's ruffled feathers, dancing with her when absolutely required and buying her enough cocktails to allow me to ultimately remain parked on the couch as much as possible. I'd switched to Jack and Coke, and my mood got worse as the guy became more emboldened with Julia. When Leah accepted another man's invitation to dance, I couldn't blame her, and I couldn't care less. I thought I'd inadvertently screwed myself when I told Leah the reason I didn't feel like dancing much was because my head hurt. Thank God she was too selfish to suggest leaving.

It was a blessing in disguise when Leah trotted off after she was asked to dance, and I was beyond caring about the friend-zone boundaries Julia and I had firmly established. I watched Ellie accompany Julia, who was visibly wobbling on her way to the ladies room and took the opportunity to find out what the dickhead, now known to me as Collin, was up to. I had a slight buzz but nothing like I should have had with the amount of alcohol I'd consumed. I approached where he was talking to yet another of his friends at the bar. *He must troll here often,* I thought. His back was to me as I took a seat near the end of the bar. He was laughing with his friend, who was patting him hard on the back.

"Oh, yeah. This is in the bag. She's really wasted, and I just slipped her an X. Dude, she's gonna be sucking my dick in an hour and thanking me for it. Maybe yours too." They both burst out laughing, and I could barely contain myself from grabbing them both and smashing their skulls together.

I paused, blinking. I needed to be certain I'd heard him correctly. Did he say he'd just given Julia Ecstasy? I turned around slowly, hoping he hadn't seen Julia talking to Leah and me earlier.

"Excuse me; did you say you had some X?" I asked lazily, my eyes hooded.

"Oh, yeah!" He was obviously an idiot, saying it so loudly. "Want some?" He moved his shoulder closer to mine so he could hide his hand behind our bodies then opened it revealing five little white pills. "Twenty bucks each."

I regarded the two men carefully, gritting my teeth as my fist closed. I huffed, wanting to lay the fucker out on the spot. "No, thanks. I don't need that shit to get my girl hot and bothered," I goaded, part of me hoping this prick would take a swing at me. Nothing would make me happier than to pummel that smug grin off his face, but I also knew I had to get Jules out of the club before that shit started fucking her up. *Christ!*

"I don't either. But it just makes inhibitions fly away." The prick leaned into the bar and smirked. "Poof. It makes bitches do some incredible shit."

I inhaled deeply, struggling to keep control as anger exploded deep in my chest. Fuck, I wanted to rip him limb from limb.

Julia would be pissed when I hauled her little ass out, but that was exactly what I was going to do.

I glanced toward the bathrooms, and Ellie and Julia were just emerging from the ladies room and heading back to the table. Collin straightened and started to walk around me. "Let me know if you change your mind, man. But make it quick, we're leaving soon."

I contemplated what my next move would be. Leah was happily dancing with another guy. I strode to the middle of the dance floor just as Collin wrapped his arms around Julia, his hands roaming her ass and back. No doubt, the drug was already working because she was clinging to him while he buried his face in her neck and reached up the back hem of her dress.

"Leah." I tapped her on the shoulder, and she glanced my way. "We're leaving."

She scowled at me, indignant. "I don't want to leave. I'm just starting to have fun. *You* go."

"I wouldn't feel right leaving you here."

"I can take care of myself. Rodney will take me home." She batted her lashes at the scrawny blond dude who was pretending to dance with her. "Right, Rodney?"

"Yeah." He nodded and looked me straight in the eye. "Yeah, sure. I can take her home."

I felt uneasy about leaving her there, but Julia was going to be a hot mess in a few minutes if she wasn't already.

"Whatever." I didn't have time to fuck around, and I turned and headed toward Julia. From behind, I tugged her arms from around Collin's neck and pulled her back against me, my right arm sliding around her waist, and pushing him away. "Let go, asshole. Time to go, Julia."

She fought my hold. "I don't want to go! I'm feeling great! I'm staying!"

"We gotta go!"

"Who the fuck are you, anyway, pretty boy? Her dad?"

"Fuck off." I easily dismissed him. "Ellie, where's Julia's coat?" Julia was pulling my arm that held her fast. My muscles flexed, but I refused to let her go. "We have to get her out of here. Now."

"Why?" she asked, confused.

"Just get her coat. I'll explain later."

Collin grabbed Julia and tried to help her get free. Ellie disappeared into the crowd then returned with Julia's coat. I used my free hand to shove hard against the cocksucker's shoulder, making him stumble back. "I said, fuck off, asshole! You can let me leave with her, or I can call the cops, after I pound your ass into the ground." I pulled out my phone. "Your choice."

By now, Julia wasn't struggling as much. "I feel strange." She was moving her hand around in front of her face, staring at it like she was in a trance, and she kept pulling her arms away so she could stare at her hands. "My hand. Everything is trailing glow-y rainbows."

"How much did she have to drink?" I asked Ellie as I tried to get Julia to put on her coat. She was too busy watching her hand to cooperate.

"Six or seven shots, maybe? But that was over like three hours, Ryan."

"Couldn't you have waited to get trashed until the rest of us were with you? Oh, screw this!" I gave up with the coat and lobbed it over my shoulder, taking a firm hold on Julia's upper arm.

"I feel so warm. Everything is so nice," Julia murmured, trying to pull away from me. "Collin! I love you! I love you, Collin."

"See? She wants to stay with me, asshole," Collin sneered. "Mind your own fucking business!" He reached for Julia again.

"Don't touch her again!" I turned around and let loose, slamming my right fist as hard as I could into his jaw. My hand slid across his mouth and his teeth gnashed across two of my knuckles. He fell flat on his ass. Most of the patrons of the bar were too inebriated to care, but a bouncer from the other side of the bar started to come toward us. My hand started to sting, and I flexed my fingers. I must have cut the skin on his teeth.

"Ryan! How could you?" Julia shrieked and tried to scramble to his side on the floor. "Collin!"

My hand was on fire and starting to bleed, but I pulled her back and easily lifted her feet off the ground. "Not happening, Jules. You're coming with me."

"What's going on here?" The bouncer was big and burly, his head shaved. He had tattoos on his huge arms and neck, and several piercings in his face.

"You'll find drugs on him." I pointed as I began to drag Julia backwards toward the door. "He drugged my friend without her knowledge. I'm getting her out of here before she gets sick. He tried to sell to me at the bar, also. I'm not going to apologize for knocking him on his ass. Nothing was broken, and I don't want any trouble; I just want to take her home."

An astonished Ellie watched it all go down and followed me out. My hand was wrapped around Julia's wrist like a vice, dragging her out through the door as she fought against me. "Stop! Leave me alone!"

I didn't acknowledge her and continued through the dark parking lot toward my black CRV.

"Ryan, I have my car here. I can take her."

"Not a chance, Ellie. I'm taking her back to my place. Aaron's at Jen's tonight, and this shit is going to make things weird. Do you feel okay? Did they drug you, too?"

"I'm fine."

"Okay, I'll call you tomorrow."

"Ryan, I don't think it's a good idea for her to go with you."

"Why not?" I ignored the implications but the look on her face spoke volumes. "Bye, Ellie." I called over my shoulder after I turned Julia and started walking.

Ellie stopped to get into her car as Julia and I continued toward mine. Julia started struggling against my hand, her nails biting into my skin as she tried to pry my fingers from around her wrist. "Why won't you let me go be with Collin?" She was starting to get angry now. "Why do you care, anyway? I'm surprised you aren't already balls deep in that skinny skank you were with! Let go, Ryan!"

Without a word, I bent and hoisted her over my shoulder like a sack of potatoes. "No, Julia. Enough!" Her dress was short, barely covering her ass that was level with my face. She kicked her feet and pummeled my back with her fists. "I'm not going to let you get used by that bastard. You can do what you want when you're lucid, but it's not happening when you're hopped up on that shit. You'll thank me tomorrow."

"You're supposed to be my best friend!" Julia cried as she bounced a little on my shoulder as I took steady strides to the far end of the lot.

"Exactly."

"I want to go back and be with Collin!"

"Quiet," I commanded without breaking my stride. "You don't know what you want right now. That fucker's lucky he's still breathing."

It was a winter night, as cold as I'd ever seen it in Northern California, other than that one freak storm Valentine's Day of sophomore year. It was maybe thirty or forty degrees, and Julia started to shiver as I deposited her onto the front seat of my CRV and buckled her in. She'd settled down like the flip of a light switch and lightly touched my jaw. I paused to look at her face. Her fingers lingered, and I wanted to lean in to her touch but resisted the urge.

I knew it was the drug that put that longing look on her face, but damn if I didn't wish it were real. "I love you, Ryan."

"Ten seconds ago, you hated me, Jules. That asshole drugged you. You love everybody right now. That's the problem." I shut the door, went around to the driver's side, and climbed in.

It took ten minutes to get to my apartment, and in that time, she was pulling at her dress, saying she was hot, then screaming and yanking at her hair, sure that cockroaches were crawling all over her.

I'd tried Ecstasy once in high school, and it made me feel fucking great, but not until after I thought I was being eaten alive by red ants, and then everything turned into a psychedelic blur. Later, I'd just felt warm and energized and very, very horny. I would have fucked a hole in the wall if that were all I could find, and I hoped to hell Julia didn't go in that direction. Given my recent and on-going struggle with my reaction to Julia, I knew I wasn't the best person to be with Julia right now. Ellie had been right, but I didn't trust anyone else to take care of her. Ellie wouldn't be strong enough to stop her if she needed to be stopped from doing anything dumb.

After I parked, Julia was still screaming. I rushed around and pulled her out of the car, grabbing both of her wrists in a frantic effort to keep her from ripping her hair out. "Honey! Julia! Julia, there are no bugs on you!"

She stopped struggling and moaned, bending over at the waist. She heaved violently at both of our feet, the liquid contents of her stomach splattering sickeningly on the cold concrete, the temperature contrast causing steam to rise. I held her propped up against my body with one arm and pulled her hair back with the other. Julia jerked violently against me for three more heaves. "Gross," she moaned. "Oh, God." Her hand pushed her hair back on the side opposite where I was holding

My nose wrinkled at the foul stench, and my own stomach protested. "Are you done?"

She nodded weakly and straightened. "I don't feel good."

I wondered if the X had fully entered her system or if she'd managed to purge some of it. At least some of the alcohol was out.

"I know. Come on." I bent to lift her into my arms bridal style. This was the first time I'd carried her this close to me. I'd given her piggyback rides, and we'd leaned in to each other often enough, I'd hugged her several times, but this was the first time I had her fully in my arms. She was so small and snuggled into my chest like a child. It felt amazing and right, as if she trusted me more than anyone in the world. Despite the vomiting, her hair smelled like shampoo, and her perfume wafted up gently.

"What did he give me?" She didn't accuse me of lying about the prick drugging her.

"X. You'll be okay."

"What will it do to me?"

"Some of it's happened already. The light show and the illusion of the bugs, though not everyone gets affected the same way. It's supposed to make you feel good, but it has side effects."

Aaron and I had the basement apartment in a big, old house close to campus, and I had to set Julia down to unlock the door. She leaned up against the wall of the house, gazing at me as if she'd never seen me before, her eyes wide and wondrous.

I pushed the door open and waited for her to precede me in, but she didn't. She just kept staring at me. I waved her in.

"God, you're beautiful, Ryan." Her green eyes were soft and full of love. My heart stopped.

It was cold, and she should be freezing. "Nah." I took her hand and pulled her over the threshold. The last thing I needed was for Julia to go all lovey-dovey, touchy-feely on me. I just didn't know how well I'd be able to resist. She was the beautiful one, *so* beautiful; even after she'd just puked her guts out, she made my heart stop. I wanted to tell her how breathless I'd been the first time I'd seen her tonight, but clamped my mouth shut. Anything that happened now was due to the drug, and I wouldn't put either one of us in that position. Julia was the most important person to me, and I couldn't trust that we'd be okay on the other side if something physical happened. I suddenly realized I wanted that look on her face to be real, not the result of a drug-induced haze.

"You *are.*" Her voice was filled with something that sounded like wonder, and her hand came to rest on my chest as she gazed up into my face. She moved in close enough for her nose to brush my jaw. "Everyone thinks so. Every girl I know says so. They all want you." I couldn't take it. I couldn't stand there one more second without touching her or turning my head the fraction of an inch necessary to make our lips touch. I closed my eyes for a beat.

"Wait here, sweetheart." I moved her to the couch and pushed her gently down, then went into my room and grabbed a pair of my sweats, socks, and long sleeve T-shirt off the stack of clean clothes sitting on the dresser.

Shit. My heart was pounding a mile a minute. I ran my hand through my hair before leaving the room and offering Julia the clothes.

"Ryan..." Her voice was soft, imploring, her hand ran up my forearm, and electricity skittered across my skin. "You're so strong."

"Jesus, Julia, you gotta change, okay? I'll give you my bed, and I'll stay in Aaron's room. You'll feel better in the morning."

"I feel good now. Different; but really good. It's like all my senses are in overdrive. I don't feel like sleeping. I want to touch... to be touched."

I wondered how the drug would interact with the alcohol and was thankful she'd purged so much out by the car.

"Well, I feel like hell. My head is killing me, and I'd really like to lie down." I knew my voice sounded irritated, but I didn't know how else to handle her and make her do what I needed her to do. And that was to get ready for bed and get behind a closed door.

Her expression fell and I felt like an asshole, but it had the desired result. Julia rose and walked away, stumbling slightly, into the bathroom. "Fine," she muttered shortly, disappearing into the bathroom, the door closing with unneeded force behind her.

I went back into my room, past the bathroom, and quickly changed into my own pair of sweats and an old gray T-shirt. I wondered briefly whether Leah got home all right, but it was beyond me to try to make two unwilling women bend to my will. It was hard enough with Julia.

I glanced at the digital clock by my bed. It was almost two in the morning. I ran both hands through my hair. I was worried about what to expect when she emerged. She seemed more re- laxed than I felt when I'd done the drug that one time. Shit, it would help if I knew more about it. Maybe puking got rid of some of it, though that seemed unlikely since some of the effect had started before we left the bar.

"Ryan?" Julia's voice behind me made me jump.

"Jesus!" My hand flew to my chest. "You scared me." She was only dressed in the shirt and the socks, and both were way too large for her. Her legs were still bare above the slouchy socks, and her hair was wet. I could see her puckered nipples and the full, round contours of her breasts beneath the thin material. I closed my eyes, shaking my head to try to clear the vision from my brain before my dick got any ideas. I wasn't one hundred percent successful. "Um... did you take a shower?"

"Yes."

"Why aren't you wearing those sweats I gave you?"

"I'm hot. Too hot."

Yeah. She could say that again.

My room was a mess. Sheet music had been knocked off the keyboard and was strewn around carelessly, mixed in with the clothes I'd just discarded and three pairs of shoes. I bent, trying to distract myself, and began picking everything up; stacking the music on the bench and shoving the dirty clothes into my now empty hamper. I threw the shoes haphazardly into the closet and turned on the bedside lamp, switching off the overhead light.

Her fingers slid down my forearm from behind to clasp around my hand. She gently tugged to turn me around, and inched closer to the bed.

"Don't do that now. Come lie down with me."

I knew it was the best and worst idea ever. My chest rose and fell as I breathed in and out. I sucked in one of those deep breaths that pushes your lungs to capacity. Julia's eyes were wide and dark, the pupils dilated—a sign of the drug—but, her expression was serene and relaxed.

"Julia..." I hesitated. "You should just go to sleep."

"I told you I don't want to sleep."

"I know." I sat on the bed and used our joined hands to pull her down to sit beside me. My other hand came out to the side of her cheek. "But I can't lie with you tonight."

Her brows furrowed and her lower lip jutted out in a slight pout. "Why? We've slept together before."

Because I want you so bad and the drug will make you willing; maybe even aggressive. I shouldn't say what I was thinking, but a version of it spilled out. "Because... I've had too much to drink and we might do something we'll regret in the light of day. Because... you're my best friend."

Her eyes shimmered and became luminous as they glassed over. My thumb rubbed along her jaw, and I leaned in to place a lingering kiss on her cheek. I let myself breathe her in, memorizing the way her skin felt under my mouth, the way she smelled, and the rhythm of her breath.

"I don't want you to be my best friend," she whispered and I knew it was honest. I felt the same way. "Sometimes."

"I know. But I am."

When I pulled back, she nodded, unspoken understanding passing between us. I stood and pulled back the covers, careful not to watch too closely as she crawled underneath.

"Will you play for me? I bet it will sound really amazing right now."

"Okay. Just a couple songs." I moved away and sat down, running my hands over the keys playing a song I knew she loved. The melody was soft, lilting, and soothing.

I played for over an hour without saying a word. When the notes faded, I glanced to the bed. Julia's eyes were closed, the covers pulled up to her chin as she curled on her side. She was so gorgeous. My heart squeezed inside my chest as I moved to the bed, my eyes never leaving her face. I wanted to kiss her but shut the light off instead, using the soft ray of light filtering in from the other room to see as I left.

"Ryan?"

I stopped without turning around. "Yeah?" I said over my shoulder.

"Coffee tomorrow, right?"

"Sure. It's Sunday, isn't it?"

~11~

The Morning After

Julia ~

I rolled over when the sun shone in my eyes. I felt like hell as I willed my eyes open. They resisted. My head hurt, and my stomach still hated me. I wanted to barf. The only pleasant thing going for me was that I was surrounded by Ryan's scent. *I must be dreaming*, I thought. But who felt like crap in their dreams?

"Ugh," I moaned softly and rolled over, my face squishing more fully into the pillow. After a couple more deep breaths, I was able to open my eyes. At first they were blurry, and I rubbed them and blinked a couple of times. I sat straight up in bed when I realized I was in Ryan's room. What was I doing in Ryan's room? My heart dropped as panic washed over me.

My stomach lurched, and I jumped from the bed and scrambled into the bathroom, but I felt dizzy and I stumbled. Somehow, I managed to make it to the toilet and threw up violently. My head felt like the top would fly off with each heave of my stomach. I was on my bare knees on the cold linoleum floor; dry heaves racking my body, when Ryan appeared in the doorway. I didn't see his face because of my position bent over the toilet, but I heard his voice, and his bare feet and gray sweats appeared in my peripheral vision.

"Julia, are you okay?"

I couldn't talk as another heave burst forth. Ryan crouched down on his haunches, pulled back my hair, and held it behind me until the misery subsided. My eyes started to tear with the efforts of my stomach. Not only did I feel like death, but also Ryan was seeing me at my absolute worst. Ryan, of all people.

"No," I finally managed when the heaving subsided. I sat back on the cold floor and leaned on the wall opposite the stool. "I think I'm dying."

Ryan wiped at my mouth with a warm washcloth and tears rolled down my face. He sat next to me, put his arm right around me, and pulled me close against his side. I leaned into him helplessly as the fingers of his hand rubbed my right arm. "You're okay."

I shook my head and buried my face into his neck. "No I'm not. I'm sorry."

"Nothing to be sorry for. You'll feel better after you eat something."

"Gross!" I felt his chin rest on the top of my head and I wanted to cry. Finally I was in his arms and it was because I was puking my guts up. "I'm sorry!" I said again, finally letting the tears flow and a sob break free. "You sh—shouldn't have to see me like this."

"Hey," he said softly, his arm tightening around me. "Stop. It's okay. What are friends for?"

I reached up and put my arm around his neck. "Ryan." My eyes were closed and tears squeezed out. "You're too good to me."

"It's mutual, Jules, don't worry about it."

"Nuh uh. I don't have to hold your hair back while you puke your guts out wearing just your underwear."

"You're not just in your underwear." He smiled gently, wiping a tear off my cheek with his thumb. He was so gentle I wanted to cry; literally wail at how perfect he was. "You're also wearing my shirt."

All I could do was nod and breathe as he held me and continued to massage the flesh of my arm. He sat with me on the floor for at least ten minutes, just holding me, until finally, I pulled back and reached for a piece of toilet paper to wipe my nose with. My head still felt like it would explode, but my stomach did feel a little better.

"You're not going to make me drink tomato juice with raw egg in it, are you?" I asked weakly. "I think I'll barf some more if you do."

"Nah." He stood up and offered me his hand. I took it and he pulled me to my feet, using my momentum to bring me into a hug. "You'll be fine. I think you should drink some water, take some aspirin and maybe have some dry toast, if you're up to it." My hands closed around his biceps and they flexed as he pulled me closer. It felt like heaven. He released me gently and reached up to push my hair behind my ear on one side of my face. "Are you?"

"Just the water and aspirin for now."

"The aspirin might make your stomach hurt, if it's empty." He took my hand and led me out of the bathroom and down the hall to the kitchen.

"Okay, Dr. Ryan." I smiled secretly. He couldn't see my face as we made our way to the kitchen because I was behind him, but I was enjoying every second of his hand holding mine. It was as if an electric current ran between our hands. It made my heart beat wildly in my chest though I knew I looked like hell. Maybe I smelled like vomit, even. The thought horrified me since I'd just spent several minutes in his arms.

He let out a small laugh with a huff. "One piece of toast is all I'll force on you."

"I should take a shower, but I don't have anything to wear but the dress I had on last night. Where is it?"

I sat down at the table, and Ryan went to get me a glass of water, returning with it and two aspirin. He held the pills out to me with a flat hand, and I took them in one hand and the glass in the other. "In the bathroom, I assume. You took a shower last night, so you don't smell like vomit. Relax."

"Did you make these?" I smiled and tried to tease as much as I could manage, remembering he'd had to synthesize aspirin with that guy Ellie dated briefly around the time I was seeing Dave. *What was his name?* I searched my brain trying to figure it out.

He laughed. "Funny. Maybe you'll live after all."

"Ryan, I'm almost afraid to ask, but did anything happen last night?"

I sat down, and he went to get the toast that had just popped up. His back was to me and I was able to observe him unseen. He had gray sweats on with a burgundy Stanford T-shirt. I was wearing one of Ryan's button-downs and was painfully aware of how the front tails pooled between my thighs, but most of my legs were bare. I didn't have a bra on and was extremely self-conscious of the way the cool air in the apartment made my nipples pucker. I could feel the fabric brush against them every time I moved, and I knew they were very visible under Ryan's shirt. I was curious how I got out of my dress the previous night.

"Plenty happened," he said steadily. "A lot of it, I didn't like."

Holy shit. Did I sleep with Ryan? "But what, exactly?" I prodded.

"You got hammered off your ass, and to make it worse, some dickhead gave you Ecstasy."

My eyes widened. "What?"

"I know. Topped off with the booze he fed you is most likely the reason you don't remember much of it."

I felt embarrassed. "Yes, I remember being at the club with Ellie, and dancing with a guy…"

"Collin," Ryan added, his face twisting wryly as he sat down next to me and put a plate of buttered toast in front of me.

"Collin," I repeated and reached for a piece of toast.

"He was grabbing your ass under your dress." Ryan sounded annoyed. "Don't you remember? Because the picture is burned in my brain."

I'd just taken a bite of the toast and I paused in chewing it. "Um," I swallowed. "No, I don't remember much after I saw you and your drape-y girlfriend sitting on the couch leering at me."

Ryan laughed. "I wasn't leering at you."

"Seemed like it to me. Your babe was, for sure. Who was she?"

"She's just a girl I met, Julia. Blow it off. It was our first date, and I won't be seeing her again."

Ryan was drinking coffee, and my nose wrinkled at the aroma of it. I usually loved coffee, but it was revolting in my current state. "Why not?"

"Because you told her to eat a donut. She was completely offended."

I grinned. "Really? Not sure what you see in that skinny, clingy-type anyway, to be honest."

"You made your disapproval known a couple of times last night." Ryan was relaxed, leaning an elbow on the table as he watched me eat.

"Just looking out for you," I smiled, the toast having the desired effect. I finally felt a little better. I stuck out my index finger and poked him in the bicep.

"Hey!"

"Tell me the real reason. I'm not buying." I took another bite of the toast and chewed, watching his face to see if I could read his emotions.

"I won't be seeing Leah again because I left her at the club to get you out of there."

My eyes widened. "Wow."

"Yeah. I don't know what you saw in that prick who just wanted into your panties."

I laughed, almost choking on my toast. "Ryan, come on. You are well acquainted with panties—a wide assortment of them. Glass houses and all that." I raised my eyebrow to make my point.

"Seriously, Julia, he drugged you. If I hadn't been there, he would have taken you out and raped you. We shouldn't be joking around about this."

Seeing his real concern, I sobered. "You're right. I'm glad you were there."

"Me, too." He reached out and took my hand, squeezing it gently. "I'm gonna wait outside the bar for that fucker next weekend, and kick his ass."

He was serious, but I thought he was adorable. "Is he really worth it?"

"No, but it will make me feel better."

I noticed a long scab on the knuckles of his right hand. "What's that?" I pointed to it.

"I slugged him once, and his teeth caught me."

"I'm sorry." I rubbed my thumb lightly over it.

"Don't be."

"So, how did I get in your shirt? We didn't... uh... Did we?"

Ryan got up and took his coffee cup to the sink. "No! You know me better than that," he scoffed. He was right. I did. "You did ask me to sleep with you, though." With his back to me, I couldn't see his face and I wondered how he'd felt about that. Just hearing him say the words, affected me. My heart sped up and heat began to pool, my lower body began to throb in a persistent ache.

"But you didn't? We've slept in the same bed before, Ryan."

"Right. When you weren't hopped up on X." He leaned his back against the edge of the sink.

"Are you telling me my big strong Ryan might have been unable to resist?" My heart thumped in my chest. I'm not sure what made me so brave, but I wanted to know the answer.

"I don't know what I would have done, and I don't want to know." He cleared his throat and turned back to me. "What do you want to do today?"

Clearly the subject was closed. "Don't you have to study for the MCATs?"

"Later, sure. We can goof off for a few hours. If you want to."

"Yeah. That would be fun. Then should I help you study? Do you need me?"

He nodded, his deep blue eyes holding mine like a magnet. "Yeah, that would be good. Should I take you home for a shower? Or, I can give you a pair of my sweats and a sweatshirt until I take you home to change."

"I choose here. The quicker I get a shower, the least offensive I'll be. I'm sure I smell pretty sour."

"No. Even last night when you were puking, you smelled like your perfume," Only Ryan would say that. "I told you, you took a shower last night before you went to bed."

"Okay, so I'll shower here, and in the meantime, you can come up with something you want to do today."

"We could drive up to San Francisco."

"Okay," I nodded. "That sounds fun." Anything that meant a day with Ryan was what I wanted. "Fisherman's Wharf would be fun, but is it too cold to walk around?"

"We'll see how you're feeling after you clean up, but I think we can bundle up enough. The sun is shining, so that should help."

Aaron burst through the front door. Sometimes he was larger than life, boisterous and loud, but he stopped short when he saw me in nothing but Ryan's white shirt. "Hey," he said hesitantly. "Uh, am I interrupting something?" He looked from one of us to the other.

"Nope." My eyes implored Ryan to keep the humiliation of the night before between us. "I just had a few too many lemon drops last night. Ryan took pity on my puke-y self and held my hair back, that's all."

"Oh," Aaron said, but he was looking at Ryan for his reaction. "Lemon drops, huh?"

"Yep," Ryan agreed. "We're thinking of taking a drive to San Francisco today. Do you and Jen want to come?"

"Yeah, maybe. I'll call her."

I took a quick shower and put on the clothes Ryan gave me. The sweatpants barely hung on my hips, and I had to keep hiking them up. Thank goodness the sweatshirt he'd given me covered any bare skin that might show. I didn't have clean underwear, so I had to go commando. I picked up the hair dryer that was hanging over the towel rack next to the mirror and turned it on, using it to dry the fog from the mirror, then put it back.

I didn't have a shred of make-up on and could do nothing about it until I got back to my apartment to change. When I went into the living room, Ryan was dressed in jeans and a nice navy blue sweater. It pulled out the color in his eyes, and the effect was stunning. He was waiting for me on the couch with some football game on the TV, and I stopped a few feet from him. He glanced up, taking in the baggy clothes, the high heels hanging from one hand, and the black, sparkly dress hanging over my arm. I hadn't taken a purse to the bar the night before, so I stuffed my ID, the money I had left, and my dirty panties in my bra. It was an absurd situation, but there was nothing I could do about it.

"Uh, this is going to be interesting. I have no shoes." I wagged the shoes in front of him.

He flashed a big smile. "Hold on." He got up and went into his room again, emerging with a pair of thick socks and a pair of his Adidas. "Try this." He handed them to me.

I huffed out a small laugh. "Ryan, these are gigantic. I'll have to shuffle like a little kid."

"Put on the socks, at least."

"Then what? They'll just get wet. I'll have to go barefoot. Just run fast."

"Put on the socks, Jules."

I twisted my face and sat down on the couch to do as he asked.

"Aaron, I'm going to take Julia home to change. I'll call you when she's ready to see if you guys are coming with us!" Ryan called down the hall to his brother.

"I called her." Aaron's voice was muffled from behind his closed door. "We're in. I'm starving so let's get breakfast first."

Ryan looked at me. "Do you feel well enough for that?"

"Yeah, I'm feeling a lot better."

He walked down the hall and cracked open Aaron's door. "Okay, Stacks in an hour."

"Done," Aaron replied.

"I probably don't need an hour, Ryan."

"Jen will, though." He rolled his beautiful eyes and my heart swelled. I was going to be with him all day long and nothing could make me happier. Maybe getting drunk was worth it.

We walked to the door and Ryan stopped. His arm wrapped around the back of my waist and he bent to slide his other one behind my knees.

"You're carrying me to the car?" I said as he hoisted me off the floor, as if I was a feather.

"Unless you have a better idea?"

I stared into his face but in that moment, could think of nothing to say. I shook my head.

"Good, open the door." I plopped the shoes in my lap and reached out to do as Ryan asked. It was cold, but I barely noticed.

"Shit," Ryan muttered. "I forgot to get my keys out of my pocket. Um..." He considered for a split second then set me down on the hood of the car. It was like sitting on a block of ice.

"Holy crap, that's cold." I started to shiver almost immediately. "Hurry! Hurry! Hurry!"

He rushed as he unlocked the door and left it open. "What does it look like I'm doing?"

He put his arms around my waist and butt then pulled me from the car. He surprised me and I squealed as I slid down and clutched at his shoulders, his hands settled under my butt cheeks. It was awkward and clumsy, but laughable, like some old Three Stooges movie. I pulled my knees up to keep my feet from touching the wet ground. Ryan chuckled. "Well? Put your legs around my waist."

I did it but couldn't help but giggle at the absurdity of the situation and Ryan laughed with me. He had to move me a few feet around the open door and into the CRV. Within seconds he was sitting me down on the seat. "I bet you say that to all the girls." I couldn't help the teasing remark.

He grinned. "Ha ha, Jules," he mocked. "You're hilarious!"

Peals of laughter burst forth from both of us as Ryan pushed my legs around and I used one of my feet to shut the door. We were still laughing when he started the car and drove the short distance to my apartment, but we didn't speak the entire way.

When he parked, we looked at each other. "I suppose we'll have a repeat performance?"

"Piggyback is easier to manage this time."

"Sounds good," I said, my voice steady. I wanted to look at him and never stop. He was beautiful in so many ways. I loved him so much I couldn't breathe and I had no choice but to admit it to myself, even if he'd never know.

"Listen, I shouldn't have invited Jen and Aaron. It should have been just us today."

I nodded and looked down at my hands then glanced back at him. "It's okay. It's still us. Always."

"Yeah, I guess." The car was still running. "What are you doing after graduation, Jules? You know I'm applying to Harvard, but what about you? I know you want to work for a magazine, but where?" The MCATs were the last thing he needed. His college GPA was a 4.0 and he had stellar recommendation letters lined up. His father was a Harvard Medical School alumnus, which would help, too. It was a shoe-in he'd make it and then he'd be gone. In less than a year, he'd be gone from me. Obviously, Ryan had thought about it, too.

I lifted my shoulder. "One of the biggest markets, I hope. L.A., Chicago, or New York. That's a long time away, though." I tried to make light of just how heavy the thought of it weighed on me.

"Not too long. Look how fast it's gone. I'm taking the MCAT next month."

"I know, Ryan." How could he think I'd forgotten any little detail about his life? Maybe he was testing me.

"When I first got to Stanford, I couldn't wait to be finished so I could get to med school."

"I think every eighteen-year-old kid thinks that way about four more years of school, but looking back, it's been the greatest experience of my life. My dad says that once you get out of school, your life flies by in a flash, so we should enjoy every second."

"Yeah, it's true."

"I'll always remember you, Ryan. You are the biggest and best part of my college experience."

He frowned. "What are you talking about? We're always going to know each other."

My heart seized, and my throat tightened. I swallowed to try to remove the large lump forming in my throat. "Life has a way of happening. You'll be busy with school."

"So? I won't be too busy for you. We'll still talk every Sunday; I promise."

I blinked at the tears stinging my eyes as I sat in his truck, engine running, in his baggy sweats, shirt, and socks. Here was my best friend, the absolute most important person in my life… in probably *ever*, and the prospect of the future didn't feel so great.

When I didn't speak, Ryan reached out for my hand and pulled it onto his thigh. "Okay? Say okay, Jules."

I nodded, still unable to look at him. He squeezed my hand; his own folded around to fully encapsulate mine. He shook it to make me look at him. "It's a year away, Ryan. Do we have to think about that now?"

"Say it."

"Okay, Ryan."

He smiled as only he could, lifted my hand, and kissed it. It was the first time he'd ever done that and I held in a gasp. "Good! Let's go! We only have twenty minutes to get to Stacks."

I smiled through my tears and groaned mockingly. "See? You and your babbling will mean I'm ugly today. I have no time to get ready."

After he shut off the engine, Ryan got out, ran around the front of the car, and pulled the door open. He turned his back. "Hop on, helpless."

I wrapped my arms around him, and his arms slid under my legs to lift me out of the car in one motion onto his back. He turned, and again, I pushed the door shut with my foot. I couldn't help laying my head down on his back the entire walk into the building; thanking God I'd met him. It wasn't long enough.

~12~

Ryan's Discovery

Julia ~

On Monday, Wednesday and Friday, my second to last semester classes ran from 8 AM until noon. I liked the afternoons free, plus the scheduling spaced out the final exams. I didn't have any classes with Ryan this semester, despite all my trying. He had way too many science and math classes to finish and had no time for electives. I was in a good place to graduate and though I had upper level classes, I didn't have to work as hard as Ryan did. We made a habit of meeting for lunch at least once a week; more if we could manage it. He had advanced Organic Chemistry at 2 PM, and we generally went to the student snack bar on Fridays. Ellie had asked to join us today, so we were meeting in the cafeteria.

I searched the crowd for the golden brown head I loved. Yes, I *loved* Ryan. I officially admitted it to myself last semester the day Jen, Aaron, Ryan and I went to San Francisco, but really, it had happened about the second time I'd laid eyes on him. After four years, Ryan was still my best friend, my calm in the storm, my rock. We were pretty much inseparable and despite our fights and the huge pull that sometimes gave us issues, we depended on each other unconditionally. There wasn't a day we hadn't seen each other since we met, other than the one silly time he said he couldn't hang out with me because of his school obligations and school breaks when we each went home to see our families. Though, after that first year, we spent most of those together too. He was gorgeous, brilliant, funny, and sensitive. We told each other everything, which was both a blessing, and a curse.

There were easily 600 students milling around the large room filled with long tables, and the din was deafening. I longed for our usual booth in the snack bar. Sometimes, I took my books to study and he'd come back to get me after his last class.

Someone shoved into my shoulder as they made their way past me. I stumbled and almost fell down, the guy's momentum slamming me into the brick wall on my right.

"Hey!" I grunted as my shoulder exploded in pain. "Watch it, will ya?" I almost dropped my backpack as my left hand moved to my injured appendage.

The man was large and oafish; his focus obviously on the food line. He looked back briefly, but said nothing, just shot a look over his shoulder at me then stopped dead when he ran into someone else. This time, he was the one knocked down when he came in contact with the solid wall that was Ryan. A scowl was firmly in place on his perfect face as he looked down on the larger man now sprawled in front of him on the floor.

"Watch where the fuck you're going, asshole! Say you're sorry."

"Fuck off. You ran into me," the downed man muttered.

"I didn't mean to me, dickhead. *Her!*" Ryan growled as he nodded in my direction. "You smashed her into the goddamn wall! She could have been seriously hurt as you hauled your fat ass to the trough!"

I almost laughed out loud and bit my lip as I looked on. Ryan stepped around the kid, who scrambled clumsily to his feet at the same time. The arm that came around my waist was gentle, concern etched on Ryan's face. "Julia, are you okay?" His hand ran over my hurt arm lightly.

"Yeah. It was an accident," I said softy, the fingers of my other hand curling into the fabric of the back of Ryan's navy blue button-down.

"The hell it was." I thrilled at the hard tone in Ryan's voice and his rush to come to my aid. It swelled my heart even though I knew he was just being Ryan. *"Say you're sorry. Now!"* he commanded of the flustered kid.

By now, we'd garnered the glances of several other students and a small crowd was beginning to form.

"Look, I'm really sorry." The guy was flushed and embar-rassed. He was out of shape, and Ryan was lean, tall and strong. Even though smaller in weight, he towered over the other man and was defined by solid muscle.

"Stop being such an inconsiderate dipshit and pay attention to where you're going. Look at how little she is!" Ryan was still pissed, and I longed to put the last few minutes behind us. My shoulder throbbed, but I was over it.

I tugged on the back of my best friend's shirt. "Come on. Let's find Ellie," I pleaded. Ryan finally turned and lifted my backpack off my shoulder.

"Are you sure you're okay? Can you move your shoulder?"

I rolled my eyes and closed my fingers around his bare fore-arm. The long sleeves of his shirt were rolled up above the el-bows, and the soft covering of hair was like silk over the strong muscles of his forearms. My fingers weren't long enough to reach much more than halfway around. He hoisted my backpack up onto his shoulder next to his own.

"I'm fine."

I noticed the eyes —mostly female eyes—on us as we navi-gated our way through the rows of tables searching for Ellie.

Women envied me; even hated me. I was used to it by now, but was still conscious of every glare. Some of them pretended to be my friend just to get closer to Ryan but I was getting good at spotting it early now.

They envied me, but I was jealous of those who knew what it was like to be held in his arms, to feel kisses from his perfect mouth, to make love with him. We were close, but there were holes that couldn't be filled without violating our friendship; a friendship I wouldn't risk. I was so green, sometimes I couldn't stand it, and worse, it had become a constant ache.

We spotted Ellie on the far side, standing on one of the chairs, waving her arms wildly.

"There she is," Ryan pointed out. "That's not weird at all." He rolled his eyes.

I laughed at her silliness. She was flamboyant and didn't give a shit what anyone thought. Not that I tried to blend in, but I certainly didn't make a spectacle of myself either.

"Took you long enough," Ellie grumbled as she plopped back down in her chair.

We each pulled out a chair, and Ryan dumped both backpacks in the empty one to his left while I took the one between Ellie and him. "I got sidelined for a minute, that's all, Ellie." I wrinkled my nose at the bowl in front of her. Cottage cheese, raw broccoli, and sunflower seeds. *Ugh.*

She stopped eating and looked at me. "Why?"

"Some dumbass plowed her into a wall."

"Ryan knocked him down," I said flatly and started tracing imaginary circles on the table with my index finger.

"No, I didn't. He wasn't watching where he was going. I just didn't move out of the way. Little bits of Newton's Laws are in there somewhere. Body in motion, outside force, *mass*," his eyebrows rose in emphasis, "velocity, opposite and equal reaction.

That's me. Outside force. Maybe a little *more* than equal reaction in this case."

"You're such a science snot," I shot back.

He laughed. "That's why you love me." He moved a hand down the front of his shirt as he sat back in his chair, smirking. "All this and brains, too." Ryan had taken and passed his MCAT with flying colors just a couple of months back. His score of thirty-eight put him in the ninety-ninth percentile. *Ridiculous.*

"Yeah. And your incredible humility is what closes the deal." My tone was deadpan and I stifled the urge to laugh but didn't quite get the job done. His smile was brilliant, and it went all the way into his eyes, only making him more mesmerizing. I soaked in every line of his face.

Ellie glanced from one of us to the other, knowingly. "Aren't you guys eating?"

"Yep." He got up and walked away leaving Ellie and me sitting at the table.

"What about you?" Ellie nudged me slightly.

"Ryan will bring me something."

"But, you didn't tell him what to get."

I shrugged. "Whatever he picks will be fine."

"You guys are like Siamese twins. We should go to The Mill tonight. A bunch of people were talking about it in my fashion merchandising class. It sounds like fun."

"Okay. Sure." The Mill was a medium-sized college bar with a DJ and dancing. It was always packed to the gills.

"Hey, girly." I looked up to find Jason Milner hovering over us. "Are you done with that assignment for Jelinek's class?" *Girly?* Was he twelve?

It was an international marketing class in which we had to research a culture from another country, write a paper on it, and then in the second half of the semester we would write another to market a product pointing out the differences in process due to culture.

"Hmmph!" I scoffed. "Yeah, right. That isn't due for two weeks. You?"

"Not yet. I thought we could work on it together."

I bristled in my chair at his obvious advances. "Um... we have different countries, Jason, so that would be impossible."

"Yeah, but Julia..." Jason began. He was good looking with dark hair and bright blue eyes. A striking combination that most women were drawn to, but I was immune. One, because when he opened his mouth it completely erased his charm and two, *Ryan*.

Ryan returned with a tray full of sandwiches, chips, fruit and cookies. He set a bottle of green tea in front of me, and looked pointedly at Jason.

"Excuse me, man, but you're occupying my space."

"Your *space*?" Jason asked sarcastically. "Your name's not on her Matthews. Besides we're talking academics." I flushed at the implications, but smiled at what happened next.

Ryan burst out laughing, over-exaggerating it by holding his stomach and wiping an imaginary tear from his eye. "Hahahaha! That's the funniest thing I've heard all day, dude! Seriously, that's a good one!" Ryan openly mocked then glanced down at me to check if I really wanted to talk to Jason. I shook my head a fraction of an inch. The look of trepidation in my eyes was all Ryan needed. "But, your *ass is still in my space*."

With a scowl, Jason stood to go, but hesitated as Ryan sat down and started doling out food. He held up some strawberries and looked at me. I nodded, and he set them down in front of me then took one and popped it in his own mouth. He picked up half of one of the sandwiches and traded with the other one so we both had part of each. None of it went unnoticed by the man now standing over us.

"I guess I'll see you in class, Julia."

"Okay," I answered back casually, absorbed in what Ryan was doing.

Jason moved to a table near us and sat with another guy. I could feel his eyes boring into my back as I began to eat the lunch Ryan laid out in front of me.

"So? The Mill tonight?" Ellie asked again.

I nodded, picking up half the sandwich. "Sure. You up for it, Ryan?"

"Uh, can't tonight, but you should go have fun."

I waited for a reason, but he said nothing, instead concentrating on his lunch. I noticed the occasional glance out of his peripheral vision at Jason who continued to look on with interest while Ellie and I made plans for the evening.

I had that sinking feeling which had become like ESP every time Ryan had a date. My heart fell like a stone into the pit of my stomach.

"Julia!" Ellie broke me out of my thoughts. "So, we'll shop this afternoon and get something hot to wear tonight."

I tried to lift the corners of my mouth in the start of a smile, but didn't quite make it and so contented myself with a nod.

"Ryan, is Aaron going out with you? If so, we'll call Jen to see if she wants to come along." Ellie was brilliant. She knew I needed the answer even if I hadn't told her how I really felt.

"Um, no. I don't know what he's doing. Maybe they'll both wanna go," he murmured softly.

The food in my mouth suddenly turned to cardboard, and I put the remainder of the sandwich down on the plate and turned to him. "Is it a secret or are you going to tell us what you're up to tonight?" I asked, trying to lace my voice with a lightness I didn't feel.

"I have a date with Samantha Cosen." He appeared uncomfortable, shifting uneasily in his chair as his eyes met mine. I remembered her. She was pretty and he'd gone out with her a time or two before. I figured that was a done deal since he hadn't pursued her further. I couldn't help the way it hurt... just as it did every time he spent his time with someone else.

"Oh." I picked up my drink and searched my brain for a way to bury the way my heart was aching inside my chest. My throat started to close, and I wanted to get out of there before my emotions got the better of me. I pushed the food away and gathered up my backpack off the chair.

"Will I see you after class? Should I meet you in the Student Union?" Ryan's blue eyes questioned, his brows dropping over his eyes slightly. He was puzzled by the sudden change in my demeanor, disappointment evident on his face. Though, his own discomfort at disclosing his plans was telling. He knew it would bother me, and I hated that I wasn't better at hiding it.

"Um, I don't think so. I have to study awhile before Ellie and I go shopping." I slung the bag over my shoulder. "What time, Ellie?"

"I'm done now. Are you sure you have to study? It's *Friday*, Julia!" Ellie encouraged.

I sighed in relief; grateful she would secure my clean escape from the cafeteria. "Yeah. You're right. I just need to drop off my stuff at the apartment."

She smiled brightly and stood up. "Me, too. See you later, Ryan." She started to put her dishes back on her tray and I took some leftovers off mine and stacked them alongside.

"I can take care of that, Jules. Don't worry about it," Ryan murmured, his eyes watching my face.

I somehow managed to smile at him. "I got it. Talk to you tomorrow." I nudged his shoulder with my uninjured one because I couldn't help myself. I hated it when we had any sort of distance between us and this was my cross to bear. It wasn't his fault I was in love with him so I shouldn't punish him for it.

"Call you later?" he asked hopefully.

"That's okay. Concentrate on your date. I'll talk to you tomorrow."

He nodded slowly as Ellie and I turned to make our way to empty the trays and then left the cafeteria.

*****

Ellie was disappointed, even pissed that I changed my mind. I didn't feel up to going out, even though it was probably in my best interest to get out the apartment and be with friends.

My heart hurt and I didn't feel strong enough to put on a happy face. Even for her.

I wandered aimlessly around the apartment after she left, wrapping my arms around myself and trying not to cry. I didn't want to watch TV. I didn't want to study. I tried to eat a sand-wich, but it tasted like dust in my mouth and I ended up throwing three-quarters of it in the trash. The clock on the cable box blurred in front of my eyes as I stared at it for what seemed like hours. My throat tightened in protest and the huge hole in my chest expanded. I felt sick inside.

Ryan! My mind screamed relentlessly. *Why didn't it get easier?*

I closed my eyes and pressed my head back into the cush-ions, trying not to let the tears that threatened to choke me spill over. I gave it a good fight, swallowing the pain over and over until I couldn't take it anymore. My lips started to tremble and the fat tears that were building in my eyes, fell in two heavy drops down my cheeks as a soft sob broke from my chest and erupted into the room.

I tumbled over on the couch and pulled my knees up, wrapping my arms around them, hoping that if I could keep the shaking sobs from becoming more pronounced, I could somehow manage to contain the misery I was feeling.

I shouldn't have bothered. My heart was broken. *Again.*

My eyes squeezed shut, forcing the tears to push out even faster. Why did it hurt so fucking bad? I knew when the sun came, up he'd call and probably come over. I'd see him and nothing would come of his date with this woman. *I knew it.* Yet every time, I was literally in hell. It was getting worse as time wore on. It was to the point I couldn't breathe, and I was barely able to keep it to myself. I wanted to wail and shout at him.

I wanted him to be with *me*. I wanted him to kiss, touch, and make love with *me*. Jealousy burned with the desperation and despair that ate away at my insides. Finally, I just gave in to the torrent of tears and cried my heart out.

Ryan, please—don't! Don't make love to her. Please, it kills me. I'm the one who loves you. I'm the one... Even if it were only fucking, I couldn't stand it anymore.

The words replayed over and over inside my head as I silently begged the man I loved to see me for who I was. My heart knew that no one could ever love him as much as I did. It wasn't possible.

Seconds, minutes, or hours passed. I wasn't sure how long I lay there crying in the darkness. Finally, my sobs ebbed, and my tears slowed to a slow stream, dripping from the corners of my eyes and leaving wet trails down the sides of my face to pool into the poor pillow beneath my head.

My eyes felt so tired. At least the crying exhausted me so maybe I'd be able to sleep. Sleep was my one true place of solace. If I was lucky enough not to dream.

I pushed myself into a sitting position and sniffed. It was dark, and the clock read just after eleven. *Not even midnight yet.* I stood and walked to the kitchen to find some candles and get some water and a Kleenex. My sore eyes couldn't take the full-blown light, but I felt the need to draw.

My secret saved me on nights like this. Over the years at school, I'd drawn his image over and over again. A world I created where he belonged only to me; my beautiful, perfect Ryan; gorgeous, yes, but brilliant and giving, funny and warm. I needed him like I needed air to breathe. No matter how many times my head tried to deny it, or I tried to push it down for the sake of our friendship, the truth rocked me to the core.

I moved around the room lighting the candles then to the drawing table Ryan had given me last year for Christmas. I pulled out a piece of the expensive linen paper I saved for his portraits and my charcoal pencils. I sat there for a moment, staring at the blank page, my fingers running lovingly along its starkness while the image I would put down formed in my mind.

When his features began to materialize on the page in front of me, calm finally settled over me. I inhaled so deeply I thought my lungs would burst; my right hand drew the outline of his face, the strong jaw, and the crooked smirk on those full lips that I loved.

Ryan was *mine*. He'd *always* be mine. My heart couldn't accept anything else.

Ryan ~

It was a nice spring night and I was sitting across from a beautiful woman at a casual Italian restaurant near campus. Maybe, the moon was out, and a soft breeze rustled the leaves of the trees that were situated around the patio where we were sitting. There could have been a conversation going on, and a waiter may have been by with an appetizer and fresh drinks.

Maybe.

My eyes skittered over the smooth expanse of creamy skin visible above the low-cut neckline of the red blouse my dinner companion was wearing, but I wasn't really seeing her. I tried to shake myself back into reality and concentrate on her words.

"Ryan? Are you with me?" My eyes met hers briefly and I forced the corners of my mouth to lift in a wry smile. I'd met her in chemistry when Professor Jannis assigned lab partners. I think it was sometime during the first semester of my sophomore year.

Since then I'd seen her at parties, had a couple more classes with her, and we might have even screwed once; I couldn't remember. I grimaced slightly at the hole in my memory. She was a nice girl; intelligent, with a taut body and beautiful features. *Very* beautiful, but the problem was; none of that mattered in the slightest. She wasn't the woman I wanted to be spending this evening with... or any evening for that matter.

I found myself yearning for long, flowing chestnut locks instead of shoulder length blonde hair; warm green eyes and not icy blue ones. Those deep green eyes saw right through me, let me be *me* and encouraged me whenever I doubted myself. I tried to swallow, but it felt like something stuck in my throat. Whatever it was, it physically hurt. My repeated attempts to push it down were pointless and I resisted the urge to claw at my neck with my hand. As the time at Stanford ticked down, I found myself more and more aware of the knife digging into my heart. I was more and more aware that soon life would take us in different directions. This was the last year. A semester and a half was all we had left. I'd done well on the MCAT, and the Harvard application had been sent. Julia had helped fill it out, and she refused to let me apply to other med schools... insisting that Harvard was my destiny. I wasn't sure anymore what my fucking destiny was. The vision of it had become obscure.

What in the hell was I doing here?

My heart pounded in my chest, a slight sheen of perspiration broke out on my forehead, while my fingers itched to pull out my phone and check for a call. I must have done so at some point because I found myself staring down at the blank screen and blinking several times to try to change the image. My heart fell.

What the fuck? What did you expect, asshole? I chastised myself. Julia knew I had a date tonight, and Ellie planned a girls' night out at one of the campus hangouts. She was bright with an effervescent personality that drew people to her. She was fun, exciting, and she thought about shit like I did. She had opinions and they were solid. Wherever she was, she was surrounded with people clamoring for some of her time. She wasn't just beautiful; she was incredible. She was *good*. People flocked to her. Men didn't just want to fuck her. They wanted to *know* her, and that fact scared the shit out of me. I'd seen it sophomore year when that user, Dave Kessler, tried to land her. I was terrified some nameless guy would sweep in and try to replace me in her life.

Julia. Her name reverberated in my brain and shivered through my soul.

Who was I fucking kidding with this shit? I ran a hand through my hair and sat back in the chair, praying the evening would end so I could check on her.

Where was she, and what was she doing? Was she home? Would she be alone? I couldn't shut off my mind, and I was tormented by the lack of answers. The tightness in my chest got worse and I sucked in a deep breath in a desperate attempt to keep from suffocating.

My thoughts were consumed with her more and more lately, but still, I tried to tell myself she was only my best friend. *Only* my best friend? Those words shaped my entire life at this point. I tried to shake it again, but nothing I did could change my feelings. *Nothing.* My eyes roamed the restaurant and longingly passed over the front entrance; the portal for my escape.

I knew I needed to get my head on straight, but my heart wasn't listening. My body wasn't listening. I was consumed; day and night. Julia was all I thought about. When I was away from her, I couldn't wait to get back to her and when I was with her, I was dying to touch her. And her mouth... Jesus, I wanted to taste that mouth. I was starving to finally kiss her. It was like I was in the deepest hell because I couldn't act on it.

"Ryan!" This time the voice was irritated and it was another mouth speaking. I forced my blurry eyes to focus on her face. It didn't matter that I wanted to bolt for the door or that it felt like my fucking skin was crawling off my body. I was here, and I owed it to Samantha to get through the evening.

"Uh, sorry, Sam. What were you saying?" I flushed guiltily and tried to carry on the most basic conversation, hoping she would want the evening to end as badly as I did. She prattled on and on about mind-numbing bullshit I couldn't recall five minutes later.

Somehow, I made it through the next two hours but the last few minutes were the worst. I'd peeled the girl off me when I'd taken her home, telling her the food made me feel ill so I could make a hasty retreat. She was disappointed; she wanted more, but it was impossible. It couldn't happen. I just couldn't do it anymore. Something had happened to change me. No longer could I act on instinct and pure animal need. *Someone* had happened, and that someone was in my heart and in my head... under my fucking skin.

I was such a coward. *Tell the fucking truth, for God's sake! Just admit it! You're head-over-heels in love with your best friend. Be a man, finally. Make her see you for more than her friend.*

I'd known it for almost three years, but somehow, admitting it put the relationship we had at risk, teetering on the precipice of uncertainty. I wasn't willing to risk the fall. I wasn't willing to risk the *loss.* I'd been forcing myself to continue with business as usual but I was precariously close to slipping up on so many occasions; so often, almost touching her face, pressing into her when we hugged goodbye, or spilling my guts on the floor at her feet. All of that was dangerous.

We knew each other inside and out. Julia and I didn't have secrets... except for how crazy in love with her I was and how desire and jealousy were eating me alive. One thing I was sure of; I did not want to lose her. I needed her. She was everything, and I... well, I was seriously screwed. I tried not to hope she mirrored my feelings because then I'd be lost. There were moments, like today at lunch, when I sensed the way she withdrew from me, when hope nudged into my heart at the same time as it ached. If we were only friends, why did I feel so damn empty when I was with someone else? Why did I feel guilty? Why did she close off like she did?

I sighed deeply as my fingers tightened around the steering wheel of my car. I realized I was sitting in front of the building where Julia shared an apartment with Ellie, but without any memory of how in the hell I'd gotten there.

I glanced up at the second-story window of their living room, and there was a low flickering light. *Candles.* I closed my eyes as my heart constricted. I knew she had boyfriends; I'd had to mentally school myself to back off, but it never got any easier. In my mind and heart, she belonged to me, and the thought of anyone else touching her ate away at my insides like acid. I'd never touched her like that, but still, it was killing me that anyone else would. That she would allow it, or want it, was more than I could stand thinking about.

The clock on my dash said 11:32 PM. Before I knew it, I was bounding up the stairs two at a time until I was standing, heart pounding, on the outside of the oak door that led to Julia's place. I couldn't hear voices, but there was music filtering softly through the walls. My fists clenched at my sides in protest.

I'd seen that idiot, Jason Milner, ogling Julia in the cafeteria when she and Ellie were discussing their plans for the evening. He'd known where they were going even though he wasn't part of the conversation.

My hand hovered over the door, and I dropped it.

"Fuck, Matthews. Make a decision," I muttered under my breath then let my fist connect with the wood three times before I could change my mind.

"Julia, it's me." I waited and heard some rustling behind the door. *Please let her be alone.* "Julia?"

The chain rattled on the other side of the door as she struggled to open it, and finally, the door flung open. She was standing in front of me, her eyes wide and questioning, her hair messed up, without make-up.

"What are you doing here? I thought you had plans." Confusion flitted across her beautiful features.

My eyes soaked in the site of her. Her hair was in a knot on the top of her head haphazardly, with tendrils escaping around her face. She was wearing pink and blue striped pajama pants and a white wife beater. I tried to ignore the expanse of bare skin and her hipbones that were showing above the waistband of the pajamas. Probably when she turned around, her butt dimples would show. Her top was skimpy and the obvious lack of bra was harder to avoid. My body reacted against my will, and I shoved my hands into the front pockets of my jeans.

I didn't wait for an invitation and brushed by Julia to come inside, my eyes scanning the apartment for any evidence of a man's presence. There was a glass of wine sitting on her art table, but no other. I smiled in relief then turned back toward her.

"Uh, crash and burn." I readily dismissed the subject and noticed the candle burning on the end table by the couch. It was the only light in the room. The music was recognizable—a compilation she'd done of Sara Bareilles, Sia, and a few other softer artists. "It's awfully cozy in here. Am I interrupting something?"

Her eyes narrowed as she hesitated momentarily before shaking her head and closing the door. Her head cocked and I noticed her hair was damp on one side of her face; her eyes were red-rimmed and swollen. Her hand came out to rest briefly on the front of my shirt as she passed.

The familiar electricity shot through me at her touch and the sweet coconut scent of her shampoo enveloped me. I longed to take her hand and press it into the muscles on my abdomen, to feel her fingers spread out over my body. I never wanted her to stop touching me but I was anxious about the obvious signs of her tears. I grabbed her hand in mine and stared intently down into her face.

"I was just drawing and trying to relax. Are you hungry? Do you want some wine?"

"Wine, sure. Are you okay? Have you been crying, Julia?" I felt my skin flush with heat at what her tears might mean. "Did you go out with Ellie? Did Milner bother you at the bar? I knew he'd show up there. Did he... *touch* you?" I followed her into the kitchen. "Did he?"

She smiled but went about the business of pouring me a glass of wine.

"No, Matthews. It's sweet of you to worry, but relax. I just... I didn't feel like going out tonight." She lifted her right shoulder in a half-assed shrug. "My uh... allergies are acting up."

She handed me the glass and we both moved back into the living room. Something felt off. She was fidgeting slightly, which wasn't like her.

"Do you need me to run out and get you some medicine? I wouldn't mind." Julia walked to the art table and began to put her things away with her back to me.

"I'm okay, Ryan, thank you. It's early. What happened on your date?" She was still putting her drawings into her black portfolio, setting it on the floor, up against the table leg, when she finished. I couldn't see her expression but the tone in her voice was hesitant.

"Nothing." I shrugged. "Just... wasn't interested, I guess. And.—" I sat down on the couch and kicked off my shoes. I didn't have to ask. If I wanted to crash here for the rest of the night, Julia would allow it.

"And?"

"*And*, I wanted to make sure you were okay. I was worried Milner would bother you tonight. He practically licked your skin today, and I know what kind of man he is. Aaron told me he's a user. I don't trust him and I don't want to see you get hurt." That was the truth, but there was more. *I can't bear the thought of him touching you. He's a manwhore, my brain protested.* "I don't want you near him, okay? Just stay away from him. There are plenty of other guys to... date."

She finally sat at the other end of the couch and pulled her knees under her. Sipping from her glass, she watched me over the rim, letting her eyebrows raise in question.

"I'm having déjà vu. Didn't you say something similar about David Kessler?"

"Maybe, they're both slime."

"Giving me orders now?" she asked.

"Yes." I smirked at her, and she laughed out loud. All was right with my world. "*Taking* orders now?"

"In this only because I agree; he's a sleaze. Just don't get used to it," she admonished with a teasing lilt.

I chuckled as I relaxed. It was so like Julia to put me at ease. "I won't. But stay the fuck away from him," I said again.

We both sobered as we looked into each other's eyes and I was aching. She looked so soft and inviting, her mouth dropped open slightly, and my breath rushed from my lungs. I wanted to reach out and touch her, to sink into her softness, to kiss her. I'd wanted it for so long... wanted it so badly I burned with it. My eyes dropped to her mouth, and I couldn't tear them away from those sweet lips. She licked them once then her top teeth appeared, biting down on the lower one.

"*Why?*" She looked at me for a few seconds more, her eyes intent on mine and I wondered if she could feel the same pull I did. She threw down the challenge and waited, daring me to tell her the truth. Knowing me as she did, I was certain she knew I was in love with her. How could she not know? I gravitated to her like the tide to the moon, but like me, she never said a word about it.

"I don't want him anywhere near you." The admission was ripped from inside my chest before I could stop it. I tried to recover by sitting back a little and reaching for the wine glass again. I cleared my throat. "Uh, he's not good enough for you."

"*Who* is?" she asked softly.

If I didn't say something fast, I was going to give in to the need and while the thought thrilled me, I was concerned what the next day would bring. "Exactly."

She looked down at her glass and nodded ever so slightly. Did she understand how consumed I was, that I couldn't take anyone being with her, save me? The skin on her cheeks infused with a rosy blush as the uncomfortable silence hung between us like a storm. She was so fucking gorgeous she stole my breath away.

"Do you feel like watching a movie with me?"

"Of course. HBO or DVD?" she asked softly.

"It doesn't matter. Anything." I grabbed the remote from the coffee table as she settled in next to me.

"You choose."

We weren't touching, but I could feel her in the air around me, her scent soaking into my skin. Contentment settled over me like a blanket, the heat radiating between us, the electricity vibrating and ready to spark at the slightest touch. The two of us together were like a combustion engine ready to fire, but my body relaxed next to hers, and I could breathe easily for the first time all evening.

It was as I needed it to be. Julia was right here. With *me* and no one else.

**If you've enjoyed this book, please follow
Ryan and Julia's story as it continues in**

The Future of Our Past

The Remembrance Trilogy, Book One.

Books by Kahlen Aymes

Titles are available in all eBook formats and paperback.

After Dark Series
1. *Angel After Dark*
2. *Confessions After Dark*
3. *Promises After Dark*

The Remembrance Trilogy
Prequel—*Before Ryan Was Mine*
1. *The Future of Our Past*
2. *Don't Forget to Remember Me*
3. *A Love Like This*

<u>Coming in 2015</u>
UnTouch Me (Stand Alone Novel)
The FAMOUS Novel Series

Stalk Kahlen

Facebook:
https://www.facebook.com/kahlen.aymes.author
Twitter: @Kahlen_Aymes
Find her on Pinterest, Instagram, YouTube and
Goodreads.

Visit Kahlen's website for Merchandise,
Signed books, Julia's Recipes, Missing Scenes,
Events, Kahlen's Blog, and Playlists:
KahlenAymes.com

For news on new releases, contests,
appearances, and excerpts; subscribe to her
newsletter: http://eepurl.com/RuW4X

Request an eBook autograph at:
http://www.authorgraph.com/authors/Kahlen_Aymes

Rights Information: McIntosh & Otis Literary,
Inc. 353 Lexington Avenue • New York, NY
10016 • Tel: 1-212-687-7400 • Fax: 1-212-687-
6894 • Email: info@mcintoshandotis.com

CPSIA information can be obtained at www.ICGtesting.com
Printed in the USA
BVOW05s2141231214

380731BV00001B/4/P